GOODNIGHT TO THE EVENING

Kathy Wile

Books by Kathy Wile:

Red Redemption
Goodnight to the Evening
Sunflower Solstice (a novella)

<u>The Kate Adams Series</u>:
Shifting Seaward
Drifting Inland
Sloping Southward

Night Visions
Psychological Potluck
The Characters of Sardis Lake
Gulf Shores Godsend

Copyright © 2020 Kathy Wile
All rights reserved.

NOTE FROM THE AUTHOR

In May of 2019, my husband and I were sitting at the ocean's edge in Estero Island, Florida in low beach chairs. The sun had recently set, and we stared out at the water in the changing light. A woman approached us from behind, saying, "You two look like you're having a wonderful time. Relaxing, saying 'goodnight' to the evening." She raised her glass in a toast, "I'm all about it. Amen to you people!" Then she departed, walking toward the western horizon. I do not know her name or where she came from, but I'd like to thank her for inspiring the title of this book.

Chapter 1

"Keep your voice down! The neighbors are going to think I'm killing you," Donovan scolded as Nina wailed in anguish. In her defense, he had just broken her heart by ending their fifteen-year marriage.

"You can't just leave me here alone! Where will I go? I don't have any family. I don't have a job ..."

"Yeah, yeah, I know. Look, I feel bad about it. Here," Donovan turned to open his suitcase. He pulled out his checkbook. "Here's $10,000. That should hold you over until you find a job, save up enough to rent a place." This amount was pocket change to him. Donovan came from old money. That, in addition to a string of wise investment choices, protected him from the drab life of a nine to five.

With trembling hands, Nina accepted the check. Her tear-stained face did little to elicit sympathy from Donovan. "You can stay here in this condo for the next two weeks, since I prepaid." Turning his back on her look of helpless devastation, he grabbed his suitcase. "Have a good life, Nina." With those five words, he departed into the night.

The shutting door caused her to jump as if the resulting sound waves carried an electrical charge. She began to shake uncontrollably, so curling up in a ball on the floor felt like the right thing to do.

Nina knew why he had left, but her amazement stemmed from her utter obliviousness to the approaching train wreck. He had met a pretty young waitress at a café they frequented, and he'd decided she would be a better companion than thirty-seven-year-old Nina. What a slap in the face, since she had been a young, pretty waitress when she met Donovan in a restaurant at age twenty-two.

Their whirlwind romance consisted of him buying her things she never dreamed of owning and whisking her away to tropical locations. He made her feel like she had never felt before: important, cherished, beautiful. Even loved.

Though she had aged a bit since then, she still looked great for thirty-seven. But a man who could have anything and was not accustomed to denying himself would see no reason to start at age forty. So here Nina lies, in a ball of well-deserved self-pity on the carpet.

Salt from all the crying eventually caused her to launch into a coughing fit, so she sat up. A single tear dove from her cheek onto the check in her lap, bringing reality back into focus. She had to clear her head. Without a plan, she would be out on the street in two weeks. Or, in this case, out on the beach, which under other circumstances, wouldn't be so bad.

For this final trip, Donovan had brought Nina to her favorite place, Orange Beach, Alabama. They had vacationed here many times over the years, and she always thought how nice it would be to put down roots here. She had just imagined those roots would be entwined with his, in the rich and welcoming soil of their own land, topped with her dream beach house.

Nina hadn't lived on her own in … well, ever. She'd gone straight from living with her parents to marrying and moving in with Donovan, a decision that had cut her off from her family completely. Her mother and father had so disapproved of him that they'd vowed to disown her if she went through with the wedding, and they followed through on their word. The hurt had killed the one part of her that existed separately from Donovan, so she had clung to him even more tightly, perhaps so tightly that the rope of her dependence eventually severed their relationship. Oh, he was definitely at fault for cheating, but maybe if she hadn't been so needy … No. Nina couldn't let herself take the blame for the dissolution of her marriage. She had been the one who fed it, cared for it, cherished it. Now, it would be like an object in a museum, existing only as a display, trapped behind glass like dinosaur bones. In short, history.

Chapter 2

Michelle Kingsley smiled playfully at her fiancée as the ocean breeze toyed with her long brown locks. Here on the deck of their favorite seafood restaurant, the view of the sunset stunned her anxious heart into serene submission. The soft, humid caress of the tropical air felt like a touch from God.

Likely, that's why she didn't hear Kevin when he somberly announced, "We need to talk." When she continued staring into the pastel wonder behind his head, he broke her reverie by waving his hand in front of her face. "Michelle?"

Her eyes slowly focused on his face. "Yes?" she asked with that blissful grin still holding her lips hostage.

Kevin squirmed and looked down at the table. "Michelle … I don't know how to make this easy on you, so I'll just say it. We can't get married."

It took a moment for the shock of his declaration to disconnect the invisible bond happiness had on her facial muscles and lower her lips like the sinking sun currently on the horizon. "What?" she asked in quiet disbelief.

Still refusing to make eye contact, Kevin explained, "As you know, I come from a long line of lawyers. My family has great expectations of me."

Perhaps the urge to gain some bit of control over the situation caused her to interrupt. She didn't have anything significant to say, but it was important to her to take part in what seemed headed in the direction of a one-sided conversation with no room for debate. "Which is why you went to law school. You just graduated with honors."

A slightly demeaning laugh escaped Kevin's lips. "Yes, I'm well aware. And now I've come here to join my family's law firm."

"We. We've come here," Michelle interjected.

Kevin shook his head impatiently. "Yes, that was our intention in coming here. But some new information has come to light. My grandfather's death changes things."

Michelle narrowed her eyes and leaned toward him. "Your grandfather died three months ago."

"But the reading of the will was delayed until yesterday. And there's a problem."

"Wait, you went to the reading of his will yesterday and didn't include me?"

Kevin just seemed plain annoyed now. "Yes, why would I?"

Feeling as though she'd been slapped, Michelle leaned back in her chair and replied, "Because I'm about to be your wife! Or so I thought."

Clearly frustrated, Kevin ran his hand through his short blond hair and continued. "The will states that I'm to inherit seven million dollars. But I can only have that money if I marry another lawyer."

Michelle inhaled sharply. "So you're dumping me for money?"

Kevin stared at her as if she'd just grown an extra head. "It's seven million dollars! Of course I'm dumping you!"

The cocoon of bliss Michelle had found herself snugly wrapped in a moment earlier had been sliced open by the sharp sword of Kevin's words, leaving her exposed and vulnerable. This new reality was too harsh for her fresh, innocent flesh. She needed a thicker skin for this, one formed from years of disappointments. Unfortunately, at twenty-two, she had yet to bear the brunt of many life-altering blows.

A long silence followed as twilight deepened. Finally, Kevin said, "I guess you'll be headed back home to Georgia."

Slowly, Michelle's gaze met Kevin's questioning eyes. "I gave up a good job back home for you. I start my new one here tomorrow, remember? At the newspaper? Or maybe you forgot I gave up everything to come here and start a life with you."

Kevin rolled his eyes. "Oh, yeah, you gave up that great job as a t-shirt designer in our tiny hometown making just above minimum wage. You'll be doing a lot better than that here, even at the paper. And will living by the ocean be such a huge sacrifice for you? That's all you ever talked about, how great it would be to move to the beach. Well, you're welcome. I got you here."

Michelle's jaw dropped. "You're unbelievable!" Shaking her head, she stood up quickly and grabbed her purse. "Enjoy your money, you greedy puppet!" She dashed off the deck and onto the sand, racing to escape his laughter as it mocked her naivety, which was tragically one of her best traits.

Chapter 3

Nina awoke alone the following morning, reality pounding her with its weighted fists. It hadn't been a dream. Donovan really did leave.

She didn't want to get up, because once life noticed she was awake, it would demand that she participate in its game of uphill battles. How could it be so impatient? Shouldn't she be given a break to mourn for her marriage?

Despite its nagging call to action, Nina decided to take today off. She splashed water on her face, changed into her swimsuit, and grabbed a towel. The balcony beckoned, so she stepped out through the door to stand in its shade as she applied sunscreen.

The warm breeze offered a welcome contrast to the air-conditioned interior. Nina spread the white lotion across her golden skin as she listened to the seagulls laughing maniacally at each other's jokes. She wished so deeply that she could join in their joyous exchange, but a chest heavy with sorrow cannot support even the airy weight of lightheartedness.

White sand like powdered sugar sifted through Nina's sandals as she walked. The color of the ocean varied here depending on the wind and tide. Today, it sparkled like clear blue liquid glass. Donovan couldn't have picked a better first day to leave Nina alone, though she was sure he would have been equally willing to leave her at the mercy of a hurricane.

Settling about three feet from the reach of the fallen waves, she spread her towel upon the sand and stretched across it. The heat of the sun soaked quickly through her skin into her bones and soothed her like a warm blanket fresh from the dryer. She found herself slipping in and out of sleep, so relaxed that she grew numb to the hurt.

A pod of pelicans flying unusually close to the sand awakened her an hour later. She silently thanked them for reminding her to turn over and bake her backside. As she rolled onto her stomach, the pain threatened to overtake her once more, but the lingering calm from her warm nap won out, and she soon dozed. Ah, the sweet dreamless rest the beach can give! Nina would be content to lose her conscious mind forever here, to melt away into the sound of the rolling surf, to sink into the soft sand, buried without a single mourner. Now that Donovan was gone, no one would even notice her absence.

Chapter 4

Michelle sat outside for several hours the night that Kevin dumped her. She reclined on a soft lounge chair, staring up at the moon and stars. Kevin had paid to rent this house for the two weeks leading up to the day of their marriage, at which time they would move into a much nicer house his family planned to deed to them as a wedding gift. Now, it looked like she would have to find a place quickly with cheap rent, if that even existed in Orange Beach. Living on the salary of a graphic designer at a newspaper meant she would also likely need a roommate.

Though she had been looking forward to having nice things and a lovely home, that had never been her focus. She genuinely enjoyed Kevin's company. His propensity for intelligent conversation and sarcastic wit kept her on her toes. She liked being challenged, and though she often struggled with feelings of inadequacy brought on by his spot-on criticism, she thrived on the motivation to be better.

Had she known that being her best still wouldn't be enough for Kevin, she would have stopped trying long ago. She appreciated the growth that his expectations brought about in her, but boy, was she mad.

Sure, seven million dollars was an amount that most people would do just about anything for, but the fact that he already had a lot of money from his family and would be making a killing as a lawyer in this wealthy area just made it that much worse. He wasn't somebody who had grown up poor and known what it was like to go hungry or without shelter. If he had been, maybe she could've understood his decision. Funny thing is that if he had lived in poverty before, he probably would have grown up to be a better person who would make decisions based on the heart and not on greed.

Michelle sniffed and wiped her cheek. Her tears burned like the anger from which they sprang. She laughed aloud. He was still motivating her, though he didn't intend to, because her rage at him would propel her forward. Ah, well. She didn't have to give him the credit for that.

Tomorrow, she would start her new job as planned. She would ask around the office to see if anyone knew of affordable places to rent and potential roommates. A smile spread across her face. "How lucky I am to have all this change to distract me. I get to start a new life after all." Then, she said goodnight to the evening.

Chapter 5

Nina could feel herself beginning to burn in spite of the sunscreen, so she arose and headed to the shower. Though the bathroom mirror revealed a bright pink tone upon her skin, she knew it would turn to tan in a matter of hours like it always did. She had been blessed that way.

As the cool water rinsed the hot sand from her skin, Nina felt grateful to have been left here of all places. Not grateful to Donovan, but to God for finally fulfilling her dream of living by the ocean. Sure, the circumstances were far less than ideal, but like the realtors say, location is everything. Even if she wound up camping out on the beach and sleeping under palm fronds for shelter, she would be here, the spot that had captured her heart and held it even when Donovan let it go.

She busied herself with getting ready. The condo was within walking distance to a few restaurants and stores. She planned to deposit the $10,000 check in a new bank account under her own name, get lunch, and pick up a paper to scan for jobs. On the way home, she'd get some groceries so that she wouldn't have to drop $20 at a restaurant every time she got hungry.

Nina chose a cream-colored dress for both its professional style and ability to reflect heat. Walking even a short distance in the blazing sun would do her in if she didn't dress accordingly. She applied very little makeup and simply brushed her blonde bob, since the humidity would do whatever it pleased to her coif.

The closest eatery to the bank happened to be Sally's Salad Shack. Nina survived the trek and ordered a salmon salad with a blackberry tea. The food didn't disappoint, especially for $9. As she chewed slowly, she browsed the classifieds of The Pelican Pica. With her red pen, she circled an ad for a cake decorator at Baked Bliss and one for a receptionist at Seaside Spa. After her last bite of salad, she headed to the restroom to freshen up and reapply her lipstick. Then, she walked the quarter mile to her next stop at the spa.

She flashed a smile at the lady behind the counter as soon as she opened the door. Exuding warmth, she approached and introduced herself. "Hello, I'm Nina Carter, and I'd like to apply for the receptionist job."

The smile quickly fell from the lady's face. "What?! What receptionist job? Robert, did you know about this?"

A clearly upset balding man in black uniform rushed to the desk, but not before the receptionist lurched toward the paper in Nina's hands. "Let me see!" She grabbed it, her eyes falling on the red circle.

Robert stopped in his tracks and shut his eyes. As the receptionist began to wail, he shot Nina a death glare. "Did you not read the part that says, 'Apply in confidence by sending resume to this address'?" he growled through clenched teeth.

All the color left Nina's face. "Oh, no. I'm so sorry. I'm just so desperate to find a job that I didn't even notice that part."

Robert pointed to the door. "Get out."

Nina took the paper that the receptionist had dropped on the counter in shock before turning to go. A few tears made their way to her eyes as she listened to the sobs of the poor woman she'd just informed of her imminent termination. How could she have been so careless?

Come to think of it, she should stop right now and carefully read that ad for cake decorator. She couldn't deal with any more embarrassment or inflict any more pain on some unsuspecting soul today. Finding the second red circle, she read aloud, "Cake Decorator Needed. Apply within at Baked Bliss. Two years experience required." Nina dropped her hand and looked skyward. She'd almost humiliated herself again. She had never done anything but waitress in her entire working life.

Nina turned and began her walk of defeat back to the condo. What was she going to do with herself? She wasn't qualified for anything but waiting tables, and all the restaurants were fully staffed with summer help. Camping out on the beach was beginning to look like a real possibility.

The ding of a bell caught her attention. She glanced in the direction of the sound and saw a sprawling souvenir shop. The large sign on top of the building consisted of letters spelling out, "Seahorse Treasures," with a seahorse in place of each "s." Large words written in red jumped from a sign on the door that announced, "Now Hiring."

Her heart leapt within her as she came closer. Underneath those precious words was even better news: "No experience needed." Nina opened the door without hesitation.

Reggae music greeted her ears. The air smelled of coconut lotion. Shelves lined with trinkets made of shells, wooden signs declaring 'Welcome to the Beach,' racks of t-shirts, and various other souvenirs stretched as far as the eye could see. This had to be the biggest souvenir shop Nina had ever seen, and she had seen a lot of them in her travels.

"Hello, can I help you find anything?" asked a faceless voice. Nina turned in a full circle before finally locating its source. A petite blond woman emerged from one of the aisles with the question still in her eyes.

"Oh, hello. I'm actually here to apply for a job."

The woman nodded and motioned for Nina to follow her. "Okay. Come on back into the office. Alice, the boss, just walked over to check on the house. She'll be back in a few minutes, I'm sure. In the meantime, you can go ahead and start filling out the application."

Nina released a sigh of relief. "Great!" Then a thought hit her. "Do you need to see a resume?" Dread filled her stomach. She hadn't thought to work one up, since her only work experience was fifteen years in the past, and she hadn't had need of one in just as long.

"Alice doesn't require one, but it couldn't hurt if you have one on you."

"I don't have one with me."

The lady smiled as she opened the gate beside the cash register. "I'm sure it won't matter. Alice can tell all she needs to know about a person just by talking to them a few minutes. She's a really good judge of character."

Nina didn't know whether that should make her nervous or happy. She guessed it all depended on what Alice was looking for in a worker.

The lady handed Nina an application and a pen. "You can sit here and use one of those books to press on while you write. I'll send Alice in as soon as she gets back. Oh, be sure to write a cover letter in the space provided. Alice likes to know a bit about prospective employees and why they want to work here before she dives into the interview. By the way, I'm Leslie. It's nice to meet you."

"Nice to meet you," Nina echoed. Leslie shut the door and left her alone. Nina took a deep breath and lifted the instrument of her fate. The ink followed her direction and sealed the words that would either be her deliverance or her downfall.

Chapter 6

Alice shuddered a sigh as she shut the door to the home she had shared with her late husband, Fred, for thirty years. She knew that she couldn't continue to take care of the property as her health steadily declined, but she also couldn't bear to sell it. If only she and Fred had children to inherit it ... But to dwell on that was pointless.

When Fred had passed ten years ago, Alice could not stand to live there without him. She had moved into a small apartment and hired someone to take care of the place. She waited two years before even going back to see it. When she did, the warmth of good memories drew her in, and she let the caretaker go. She checked on the place daily and tended to the yard and plants as well. Doing so made her feel closer to Fred.

Two months ago, Alice had collapsed at work. At the hospital, she learned she had congestive heart failure. The doctor had guessed she would live another six months to a year. It was all the same to Alice. She knew her heart had broken the day Fred died, and it had been trying to get her to him ever since.

She just wished she knew what to do with this house. She would love to find some nice couple to leave it to, but in her line of work, she dealt primarily with tourists who would be heading back home in a week or so. If Leslie and her husband weren't planning to move to south Florida soon, she would've given it to her.

Alice breathed a prayer that the home would wind up in the hands of someone who would treat it with the love and care it deserved. Then she began the slow walk back to the shop, tackling the steps down to the sand one at a time with several breaths in between. These days, even the short distance between the back of Seahorse Treasures and the front of the house got her winded. She would have to sit for fifteen minutes upon arriving just to catch her breath. But if she couldn't, that would be okay with her.

Chapter 7

Michelle pulled into a parking space beside The Pelican Pica. Excitement and nervousness bubbled inside of her, making her hands shake when she reached for the car door handle. As she walked up the ramp, she noticed the big wooden sign in the shape of a pelican with a newspaper in its mouth gracing the front entrance and giggled. Sure, a pica is a unit of type size, but it's also the name of a tendency to eat substances other than normal food. She wondered if the owners had incorporated this play on words into the sign.

Puns rarely went unnoticed by Michelle. The heightened state of her nerves made wordplay seem even funnier. She took a moment to calm herself and put on a serious face before opening the door with the paper munching pelican on it. Oh, no. A snicker escaped her lips. Good, no one was in the lobby to hear.

On second thought, no one was in the lobby. It was already 8 a.m. Shouldn't someone be here to greet customers? She needed to tell the receptionist that she was here for her first day of work. She didn't know which cubicle would be hers, and she didn't want to just walk back into the "Employees Only" section and get settled at the wrong desk.

Michelle took a seat. She would wait here for a few minutes to see if anyone showed up. An eerie quiet permeated the halls. If not for the unlocked door and the overhead lights, she would think they weren't yet open for business.

She picked up a magazine and began mindlessly scanning its pages. She couldn't focus on anything right now, but she had to do something with her hands. They were becoming rather fidgety.

So muffled that she thought perhaps she'd imagined it, a cry escaped one of the rooms down the hallway. It was followed moments later by what sounded like sniffling. Alarmed but too new to the place to pry, Michelle remained seated and strained to hear.

A door opened and voices sounded, but she was still too far away to decipher what they were saying. Michelle expected to see someone come to the front. Perhaps they'd been in a meeting, but someone always occupied the front desk at a newspaper. Her friend had worked at one, and she had only ever left for short bathroom breaks and lunch. Even then, someone stepped in to fill her spot until she returned.

After several minutes passed and no one surfaced, she stepped to the front of the hallway and called out, "Hello?" She heard more muffled voices and things being shuffled around, but no one replied. Cautiously, she took a few steps toward the first office.

Before she could appear in the doorway, a man wearing a white shirt and a blue tie rounded its corner carrying a box full of office supplies. "Excuse me," he said, barely glancing at her as he continued at a fast pace toward the lobby.

Wanting to say something but sensing his foul mood, she kept quiet and waited for someone else to appear. She didn't have to wait long. Four more people carrying cardboard boxes stuffed with everything from potted plants to staplers and coffee mugs came her way. Their eyes appeared glossed over and their gazes fixed. They didn't even glance at her.

Desperate for answers, Michelle touched the arm of the last woman in the group. "Excuse me, I'm Michelle Kingsley, and today is my first day here. Can you tell me where I need to …" she trailed off as the woman began shaking her head.

"The paper is finished. They just told us this morning that we are all without a job." A sob escaped her mouth with that last word.

Michelle's jaw dropped. "I'm so sorry. What happened?"

The woman put the box down on the floor, the weight of it too much to bear in tandem with her newfound sorrow. "We've known for some time that both ad sales and readership have declined, but we've taken steps to repair the damage. We've offered deep discounts for people who sign up to advertise for extended periods. We've cut subscription costs. We've kept our online subscription costs low, and we've encouraged advertisers to take advantage of an online presence." She paused and put a finger to her quivering lips. "But it wasn't enough," she squeaked out. This poor woman had obviously felt a deep dedication to the paper. She buried her face in her hands and wept.

Michelle put a hand on her shoulder. She wanted to hug her, because she obviously needed comfort, but this poor stranger might feel awkward being held by someone she'd just met. A great relief washed over Michelle as the woman who had interviewed her approached and took the crying lady into her arms.

The interviewer and Michelle shared a knowing glance. With a nod from her, Michelle understood that she'd been dismissed and was free to go. She took a few quiet steps away from the situation before succumbing to tears herself. For just a moment, she shared in the collective despair of the office, like an accidental visitor happening upon the funeral of a person she didn't know, unattached yet sympathizing with those who grieved.

As she shut the door behind her, the pelican who moments ago had seemed so hilarious dropped to the floor. She bent to retrieve it, and she heard a voice say, "You can take it if you want."

She glanced up to see a white-haired man in a suit smiling at her. "Oh, won't someone who has been here a long time want to keep it?" Surely a loyal employee would like to have it to remember the place by.

The man shook his head and laughed. "We've made fun of our logo for as long as it has existed. We actually tried several times to get the owners to consider a name and image change, even going so far as to have a contest to develop a new design. They wouldn't hear of it. You take it. I saw how much it amused you."

Michelle gasped. She hadn't been aware of anyone watching her.

"I was in my car as you walked to the door. No one has so much as noticed that sign in years, but it delighted you. On behalf of The Pelican Pica, I want you to have it."

She looked down at the bird in her hands and smiled. "Thank you. I'll treasure it. I'm Michelle, by the way."

"Mark Rutgerz. Nice to meet you. If you'll excuse me, I've got an early retirement to plan." With a warm smile, he departed.

Michelle gently placed the pelican in her back seat. She lowered herself into her car and sat staring at the building where she would have formed a future. She felt as if she had been taken under by a rogue wave. Nothing she came here for existed anymore. She found herself without a fiancé and a job, and soon she wouldn't even have a place to live. The force of the wave's final blow knocked her thoughtless. She sat still in this state of nothingness, losing only time.

Chapter 8

Ten minutes had passed since Nina had taken the pen in her hand and summarized her situation. She had been honest about her need to find work right away and even mentioned that her prior work experience consisted of waitressing and nothing more. There was no need to pretend, especially since this boss could apparently see through a person quickly. Nina's nerves became more active with each passing moment of silence. Her leg bobbed up and down as she counted the beads of her necklace like a rosary.

Finally, a new voice travelled down the hallway. Cheerful and robust, this voice didn't sound too intimidating. As Leslie and Alice came closer to the office, Nina could hear Alice breathing heavily, as if she'd just been for a run. "Get me a chair, dear." Wheels rolled across the floor outside the door. Alice settled into it and exhaled loudly. "Let me look over her application while I catch my breath."

Leslie mumbled something and tapped on the office door before opening it. She stuck only her head in and smiled. "All done?"

Nina nodded and handed her the papers.

Leslie took them and said, "Give her just a few minutes to look over this, and she'll be right with you."

"Might take more than a few, hon. But don't worry. It's not you, it's me. Just trying to get air into my lungs," Alice said with a rasp from the other side.

"Okay, thank you," Nina answered, unsure of the appropriate response.

While she waited, she practiced some deep breathing exercises. It was weird knowing someone just outside the door was appraising her without ever having met her. She hoped Alice caught her breath soon, because she couldn't take much more of this suspense.

The sound of chair wheels slowly rolling toward the door broke the silence. Alice turned the knob and wheeled herself toward Nina. With a smile and an outstretched hand, she said, "Hi, I'm Alice. Nice to meet you."

Something about her demeanor instantly put Nina at ease. Alice had straight, sleek gray hair that hung to her shoulders, except for the bangs. She wore glasses with rims of the same shade, and her smile revealed what must surely be false teeth, because they were too pearly and perfect to belong to a woman of her age. Nina returned the smile, echoed the greeting, and introduced herself.

After the handshake, Alice rolled behind her desk and looked down at the application. "So, Nina, your situation may be the most unique of any prospective employee I've ever encountered." She let the papers drop to the desk and made eye contact. Softly, she asked, "How are you holding up?"

Nina bit her lip to hold back tears. Alice was the first person to ask her that since Donovan had left. Of course, she was also the first to learn about what had happened, but just hearing the concern in the voice of another human directed toward her was enough to make her come undone. She held it together, though, save for a sheen of moisture veiling her eyes.

"It would be a lie to tell you that I'm okay, but I believe I am going to get to a place where I am. This job would be the first step in that direction."

Alice gave a sympathetic smile and said, "Okay. Just a few questions for you. Number one, do you prefer stocking shelves or dealing with customers?"

"I'd probably be better dealing with customers. I'm not very good at lifting heavy boxes or climbing ladders."

Alice grinned and jotted something down. "Alright. Next question … what days and hours are you available to work?"

Nina quickly answered, "All of them."

Bewilderment crossed Alice's features. "Well, I wouldn't make you work more than forty hours a week, unless you just wanted to."

"Nothing is more important to me right now than saving up to get on my feet. The condo my husband rented is only paid up for the next two weeks. After that, I'm on my own. So yes, I can work as many hours as you'll let me."

Alice's jaw dropped. "You mean you're about to be without a roof over your head?"

Nina looked down at the floor. "Yes, ma'am. He gave me some money to get started, but I've got to find a place with cheap rent quick."

A light came on in Alice's mind. She could solve two problems with one answer. "Child, I've got just the place for you."

Chapter 9

For about an hour, Michelle meditated on the black hole that had consumed her future. Then she got out of the car and began to walk. She had no destination in mind, but she needed more air than the confined interior of her sedan offered.

To put distance between herself and the now defunct Pelican Pica, crossing the street seemed like the right thing to do. She slowly moved westward down the sidewalk, surrounded by strangers thrilled to be on a beach vacation. Despite the great difference between her mental state and theirs, it felt nice not to be alone right now.

The warm breeze that only last night had filled her with serenity bordering on bliss now lifted her hair off of her neck and kissed her cheek. This offered her some small measure of comfort. It seemed as if the very air around her bore witness to her string of misfortune and breathed its condolences across her skin.

She walked until the heat of midmorning became too much. She determined she would stop at the next place of business for a bottle of water and an air-conditioned moment before heading back to her car. Right past a cluster of sea oats, she spotted a large souvenir shop that would surely sell something cold to drink.

The heat was such that she didn't pay any attention to the name of the place. She saw a refrigerator full of bottled drinks through the window, and that was all that mattered. She went inside and bought two waters at the counter. The cashier looked at her with concern as she guzzled the whole first bottle without taking a break. As Michelle twisted off the top of the second one, the lady commented, "Honey, you look awfully flushed. Do you want to sit down a minute in the breakroom where it's cooler?"

Grateful for the offer, Michelle nodded her head. "Yes, that would be amazing."

The lady led her through a doorway and into a room where the air conditioner blew full blast. "Sit down in here for a while."

"Thank you so much. I walked here from the newspaper office, and I think I overdid it."

The woman's jaw dropped. "You walked all the way from The Pelican Pica? That's over two miles! Did your car break down or something?"

Michelle sighed and cast her eyes downward. "No. I was supposed to start a job there today, but the owners decided to shut the place down. I came in and everyone had all their stuff in boxes. They were walking out in tears. It was awful."

The woman gasped. "I can't believe it! They've been there for as long as I can remember." She shook her head in disbelief. "That's just terrible."

Michelle slowly sipped her second bottle of water. She wiped a droplet from her lip and continued, "So now, I've got to start all over. I just moved here from Georgia, expecting to get married in two weeks, move into a nice house, and begin a career as a graphic designer. Now it's a no-go for all three."

This brought the poor cashier nearly to tears. "My goodness, you poor soul! Well, you may have noticed the sign on the door, but in case you didn't, we are hiring."

Michelle tilted her head to one side. "Are you? What would the job entail? I'm more of a behind-the-scenes worker, not too keen on dealing with the public."

"We have a stocker position available. The most you'd deal with people would be to maybe point them in the direction of what they're looking for. Otherwise, you'd be putting stuff on shelves, rearranging things that have been shuffled around, keeping track of boxes that come in off the delivery trucks, inventory, that sort of thing. Is that something you'd be interested in doing?"

She got more excited with each task the lady listed. Michelle loved physical work, and this sounded like a good way to stay in shape while making money. "Absolutely! Where do I sign up?"

Voices carried from a room down the hallway. A pretty blonde lady and an older woman with shiny gray hair walked past. "It looks like Alice has just finished up an interview with someone who was interested in the cashier position. I'll go get you an application, and I'm sure she will be available to talk with you in just a few minutes."

As she turned to leave, Michelle called out, "Oh, by the way - I was too overheated to pay attention as I walked in – what is the name of this place?"

With the proud smile of a happy employee, she replied, "Seahorse Treasures."

Chapter 10

As the door swung shut, Alice called out, "See you in the morning, Nina!" Hoping for a chance to sit and breathe a moment, she slowly made her way toward the back. Leslie thwarted her plan when she met her at the hallway entrance and said in a sing-songy voice, "We've got another one!"

Alice took a long, slow breath as she watched the application in Leslie's hands wave back and forth like the flag of a foreigner. She didn't know if she had it in her to meet and interview another stranger today. She never talked about it, but the burden of the part she played in determining someone's future overwhelmed her at times.

She stalled, taking a seat behind the front counter and asking Leslie, "What's this one's story?"

Leslie handed over the application and answered, "She's out of a job as of today, her fiancée just broke off their engagement, and she walked two miles in the hot sun to get here. Well, she actually just stumbled across us while buying some water, but still, it's impressive."

Alice's eyes widened. "Another brokenhearted soul? Don't tell me she's not from around here."

Leslie nodded. "She's from Georgia. Moved here to start a new life with her fiancé."

A cold chill came over Alice. Two jobless, deserted women in one day? It didn't seem feasible.

Looking over the application, Alice noted, "This one's young. To me, that means she might not stick around long. Especially if she's on her own, she'll be looking for something better in the future." She put the papers down and huffed out a breath. "But we could use her for as long as she needs us."

Leslie gave her a knowing smile. "You're almost too kind, Alice. But I agree. Temporary help is better than no help at all. And it's always nice to know you're making a difference in someone's life."

Alice looked down the hallway and sighed. She didn't want to get up from her seat. She had just caught her breath again after saying goodbye to Nina, and walking to the office would take it away once more. But she didn't want to interview the girl out here in public, so she had no choice. Carefully, she rose from her perch and took deliberate steps.

She paused with her hand on the doorknob to her office, breathing in and out a few times to give herself a head start in the race against her own heart. It seemed more and more pointless to run from the inevitable, but right now, she had an interview to conduct, and she wasn't one to shirk her duties.

Giving her best smile in spite of the situation, Alice greeted Michelle. "Hi, I'm Alice. It's nice to meet you."

Michelle stood and took Alice's hand. "So nice to meet you. I'm so glad I came by here today."

Alice's breaths shortened as she shuffled to her chair. "Forgive my breathlessness, dear. I've got heart problems, and there's nothing I can do about it." She again offered a shining smile to show she had accepted her situation, giving Michelle permission to do the same.

"Oh," Michelle began, unsure of how to respond.

Before she could formulate a condolence, Alice continued, "I see you were scheduled to start work at the paper today. I'm sorry that didn't work out for you. It's a shame what's happening to newspapers these days. I've been an avid reader of The Pelican Pica for as long as I can remember, and I'm sad to see them go. But, life goes on. You need a job, and we need workers. I assume Leslie has gone over the description of duties with you?"

"Yes," answered Michelle, "and it sounds perfect for me. I love to keep busy, move around a lot, and the job at the paper, though it would have been in my field of study, wouldn't have let me do that. I'm actually glad to have the chance to do something other than sit at a desk all day."

Alice grinned. "Way to go. Put a positive spin on it. Now, tell me, how long do you think you'll be in town? Leslie explained your situation, and I'm wondering if you are just looking to save up enough to move away or if you think Orange Beach is for you?"

Michelle emphatically stated, "I'm staying here. I adore this town, and I love the ocean. Despite the circumstances, I'm thrilled that I wound up here, and I have no plans to leave."

That satisfied Alice. "Great! Can you start tomorrow?"

"Yes! Oh, thank you so much." Michelle stood to shake Alice's hand once more. "I am so looking forward to working with you."

Alice laughed heartily. "I appreciate your enthusiasm. We have another woman starting tomorrow as a cashier, and she has also just been through a difficult breakup. Maybe you two can help each other through this."

A look of compassion came over Michelle's face. "Maybe," she said with a sympathetic tone.

Alice sat back down. "I would walk you out, but I need to sit still for a while. I'll see you tomorrow."

As Michelle said goodbye and shut the door behind her, Alice smiled to herself. It looked like her house might be getting more than one tenant.

Chapter 11

Nina sat on the sand thirty minutes before her first shift at Seahorse Treasures. She held her eyes shut and let the sea breeze calm her nerves. No matter what happened, as long as she stayed in Orange Beach, she would have the comfort of this coastal caress. It strengthened her like a motivational speaker, though its message came through silence.

After five minutes of meditation, she opened her eyes and looked around, blinking as if coming out of a dream. The clouds cast the world in pale gray, but the beauty of the ocean and all its accessories shone with an intrinsic light that even night failed to dim. Nina took a sip of her espresso, hoping to spark her own inner light. If she could do so by osmosis, then sitting here a few moments longer would accomplish it.

Nina stared and sipped, her mind cleared of all thoughts. Starting fresh certainly offered this benefit. Everything in her life was now an unknown. She couldn't worry when she didn't even have a grain to build a pearl around.

A car door slamming across the street in the parking lot of her new workplace caught Nina's attention. She turned to see a young woman with waist-length brown hair walking toward the door. Nina glanced at her watch. The store would open in ten minutes, so she stood to dust off the sand and head on over.

Alice had told her to go around back and knock on the Employees Only door if she arrived prior to opening time. As she approached the back of the building, she was surprised to see the young lady knocking on said door. Before she could question her, the door opened and Leslie appeared.

"Hi Michelle, Nina. Come on in and I'll get you started."

Nina followed Michelle into the building. Though Nina stood at an above average height of 5'9", Michelle struck her as rather short. Nina seemed to tower nearly a foot over her.

Leslie led them into the office. She turned to face them and said, "Nina, this is Michelle. Michelle, Nina."

They shook hands and said the obligatory nice-to-meet-yous. Then Leslie reached into a desk drawer and pulled out two keys. She handed one to each of the women. "These are in case you are the ones to open and close for the day. Shifts vary, so it won't always be one of you, but keep these on you every day anyway." She reached into her back pocket and produced two laminated cards. "These are your time cards. Clock in behind the checkout counter. There's a slot next to it where you can keep them. Follow me and we'll get you clocked in for the day."

Once they had scanned the bar codes on their cards, Leslie sent Michelle to the stock room to train with someone named Barry. Nina stayed at the counter and learned to work the cash register. She had used a similar one at the restaurant, so it didn't take her long to grasp. Then Leslie covered the return policy, the preferred greeting to customers, and what to do in an emergency. Within fifteen minutes, Nina had her first customer. Leslie stayed by her side to supervise. The transaction went smoothly.

No other customers had entered the shop yet, so Leslie gave Nina a tour of the floor. "Take any extra time you have between customers today to familiarize yourself with the layout of the store. You're gonna get plenty of questions about where to find certain things. It's fine to tell people that today is your first day and you're not sure, but now's a good time to start memorizing where things are kept.

Nina felt a clash of pressure and peace. She wanted to perform well on her first day and learn as much as she could, but she tended to put stress on herself to be perfect all at once. Though she knew that wasn't possible, it did seem that things were coming naturally to her so far. The layout of the store made sense, with swimsuits next to beach towels and umbrellas, clothing next to jewelry and sunglasses, and sunscreen next to over-the-counter meds, so it would be easy to burn their locations into her memory.

Leslie said, "I'm going to step into the back to make a phone call. If you need me, I'll be in the office."

"Okay, thanks." Nina continued to walk slowly about the place, studying each object and its position relative to other items. As she browsed, she thought about the conversation she'd had with Alice regarding her house yesterday. Alice wanted her to move in and take care of the place as soon as her paid time at the condo ran out. Nina could hardly believe this miracle, for there was no other word to describe it. She hadn't even expected to find a job this easily, but to be given lodging as well just seemed too good to be true. To top it off, Alice didn't even want to charge her rent. She said if Nina could just pay the utilities, that would be enough. Alice felt that Nina would be helping her out by making sure the house and yard stayed in good condition, but Nina hardly thought that would be much work, certainly not enough to earn what she would've paid in rent. She didn't want to protest, though. Her only question to Alice had been, "Are you sure?"

Nina heard a door open and saw Michelle turning the corner to the hallway. As she walked out of sight, Leslie called out, "Nina, could you come here, please? Alice wants to talk to both of you."

Nina walked into the office to find a smiling Alice seated behind her desk. "Sit, please. I have a proposition for the two of you."

Equal amounts of dread and anticipation filled Nina. She glanced at Michelle, who didn't seem worried at all. A big smile covered her face, and excitement radiated from her. Ah, to be young and full of hope again! Nina both envied and pitied her.

Looking at Nina first, Alice began, "Nina needed a place to live, and she has agreed to stay in my old house behind the shop. I need someone to take care of it, as it belonged to my dear late husband and me and means a lot to me. I'm no longer in good enough health to maintain the place. I've offered to let Nina stay there rent-free, paying only utilities. I understand that you, Michelle, will also soon be out of a place to live. So, Nina, if it's alright with you, I'd like to see if Michelle would be interested in being your roommate."

Nina hadn't expected this. She wasn't crazy about the idea of living with a stranger, but she also wasn't in any position to refuse. So instead of answering outright, Nina turned to Michelle and said, "If I may ask, what has happened with where you were staying?"

Without a shred of hesitation, Michelle replied, "My fiancée called off our wedding that was just two weeks away. I have to get out of the rental house by our former wedding date." Then she nodded her head as if to say, "Yeah, he's that awful, and it's that bad."

"Oh, wow." Nina's heart ached for the girl. Overcome with empathy, she offered, "Of course you can be my roommate."

"Wonderful, then. Michelle, do you accept? Same terms as Nina?" Alice looked at her with eyebrows raised in anticipation.

Michelle's grin widened. "I would love to! You have a deal." She stood to shake Alice's hand, her short frame not having very far to rise from the seat. Then she turned to Nina and put a hand on her arm. "Thank you for letting me live with you. I'm a good roommate. I keep things clean and don't make much noise."

Nina smiled at her description of herself. "You're welcome. Oh, by the way, I was just dumped by my husband of fifteen years, so we have some pain in common."

Michelle gasped. Her big blue eyes popped as she whispered, "My word!"

Alice interjected, "I think you two will have a lot to talk about." She pulled two keys attached to seahorse key rings out of an envelope. "Here are the keys to the house. I'll walk you through later today, but those are yours to keep."

Both ladies thanked her. Then they went back to their prospective posts and finished their shifts. Alice was waiting for them by the time clock at the end of the day. She jingled a key ring matching the ones she had given them earlier. "Let's go check out your new place."

Chapter 12

The three women walked the sandy path to Alice's house. A sprawling vine off to the side with purple flowers prompted Nina to ask, "What's this plant called?"

"Railroad vine," answered Alice, "also beach morning glory. It's great at keeping the dunes from shifting all over the place. I know morning glories are considered invasive inland, where they choke out gardens, but here in the sand, they're helpful."

She continued her nature lesson, "And this succulent vine you see here is sea purslane. Like railroad vine, it can survive dry conditions, and it prevents sand shifting. This little beauty is also edible and a good source of vitamin C."

Nina and Michelle said, "Ah," in unison.

"You won't have to do any maintenance on these. They can survive almost anything."

Nina hoped she shared that trait. She had taken the most severe blow of her life, yet here she stood. She had the two things she needed most, a job and shelter. With those bases covered, she felt free to flower.

They approached a moderately sized home on stilts surrounded by palm trees and flowering bushes. Alice saw Michelle running her fingers through the palm fronds and said, "I'll give you a rundown of plant care later. For now, I just want to show you the house."

Alice stopped at the base of the wooden steps leading up to the door and sighed. "This is the main reason I can't take care of the place any longer. Girls, this is going to take my breath away for quite some time."

Michelle stepped in front of Alice and offered, "If you'd like, you could just wait here and we could go up. I hate for you to suffer just to show us around."

Hating to admit defeat but hearing the wisdom in her words, Alice thought out loud, "What if one of you calls me on your phone and we do a video chat once you're inside? You can point the camera at your view as you walk, and I'll mention anything I see that needs discussing?"

Nina pulled out her phone. "I'll do it." Then she followed slowly behind a spry Michelle, who leapt up the steps like an excited pup. As Michelle put the key in the lock, Nina started the call.

They stepped into the mud room, or in this case, the sand room. His and hers beach towels were folded neatly across a long rail, and a beach umbrella rested upside down in the corner. Shelves for sandy shoes lined one wall. Alice said, "You can remove your shoes and put them on the shelf if you want to avoid getting the floor sandy. It's up to you."

She looked at Michelle, who shrugged and reached down to slip off her sandals. Nina did the same. Barefoot, they continued into the kitchen, which was bright and had plenty of counter space. A big island stood in the middle of the open room, and to the left, a large dining area wrapped around to the space adjacent to the sand room. "As you can see, you have lots of room for preparing meals and eating them. Fred and I spent a lot of time in the kitchen, and we loved having coffee and chatting at all hours right there at that dining table."

"It's beautiful," said Michelle, running her hand across the white and gray marbled surface. She stopped at the window over the sink and took in the view of the pond in the backyard. "I'm going to really enjoy this."

Nina pointed the phone at the living room, which was open to the kitchen and dining room. Three beige couches formed a nice seating area, leaving the fourth end open for a view of the big television. White shelves held large seashells, and Alice commented, "Fred and I found each and every one of those shells on our sunrise walks. I won't have any of those artificial ones in my house. I can remember the day when we found each shell, what we talked about, how the weather was ... Oh, how I do go on. Just know that your décor is one of a kind."

"I appreciate that. It adds a touch of intrigue," Nina commented.

"Now, on to the bedrooms," Alice recovered. She got a little misty-eyed thinking of beachcombing with Fred. She sure hoped that in the afterlife, they could hunt for treasures on the beaches of heaven. Her heart warmed at the thought that she wouldn't have to wait very long now.

In the hallway, a large landscape painting caught Nina's attention. She stopped to get a closer look. Pastel pinks and purples kissed the sky over a bright red setting sun. Touches of cloud wisps edged in gold so bright it almost hurt her eyes fanned across the expanse. The white breakers glowed with colorful reflection, as did the seagulls lining the beach as if gathered in reverence of the day's final performance.

"Nina? Everything okay?" Alice's voice reminded her she had been distracted.

"It's ok. I'm just admiring this painting. Do you know who the artist is?"

"No, I don't. Fred bought it at an estate sale. It is a beautiful work of art. The person who painted it knew how to paint light, that's for sure."

"Mmhmm," Nina agreed. She turned the phone toward the doorway with a waiting Michelle in it and caught up. "Sorry," she whispered, but Michelle waved off her apology as unnecessary.

"This first doorway is to one of three bedrooms," Alice narrated. It was a little small, but there was enough room to walk around the bed on all sides. A dresser with a big mirror sat against the wall facing the doorway, greeting whoever entered with the visual equivalent of a mockingbird.

"The room at the end of the hallway is the master. Nina, since I offered you the place first, this can be your room." Nina glanced at Michelle, who nodded emphatically. If she turned out to be this agreeable about everything, she would be a dream housemate.

As Nina panned the camera about the pretty pale blue space, Alice had remarkably little to say about the room she and Fred had shared. Perhaps the memories were too painful.

"The master comes with an attached bath, but as you'll see in a minute, Michelle, so does the next bedroom. Also, it's larger than the first."

Michelle got excited and ran to her would-be room, leaving Nina to make the decision of whether to take Alice with her to see the bathroom or direct her toward the runaway. Slightly annoyed, she chose the latter.

Noticeably larger than the first bedroom, this second guest room had a view of the backyard and a queen-size bed. The mauve décor complemented Michelle's skin tone and hair color, and she looked more than content as she turned slowly in a circle to take it all in. Through her smile finally came the words, "It's perfect."

"I'm glad you like it. On your way back down the hallway, notice the first door on your right. That's the guest bath. If you will go out the back door, I'll meet you around there and show you the rest of the yard."

They headed out onto a nice deck and saw a well-maintained backyard full of palm trees and a few plants Nina recognized, like hibiscus and climbing shell vine. A fountain circulated the water in the center of a pond just beyond the yard. It all looked delightfully tropical.

Alice rounded the corner of the house slowly, her breathing ragged. "Could I trouble you for a chair?" she asked. Michelle rushed over with a canvas camping chair from the deck and Alice let herself fall into it. "Whew! Getting old is not for the faint of heart!" She laughed at her own joke, which managed to elicit merely smiles of pity from her two tenants. "Tell you what. The plants are good for now. How about I give you their care instructions tomorrow at work? I need to catch my breath before I drive home."

Ever helpful Michelle offered, "Do you want us to go get your car? Nina could drive you home and I could follow in my vehicle."

Alice laughed. "Oh, I've seen your car. You're not going to be driving it out here."

"Huh?" Michelle didn't know whether to be offended or just confused.

"You'd need a big four-wheel-drive vehicle to get across this sand. I always parked my car at Seahorse Treasures and walked home, unless the weather was just dreadful, and then Fred would pick me up in his Jeep Wrangler." Looking at their astonished faces, Alice said, "I'm sorry. I probably should've mentioned that. I hope it's not a dealbreaker?"

Nina and Michelle both shook their heads adamantly. "We don't mind walking," said Michelle, the self-appointed spokesperson for the pair. Nina, however, agreed.

"Great, then. Move in as soon as you're ready. I understand you'll probably want to stay where you are until your time is up, but just know that I'm okay with you moving in sooner if you like."

The rumble of an engine approached, and they all turned their heads to see a Toyota 4Runner rolling with ease toward the front of the house. "That would be Barry," explained Alice. "He is so thoughtful. I told him I'd be showing you two the house today, and he has taken it upon himself to give me a ride, I see."

A door shut and a man with wavy dark brown hair that fell in layers nearly to his shoulders appeared. He had the golden skin of a beach dweller. "Miss Alice, are you ready to go?" he asked before his gaze fell upon Nina. He took her in with his mysterious eyes. Even in her current state of low self-confidence, she could tell he was completely awestruck.

Picking up on the obvious, Alice said, "Barry, I don't think I've introduced you to Nina yet. Nina, this is Barry. He's been working in the stockroom with Michelle all day, so you probably haven't even seen him."

Smiling at the compliment of his admiring stare, Nina offered her hand. "Nice to meet you, Barry."

He shook his head almost imperceptibly to clear it. Coming to his senses, he took her hand and said, "Likewise, Nina." He released her hand slowly, as if reluctant to break contact. But he continued to look into her eyes.

Michelle sensed that he might be making Nina uncomfortable, so she jumped in front of her and said, "Alrighty, then. Alice, can we help you to Barry's vehicle?"

Alice started to rise, but Barry rushed over to lend a hand. He stooped to put his arm around her and lead her as slowly as she needed to be led. He smiled at Nina as they passed, and as soon as the engine started, Michelle burst into laughter. "I think someone has a crush on you."

Nina replied, "Yeah, I got that vibe. But he's young, isn't he?"

"Thirty-four." Michelle wagged her eyebrows at Nina.

"Really? Wow, he looks like he could be mid-twenties, easily."

"Ahhh, are you interested?" Michelle teased.

"What, me? No, no I'm swearing off men for the foreseeable future."

Michelle gave her a doubtful look. "Well, you're gonna have a not-so-secret admirer on your hands, I'm afraid. I can just hear him now – 'Is she seeing anyone? Do you think she'd go out with me? Maybe we could double date.' Really, you might have to go out with him just to get him off my back."

Nina let out a long, ragged sigh. "My divorce isn't even final yet. Give me some time." Then she walked off toward the shop, not giving Michelle the chance to argue. The thought of being with anyone but Donovan was alien to her. Though her hurt and anger were enough to propel her toward the higher ground of being over him, there were so many things she hadn't even dreamed of having to deal with, chief among them dating someone new. She had just completed her first day of work, something else she hadn't envisioned. She'd also just accepted a new home that came with a new roommate. She had definitely had enough "firsts" for one day.

Chapter 13

Nina stood in the center of the condo, looking around the room at her very few belongings. She would like to have had all of her things from home, but the pain of going back to retrieve them wasn't worth the continued ownership. Nina accepted the idea of starting fresh in every area. She would be okay with shopping for cheaper clothing and shoes and with building a new wardrobe slowly as funds allowed. The garments might not match the quality of her old garb, but they would be purchased with money she had earned, enhancing their value.

She spent some time weighing the option of moving into Alice's house immediately. The thought appealed to her. Leaving the last thing Donovan had paid for behind would mean becoming independent sooner. However, once she moved into the house, she would be responsible for utilities. Staying in the condo another week meant saving money.

Her phone rang. A glance at the screen revealed Michelle's number. Nina answered, "Hey, Michelle."

"Hey girl. I don't know about you, but I'm ready to get out of my ex-man's rental. So I'm gonna go ahead and move into Alice's today."

Nina smiled to herself. "I considered the same. But I think I'm gonna hang around for the rest of the week and enjoy the free electricity."

Michelle replied, "I hear ya. Yeah, I thought about taking advantage of it, too, but I just can't stomach the idea of him driving by, seeing my car out front, and thinking he's doing me a great favor, you know?"

"I get that." Nina didn't have to worry about that with Donovan. He'd made it pretty clear with his last comment that she wouldn't even be crossing his mind again. She could enjoy the beach knowing their ties had been irreconcilably severed.

A knock at the door jolted her. "Michelle, I'm going to have to let you go. Someone is at the door."

"Okay, no problem. See you at work."

Nina peered through the peephole and saw a man in a suit holding an envelope. As soon as she opened the door, he asked, "Nina Carter?"

"Yes?" she replied warily.

The man handed her the envelope. "You have been served." With that, he turned and walked away.

Nina tore into the envelope. Divorce papers stared her in the face, the final nail in their marital coffin.

Just a few days ago, the sight would have elicited tears of grief from her heavy heart. Now, she surprised herself as a laugh escaped her parted lips. She leaned against the doorframe and suddenly found herself caught up in a maelstrom of laughter. When she found her breath, she wiped her eyes and said to herself, "It's not funny. Oh, it's not funny." Then she doubled over and erupted once more.

As soon as she could stand up straight, she shut the door behind her and headed toward the balcony. She grabbed a pen and a bottle of coconut pineapple juice on the way. A lounge chair she had set up on the sand at the base of the steps looked like it had been prepared precisely for this moment. She leaned back, sipped her tropical drink, and read through the legal jargon until she reached the blank line requiring her signature. Donovan's line had, of course, already been filled with his sweeping pen strokes. For just a moment, Nina admired their elegance. Then, she thought of how lucky she was to be released from a man who no longer wanted her, and she signed her name with gusto. Her pen strokes, though not as beautifully scribed as his, were filled with more enthusiasm and long, liberating tendrils.

The deed done, Nina clicked her pen shut. A smile came, unforced and unstoppable. As the sea breeze caressed her face, she felt as safe and content as a small child. The weight of her broken heart shifted in the wind and blew away like the ashes of something unrecognizable.

Inside the envelope with the divorce papers was a business card of a law office, with the words, "Please mail papers to:" above the address. Evidently, Donovan was eager for the divorce to be finalized as soon as possible, because he had anticipated the fact that vacationing Nina wouldn't have an envelope and stamp on hand. He, or perhaps the lawyer, had included a return envelope with postage already in place.

Nina didn't waste any time. She sealed the papers in the envelope, wrote her future return address in the top left corner, and marched to the nearest mailbox. She had no clue where the post office was, but she imagined it would be further than she could walk. In hopes that whoever owned this mailbox wouldn't mind, she shoved the envelope inside and raised the flag. Hopefully, the mailman hadn't already run and would pick it up today before the person checked their box.

Chapter 14

Michelle threw the last of her bags into the back of Barry's 4Runner. "Ready to roll," she announced. It felt weird being unable to drive her own car up to the house, but that seemed a small price to pay for the rent-free lodging.

True to the gentleman Alice said he was, Barry had offered to help Michelle move in. Michelle had a feeling that he would do the same for Nina. As if on cue, he asked, "So where's Nina? She moving in today, too?"

Michelle cast him a sideways smirk from the passenger seat. "I had a feeling you'd ask that. She'll be moving in after next week." She giggled a bit.

"What's funny about that?"

She punched him lightly in the arm. "Oh, Barry, you wouldn't make a good poker player. It's so obvious you've got a crush on her."

His face turned red and his voice serious as he asked, "What makes you say that?"

He stared straight ahead while driving, so he didn't see the playful look in her eyes as she answered, "Oh, I don't know, maybe the way your eyes shone the other day when you met her. You couldn't take them off of her. It's like you were suspended in time. Or maybe it's the fact that your cheeks are bright red right now. Probably both."

Barry shook his head. "She's out of my league, bigtime." He pulled up as close as possible to the base of the steps and turned off the engine.

"You're too modest, Barry. Look at you. I don't know if you've noticed, but you're pretty darn cute. I'd date you if you weren't so old."

The shocked look on his face elicited a fit of laughter from Michelle. "Come on, I didn't mean to make you uncomfortable. I'm just trying to build your self-esteem."

"Oookaay," he said slowly. Having no good response to that, he got out of the vehicle and began unloading her luggage.

As he placed bags on the stairs, Michelle grabbed them and lugged them to the top of the steps. She had no problem lifting heavy objects. She really had just needed the ride.

Once he had unloaded the last bag, he walked it up the steps to the deck. Michelle had already carted most of the luggage inside. She stepped out of the doorway and announced, "I can take it from here. Thank you so much. If you ever need my help with anything … Hey, maybe I could drop subtle hints to Nina about how awesome you are!"

Barry stared at the floor. The redness hadn't had a chance to fully vanish from his face, and now she'd caused a fresh flow. He didn't know Nina's situation or why a woman as captivating as her could be single. He only knew he was enamored with her. Finally, he brought his gaze up to meet Michelle's. "That'd be great."

Michelle smiled. "Will do. I'll let you know how it goes."

With that, Barry bounded down the steps and left. Michelle went inside to unpack. Most of her stuff could stay in her bedroom and bathroom. Kevin had kept the gifts they'd received at their shower, like the coffeemaker, the toaster, and other items meant for their new home. Fortunately, Alice's house came furnished with all the appliances they'd need.

Michelle thrilled at the prospect of playing matchmaker. Although Nina said she needed time, and certainly she'd want to finalize her divorce first, there was no harm in her getting to know Barry in the meantime. She would be sure to mention him a lot. If she could be sly enough, she might even manage to get the three of them together for lunch or other outings. No one would consider it a date if she was there.

She had to go about this carefully, however. Nina would run if she smelled a setup. This would be easier if Michelle hadn't already teased her about Barry's admiration. She would have to take her time and not overdo it.

After hanging the last dress in her closet, Michelle headed out to the back deck. She lounged in a chair and listened to the seagulls laugh. A great blue heron stalked a fish in the pond. She watched in amusement as it waded slowly, then stood motionless, patient until its target reached the perfect spot for the harvest. The heron stabbed so quickly that the prey didn't have a chance to flee. The bird guzzled the fish like a tasty drink.

Michelle took notes on the heron's hunt. Approach slowly, wait patiently and still enough to avoid detection, strike only when the moment is perfect, or else risk losing your goal altogether. "Got it," she said aloud. "Thanks, my feathered friend."

Chapter 15

The weekend had arrived, bringing with it a steady flow of customers. Nina hadn't sat down all morning. The line at the register remained at least three people long.

It amazed her how many people bought sunscreen. That seemed like something you should buy ahead of time and bring with you, but evidently, a lot of beachgoers doubled as procrastinators. Several who purchased sunscreen were already lobster red and also bought aloe vera gel. Nina had to resist the urge to lecture them on the importance of sun protection and the danger of skin cancer. She needed to keep this job, and if people were obstinate enough to allow themselves to burn, they probably wouldn't listen anyway.

At about 11:30, the line dwindled to one last person. She approached the counter with a beach umbrella in hand and said, "Hey, I think you're out of sunscreen. The guy in front of me grabbed the last bottle."

"Okay, thanks for letting me know. I'll see if we have any more in stock. Did you need some?"

"No, I brought four bottles from home. I didn't want to chance it, you know?"

Nina smiled. "I understand. I wish more people were proactive about protecting their skin."

The lady said, "I come from two generations of skin cancer, so I tend to overdo it with the sunscreen. You can't be too careful."

"Amen," agreed Nina. She finished checking the customer out and walked over to the shelf to double check. Sure enough, not one bottle remained. She walked behind the desk and took a much needed load off. From the chair, she reached for the phone.

Michelle answered, "Stockroom."

"Hey Michelle. We need a restock on sunscreen. Can you help me out?"

She heard rustling and mumbling, followed by, "We'll get it out to you in just a minute."

Nina shut her eyes and leaned back in the chair. This had been the busiest day she'd experienced yet. She hoped Leslie would be back from her doctor's appointment soon so she could take a lunch break.

The sound of a box hitting the floor brought Nina's eyes open. Barry stooped over an open cardboard container. He filled the shelf with several types of sunscreen. Nina looked around for Michelle, but she must have been busy with something else and sent Barry in her place.

Ordinarily, Nina would have approached a coworker for small talk. However, she felt the need to keep her distance in this situation. She didn't want her friendly intentions to be misread.

Barry finished stocking and picked up the empty box. He turned toward Nina at the front desk. He wanted to avoid awkwardness, so he simply waved and smiled from this distance.

She returned both, and he felt his heart leap within his chest. Before he could embarrass himself or face rejection, he walked back through the door to the stockroom.

Michelle was waiting for him. "How'd it go?"

"I waved and smiled, she did the same. End of story." Barry moved past her and busied himself with boxes.

"You didn't even speak? Not even a hello?" The disappointment was evident in her voice.

"I'm lying low, Michelle. I'm not a forward kind of guy, and I don't want to blow this."

"I agree we have to be subtle, but you gotta work with me here, Barry. I need you to at least get out a simple 'hello'."

Barry gave her a slightly annoyed look. "Maybe later." His eyes suggested no room for discussion.

Michelle threw up her hands and went back to work. Perhaps this particular matchmaking job would be more of a chore than a joy. She reminded herself of the heron. How often did it get to eat? Probably not every time it tried. Most likely only when it persisted despite several failed attempts.

Chapter 16

Moving day had finally arrived. Though Nina had only a couple of bags, Michelle had offered to pick her up at the condo so she wouldn't have to lug them down the street.

Nina peered through the curtain as Michelle pulled into a parking spot. She opened the door and wheeled her baggage outside, leaving the key on the dresser. Her nerves caused her hands to quiver and her stomach to cramp with a mixture of excitement and a sense of finality, a bit of unease at the unknown. She hadn't eaten breakfast or even had coffee because of it.

She put her bags in Michelle's open trunk. As she opened the door, Michelle pulled down her big sunglasses and said, "Hey, roomie! Happy first day of your new life!"

Clearly, Michelle had already caffeinated. Nina could only manage a weak, "Thanks," as she buckled her seatbelt.

Taking note of her less than enthusiastic tone and her trembling hands, Michelle said, "I hope you're not upset that you have to live with me. I promise I'm clean and quiet."

Nina laughed lightly. "No, not at all. It's just a pretty significant day. I don't always do so well with change. My mind is ready for it; my body just hasn't gotten the message yet."

"Understood." She backed out of the parking lot and onto the street before mentioning, "Hey, Barry is gonna give us a ride from work out to the house so you don't have to wheel your bags through all that sand."

"Okay." Nina didn't even argue. The thought of dragging heavy things in her current state made her more agreeable to the idea.

They pulled into the backside of Seahorse Treasures, finding Barry already there with an open trunk. Nina and Michelle each took a bag. As they approached, Barry reached forward for the luggage and said, "Good morning, you two! Happy moving day." He smiled as he accepted the bag from Nina without a lingering stare or a brush of his hand against hers. He took the other one from Michelle. "I hope you're hungry, because I brought breakfast."

"Yes. Wow. Thank you," Nina replied.

"No problem. Shall we go?"

Dual nods from the ladies sent him to the driver's seat. Michelle took the passenger's seat so Nina wouldn't feel uncomfortable. She then proceeded to talk for the entire short drive.

Barry pulled to a stop near the steps. "You guys grab breakfast, and I'll grab the bags." A minute later, the three sat around the dining room table with a spread of sausage biscuits, blueberry muffins, and coffee before them.

As they ate and chatted, Nina noticed that Barry's demeanor had totally changed. He didn't seem nervous at all, and any signs of a crush that he had so obviously exhibited before had disappeared. She wondered if he had given up hope. He seemed suddenly gifted at small talk and lighthearted joking. Maybe he had been all along and she didn't know it. They really hadn't spoken, other than saying, "Hello, nice to meet you," on the day he came to pick up Alice.

Michelle finished her biscuit and asked, "Barry, I was hoping I could get you to look at the bottom step out back. It seems a bit wonky. Can you come check it out?"

"Sure," he answered. They walked away, leaving Nina alone at the table.

Michelle shut the door behind them and turned to Barry. "Who are you?"

"Pardon?" he asked.

"This newfound confidence, this not staring puppy-dog-eyed at Nina, this … this normal guy! What's gotten into you?"

He shrugged his shoulders. "I'm done."

Michelle's jaw dropped. "You're done? What, like a switch, you can just turn it off?"

He heaved a sigh. "Oh, I'm still fascinated with Nina. I just decided not to dwell on it."

Michelle mumbled incoherently, staring with expectation of further explanation.

"Look, if I let myself get caught up in my feelings, I'm gonna bumble around like an idiot. I've got to be able to be around her to get to know her. I'm just kinda okay with that potentially not happening. It's the only way I can continue to function. And if there is going to be even a grain of hope for us, I have to be someone she feels comfortable talking to, not a creep who stares and waves from a distance."

A light came on in Michelle's eyes. "Ah, I get it. You're making sense. Go on."

Barry shrugged again, crossing his arms in front of his chest. "That's really all there is to it. Now, am I going to look at this step or what?"

Michelle blinked as if she'd forgotten her reason for calling him out here. "Oh, there is no step. I mean, there is obviously a step. If not, that would be a problem; but the step is fine. I just needed to get you alone for a minute."

"Get me alone, huh? I thought I was too old for you," he said with a gleam in his eye.

She punched him in the arm. "Come on back inside, geezer."

He laughed heartily as she opened the door. The sound reached Nina's ears. She noticed what a pleasing tone he possessed. One thing she could not tolerate in a person was a fake or irritating laugh, and he had neither.

"How's the step?" Nina asked.

"It's fine. It just had a loose screw," Barry answered. Michelle coughed to avoid laughing. Nina didn't notice.

"That's good. Thank you for checking it out."

"No problem. Well, I guess I should get out of here. Ladies, it's been fun. We should do it again sometime." With that, he exited rather quickly.

Michelle took Nina by the arm and said, "Hey, let's go check out the pond. We've got a lot of wildlife out there. It's pretty cool to watch."

Nina had hoped to get settled in first, but before she could protest, Michelle dragged her to the deck and down the steps. They stood in front of the water. Michelle pointed out a family of turtles sunning on a log. A heron stalked prey near the opposite shore.

"If we stay quiet, more animals will come," Michelle suggested. So, they stood in silence, listening to the noises of nature, waiting for new sounds to surface. Their state of serenity was soon interrupted by a strange howl.

They looked at each other in alarm. The howl came again, this time more urgent. Michelle pointed to the shed in the lot behind the pond. "I think it's coming from there."

They began walking around the shore toward the shed. An awful clamoring suddenly sounded inside the structure. Then all was quiet.

A man probably in his thirties with short but shaggy brown hair rounded the corner of the building. He had a Jack Nicholson smile that Nina found discomfiting. He met them halfway and explained, "Don't worry. It's just my old hound dog wanting to get out. I had to put her in there because she broke a leg and needs to stay still and let it heal. Vet's orders."

The creepy smile never left his face as he approached them with his hand extended for a shake. "Mike Waters. Nice to meet you."

Though neither of them really wanted to, they shook his hand out of politeness and told him their names. He looked back and forth between them several times before glancing back at the shed. "Don't worry about ole Gertrude in there. She's got plenty of food and water and a nice bed. She just doesn't know how to appreciate it. Just like a woman." He cackled way too long and hard at his own unfunny joke, causing Nina to suppress a shudder.

Neither of the women really knew what to say to end this awkward exchange and escape. Both were relieved when Mike finally stopped laughing, took a deep breath, and said, "Well, let me get back to her. She probably needs to go to the bathroom by now. That's one thing her luxury suite didn't include." He grinned an impossibly wide grin and waved goodbye.

They walked quickly back to the house. Once they'd gone inside and shut the door, Michelle turned to Nina. "Alice didn't mention this house came with a psycho neighbor!"

Nina shivered. "Alice is so sweet, she probably thinks he's charming. I'm sure she would've warned us if he was actually dangerous." She said this as much to reassure herself as to comfort Michelle, but she didn't know how much she believed it.

"I'm looking him up online just to make sure." Michelle retreated to her room to do research.

Nina took this opportunity to head to her room and unpack. "I'll be in here getting settled if you find anything."

"Ok."

As she looked about the room, she noticed a few nails on the otherwise blank walls. "If only I had some art to hang." Then she remembered the painting in the hallway. There was no reason to leave it out there. She approached it with respect, handling the large gold frame with care as she lifted it off the nail. No glass offered protection. It merely rested in the grooves of the frame. Slowly, carefully, she reached the nail on the wall across from her bed and hung it in its new home.

She had gotten all of her clothing either folded or hung by the time Michelle finally entered the room and announced, "Mike Waters has no social media of any kind. I can't find a number or address for him. It's like he doesn't exist."

"Unless that isn't his real name," Nina offered.

Michelle shivered. "I don't like this." Her big blue eyes looked childish with innocence and fear, pulling at Nina's heartstrings.

"Let me call Alice." Nina dialed her number and put her on speakerphone.

"Hey, girls! How are you liking your new place?"

Alice sounded so happy that Nina almost hated to ask. "Hey, Alice. The place is great. We were just wondering what you could tell us about our neighbor, Mike Waters."

"Ah, you've met Crazy Mike," she observed. "Well, don't worry, he's harmless."

Nina and Michelle shared a look. "But you admit he's crazy," Michelle commented.

"He's a bit eccentric. That huge grin doesn't help matters. But as far as I know, the weirdest thing he does is collect frogs."

Nina's eyes widened. "Frogs? Why?"

"Oh, he says he likes to keep them as pets. I've seen him down by the pond at dusk catching them before, but I didn't see any harm in it, so I left him alone. Did you girls see him frog hunting? Do you want me to ask him to stop?"

"No, he wasn't frog hunting. His dog was making a lot of noise inside the shed, so we walked over to check it out. That's how we met."

"Hmm, I didn't know he had a dog. He must've gotten her recently. Ah well, I wouldn't worry about it."

Michelle and Nina shared a look of surprise. Finally, Nina said, "Ok, that's all we needed. We'll see you at work. Thanks!"

"Have a good first day in the house. See ya!"

Nina slid the phone back in her pocket. "I don't care what she says. A man who catches frogs from a neighbor's pond to keep as pets does not strike me as harmless."

Michelle nodded. "I agree. Maybe we should just watch the wildlife from the deck, a safe distance from him and to the back door."

"Agreed. It wouldn't hurt to invest in a pair of binoculars to use at the kitchen window. I've never been one to spy on a neighbor, but something tells me we should keep ourselves informed in this situation."

"I just saw some in a box at work today. Probably for bird watching, but hey, we get a discount. I'll buy them tomorrow."

"I'll throw in half." Nina glanced out the window and saw Mike waving at the shed from just outside his front door. "He collects frogs, and he waves at dogs."

Chapter 17

A loud thump on the desk jolted Nina. She whipped her head around to find Michelle opening a medium size cardboard box. "I got them. Can you ring me up?" She held up a pair of gray binoculars that would be well camouflaged in the shadows of the house.

"Yes." Nina scanned them in. "$20.00, which means I need $10 from you." Nina pulled a ten out of her pocket. She had stopped by the bank yesterday and gotten several different bills out in anticipation of this.

Michelle handed her the other ten. "So how are we gonna do this? Is one of us going to watch him at all times?"

Nina shook her head. "Oh, no. I don't want to waste my life away in a paranoid stakeout. How about we keep them in the kitchen, and whenever one of us goes in there for something, we take a peek?"

"Ok. Yeah, you're right. We don't want to get so caught up in watching him that we forget how to enjoy our new lives. Hey, speaking of, how about we go for a beach walk tonight? Maybe build a fire, roast some hotdogs?"

"After dark?" Nina knew that Orange Beach was relatively safe. Lots of families take their yearly vacations there, and even at night, you can find parents with their children on the beach, searching for sand crabs with flashlights. However, what if Mike decided to expand his hunting ground to the beach, perhaps for something more than just frogs?

Michelle appeared lost in thought a moment, staring at the wall behind Nina. Then a light came on in her mind. "I can ask Barry if he wants to come with us."

Nina started to object, but then she recalled how normal he had seemed yesterday. "As long as you don't go sneaking off and leaving the two of us alone."

"Why would I do that? That's ... no, I won't." If Nina hadn't said that, she most certainly would have.

"Okay then. That sounds like fun. I haven't done anything social since before Donovan and I came to Orange Beach. It'll be nice."

A smile lit Michelle's face like a candle. "Great! I'll go tell him now." She rushed through the stockroom door. She was breathless by the time she reached Barry.

He gave her an odd look. "You okay?"

As he heaved a box upon an overhead shelf, she noticed the rippling of his arm muscles. He had the big veins of someone who worked out just enough to stay in ideal shape. She thought to herself, "*Nina is gonna fall for him eventually. It may take time, but she'd be crazy to pass him up. I wonder if he has a younger brother ...*"

She took a deep breath and managed the words, "Nina and I are having a beach bonfire tonight. Do you want to come?"

Barry stopped working and looked into Michelle's eyes, trying to gauge her seriousness. "Does Nina know you're asking, or is this invitation just from you?"

Michelle nodded emphatically. "She knows. She thought it'd be a good idea."

Barry didn't trust his luck. "Why?" he asked cautiously.

"We have a crazy neighbor and she doesn't feel safe."

Understanding and disappointment came over Barry's face. "So I'd be security."

Michelle bobbled her head from side to side. "Well, yeah, but also, it's a good chance to get to know each other. She did say she was looking forward to socializing."

Barry thought a moment, then threw his hands up. "What the heck? What have I got to lose? Let's do it."

"Great!" exclaimed a breathless Michelle. "Would you mind meeting us at our house at 8:00 so we can all walk over together?"

"I'll be there." Then he went back to heaving boxes.

Michelle ran to tell Nina. "It's on!" she yelled as she burst through the door once more.

"Okay," said Nina in a small voice.

"Try to contain your excitement," Michelle quipped.

Nina just smiled and went back to work. At least she'd agreed to the outing. Michelle took it as a sign of progress.

Chapter 18

At 7:55, the two women waited at the kitchen table for Barry. They had the hot dogs, buns, and marshmallows in a bag ready to grab. Barry had volunteered to bring chips and drinks.

Nina had that nervous flip in her stomach again. She had gotten used to being alone these last two weeks. She wasn't quite sure she remembered how to be around people. It was too easy to withdraw into her own mind and dwell on what her next steps in life should be. Though she didn't know if she'd be able to keep herself in the present, she needed to try. The possibility of failure, of breaking down in tears in front of her new coworkers, of embarrassing herself unsettled her insides.

Michelle got up and walked to the front door. She had to stand on her tiptoes to peek out the window. Putting her hand on the doorknob, she announced, "He's here."

Nina felt one long heartbeat pulsate downward into her stomach. She stood quickly, and for a moment, thought she might pass out. She lowered herself back into her chair as Michelle let Barry in and turned to grab the food.

"Are you ok? You look pale." Michelle approached Nina, who was taking ragged breaths and staring down at the table.

"Yeah, just a little lightheaded. I'll be fine." She stood slowly this time, careful to measure her strength with each inch.

"You probably need food. Here, eat this." Barry handed her a bag of hickory smoked barbecue chips.

She took them and said, "Thanks."

"Hey, let's all sit a minute before we head over." He took a chair and passed Nina a soda. "You look like your blood sugar could use a jumpstart."

Nina hadn't eaten anything all afternoon. She normally snacked when work slowed down, but today, she had been too nervous. "You're probably right." She popped open the soda and tore into the chips.

"Well, I'm not gonna make you eat alone." Michelle grabbed chips and a drink as well.

"I'm not gonna be the odd one out." Barry joined them.

Nina finished her chips first. She could've easily downed another bag, but she wanted to save room for hotdogs.

"Better?" Barry inquired.

Nina smiled through napkin wipes of her orange dusted lips. "Much. Thanks."

They collected their picnic and stepped into the darkness of the front deck. Before they reached the first step, a mournful howl filled the air. Barry stopped them by holding out his hands to block the stairway. "That didn't sound like a coyote," he whispered.

Michelle quietly said, "That's our weird neighbor's dog. He's keeping her in a shed while her broken leg heals. She sounds pitiful, but we aren't in danger from her."

"What kind of dog did he say she is?" Barry asked.

Nina chimed in, "Some kind of hound."

"Huh. Well. I guess hounds do make a variety of strange yelps." He lowered his arms and started down the steps. Though the sound had given all three of them chills, they had no valid reason to fear. They did walk more quickly than three people crossing the sand to enjoy a bonfire normally would.

The wind picked up as the land rose slightly toward the pavement. They crossed a highway devoid of headlights. Barry took the lead. "I've got a spot set up for us."

Their flashlights revealed a large hole in the sand filled with strategically stacked driftwood. "When did you have time to do this?" Michelle asked in amazement.

"I got off at 6, so I just came straight out here to get it ready."

A surprised Michelle asked, "When did you have time to go shopping for chips and soda?"

"I'm a dude who lives alone. I have a pantry full of chips and soda."

Nina inwardly cringed. He seemed physically fit enough to give her the impression he cared about his diet. Despite their plan to eat junk food tonight, she had taken him for a vegetable and lean meat eater.

Because Donovan had spared no expense, she had gotten used to dining on organic everything. Nina loved salads, seafood, and sushi, the three S's that never grew old for her. She had still been eating from those categories these past two weeks, though in smaller portions and from cheaper restaurants and grocery stores. Surprisingly, the sushi from the local food market wasn't half bad.

Michelle spread a couple of blankets down on the sand, and everyone set the bags they'd been carrying on top of them. Barry pulled a lighter from his pocket and clicked the blaze to life. Nina lowered her body to the blanket and found herself mesmerized by the fluidity of the growing flame. It leapt up like a wave crashing against a rock, filling the inky black space with neon orange.

While Nina lost herself in thought, Michelle and Barry speared hot dogs with roasting forks. Michelle sat down to Nina's right and Barry to her left. After a few minutes of silence, Barry quietly said to Nina, "You know, staring at fire too long is bad for your eyes. How about looking away for a moment and grabbing us a plate for the hotdogs?"

Nina stirred from her reverie. "Sure. Sorry. I haven't been much help tonight."

"It's okay. What better place to get lost in thought? I come out here by myself sometimes, light a fire, and think for hours."

That confession surprised Nina. "Really?"

"Yeah. Hey, I may eat junk food sometimes, but that doesn't mean I don't feed my mind. You know how they say dreams are your brain's way of working through problems? Well, I prefer to do that when I'm awake. And it helps. Whenever I do have dreams, they are light and happy. None of this wading through snake jungles and running from tornados that so many people I know have to do at night."

The light from the fire was bright enough to illuminate the serious look in Nina's eyes as she stared at Barry. "I run from tornados every single night."

He spread his arm out toward the blaze and announced, "Here's your therapy."

She looked into the fire's orange iris. If she weren't flanked on either side by people who two weeks prior had been strangers to her, she could lose herself there and work through some issues that had been nagging at her subconscious. Though they seemed to mean well, she couldn't totally relax in their presence.

"It is best to do it alone. And with people like weird neighbor guy and houndzilla out there, it might not be safe to get lost in thought and become less aware of your surroundings." Barry and Michelle worked the hotdogs off of the forks and onto the plate. "After we eat, Michelle and I could sit over there and give you some space. You'd have the safety of company without the intrusion."

Nina nodded. "Yes, thank you. I'd like to try that in a bit."

She had underestimated him. He was proving to be quite mature and sensitive. Nina knew she had a lot to learn. For years, she had been surrounded with fakers who feigned concern to get what they wanted, or the arrogant who spoke nonstop of their riches and accomplishments. Here and now, she tried to think of one single person who had expressed real interest in her emotional or mental state, and she could not.

"Here you go." Barry passed Nina a plate complete with bun and hotdog. "Fuel for the mental fire you're about to light," he explained with a gleam in his eye … or was that just the dancing reflection of the flame?

As they ate, Nina only halfway listened to Michelle and Barry's lighthearted banter. She felt like a child fresh out of the bath, hair still wet, sitting on her bed as the adults talked of things that had no relevance to her in the room nearby. She felt herself getting sleepy, and though she knew her mom would complain that she hadn't blow-dried her hair before putting her head on the pillow, she couldn't resist the urge to lie down.

Caught up in this flashback, she put her plate aside and stretched out on the blanket. Barry and Michelle immediately hushed. They managed to pick up the second blanket and move to the other side of the fire without waking her.

They talked only loud enough to be heard above the waves, even though Nina seemed to be in a state of rest deep enough to allow them to talk at regular volume. After an hour had passed with no sign of consciousness, Michelle finally asked, "What should we do with her? Do I need to wake her up so we can walk back to the house?"

"No, no don't," Barry said softly. "She's so beautiful."

Michelle looked at him intently. "You're fading in your resolve."

"This doesn't count. I'm not staring from across the building. I'm taking a genuine look at this wonderful, tortured human who only wants to trust the fire to burn out her nightmares. I think she needs someone to be there for her now more than ever. I can help her."

Michelle sighed dreamily and rested her head against his shoulder. "How'd you get to be so wise, Mr. Barry? Oh, yeah. I forgot. Wisdom comes with age."

He patted her on the head like he would a little sister. He wasn't offended at all by her frequent jabs at his age. Like the rest of his family, he could appreciate playful banter as a sign of closeness. He doubted he'd ever spar like that with Nina, though. She seemed too damaged. Her bruised spirit screamed, "Handle with care!"

Something in the pit protested with a loud snap as the fire consumed it, causing Nina to stir. She sat up with sleepy eyes and tried to focus on Barry and Michelle through the orange fingers rising in the space between them. "That was nice. I think I need to go to bed now."

"No tornados?" Barry asked.

"No. Just a rather comforting flashback to my childhood. Nothing important, just relaxing." She rose from the blanket and dusted the stray grains off her long legs. "What can I tote?"

Barry stood. "How about you just carry these blankets, so you can stay in the mindset of going to bed? We can get the rest."

"Okay. I appreciate it," she mumbled as she shuffled toward the road. They caught up with her and flanked her to keep her from bumping into anything or tripping over a vine.

Barry put the load he'd been carrying in the house. "I'm going back to put out the fire. Thanks for the invitation. I enjoyed it. Hope we can do it again sometime."

Nina wanted nothing more than to collapse in her own bed, but she couldn't let him leave without saying something. "Barry, you helped me. I'm not sure how, but I think I'm going to get okay."

Barry smiled at her clear struggle to say what she wanted in her sleepy state. "I'm honored. Let me know if you need more help getting okay."

She nodded, her eyes already closing. "Night," she mumbled while feeling her way down the hall toward her room. As he heard the bedroom door close, he inwardly celebrated the fact that she no longer seemed to be shutting him out in the way that mattered.

He turned to Michelle. "I think we've made progress tonight."

"Seems so." She smiled and patted him on the cheek. "Goodnight, Barry."

"Goodnight." He walked into the night to douse the flames, but upon reaching the pit, he decided to take his own advice. He sat before the fire and let the thoughts flow. He had a lot of new things to think about tonight, and a lot of dreams to prevent.

Chapter 19

The next morning, Nina and Michelle had their coffee in the kitchen with the window raised. A cool front had blown through in the middle of the night, so the air was just about as pleasant as it gets in summer on the Southern coast. Nina shut her eyes as she took a long, hot sip of coffee. The peace that had come over her at the bonfire persisted, and she was so very grateful.

The sound of a car door slamming caused the women to look at each other. They rushed to the window and saw Mike pulling out of his driveway. Michelle grabbed the binoculars to get a good look at his vehicle.

"He's got suitcases and boxes stacked up high in the backseat. It looks like … is that a lamp in the front seat? It looks like he's skipping town!"

Nina took the binoculars and confirmed it. "That's definitely a lamp and a car full of belongings. I hope he has his dog in there!"

The car rounded the corner and disappeared. Michelle and Nina stepped out onto the deck. Two seconds later, a panicked cry sounded from the shed. "He left his dog!!" Michelle yelled.

Nina looked down the road through the binoculars once more. "Well, we can't catch him. He's out of sight. What should we do?"

"Maybe someone else lives there with him. Let's go knock on the door and see if anyone is there to take care of her."

Both of their hearts pounded as they walked with purpose toward the house across the pond. Nina's long legs helped her reach the door first. With a trembling index finger, she rang the doorbell. She could hear it echo inside the house, but no one came to the door. Michelle knocked, but still no one responded.

"I think I hear frogs," Nina commented. Michelle motioned for her to come around back with her. When they rounded the corner of the house, they both gasped at what they saw. The entire backyard was a swamp. Shallow water dotted with lily pads and garnished with random logs and marsh grass spread across his entire property. A mesh fence that must've been at least eight feet tall curved inward toward the water. The gaps were only large enough to let airflow and maybe mosquitoes through, so the frogs were well contained.

"Seriously creepy!" Michelle whispered.

Nina stood still, in shock at what he had created. "Why?" was all she could say.

"I don't know, but I do know that dog needs our help. Let's go see if we can get into the shed."

"Wait a minute. Should we do that? What if she bites? Mike said she was wounded, and he's been keeping her in the dark for who knows how long. How is she going to react to a couple of strangers? She's probably going to be blinded by the light once we open that door, and that may scare her even more."

Michelle sighed. "You're probably right. Well, let's just see if we can peek at her through a crack. Then we can call animal control."

"Okay." They approached the shed with caution. Once they'd gotten within a foot of the enclosure, they could hear Gertrude whimpering pitifully.

Michelle took the lead. She pressed her eye against a small crack in the door. The padlock prevented them from entering even if they wanted to do so. "I can't see anything," she whispered to Nina. "Let's go back to the house."

The whimper ratcheted up into a wail. Chills ran down both women's spines. "Walk fast," Nina advised, grabbing Michelle's arm and urging her forward.

Then the wail formed into a word, "Help!"

Chapter 20

Nina and Michelle looked at each other in disbelief. "Did I just hear what I thought I heard?" Nina asked.

Michelle didn't have to answer as the cry came again, this time unmistakable. "Help! Help me!"

Both women ran back to the shed. "Hello? We're here. We're gonna get you out of there." Michelle tugged uselessly at the lock. "Do you know where he keeps the key?"

"No." Her defeated voice was barely audible.

Nina was already calling 911. Michelle tried to get more information out of the person inside, but every question she asked was met with only more whimpering and sobbing.

They didn't have to wait long. The police and an ambulance whipped into the driveway five minutes later. One officer cut the lock with bolt cutters, while the other stood next to the door, gun drawn and ready for whatever might happen. With the lock removed, the first officer pulled open the door and shone a flashlight into the dark corners while the second walked stooped in front of him, gun aimed to defend.

A woman with blonde mermaid hair cowered in the far left corner. She shut her eyes tightly against the light. Her expression seemed frozen in pain and terror. She appeared to be crying, though tears no longer flowed.

This pitiful sight prompted the officer with the weapon to put away his gun. He held the flashlight for the other, who brought the bolt cutters in to free the woman from the length of chain that bound one arm to the wall. She shrieked with happiness as the chain fell to the dirt floor.

"Are you hurt?" they asked her.

"No, no, no. Just thirsty." Her voice shook as she spoke in a hoarse tone. The officers attempted to walk her out, but she took one step and collapsed.

"We need a stretcher!"

Two EMTs rushed inside and emerged a moment later with this poor dirt-streaked lady trembling on top of the gurney. As they loaded her into the ambulance, she made eye contact with the women. "Thank you," she whispered as she pointed one shaking hand in their direction.

As the EMTs were shutting the door, Michelle heard one of them say, "She needs fluids, now."

"Got some questions for you two." Officer #1 stepped in front of them. "First and foremost, how did you know she was in here?"

Michelle spoke first, "We've been hearing what sounded like howling for three days now. The guy who lives here told us it was his dog, and he was keeping her in the shed so her broken leg could heal. Today was the first time we've actually heard her speak."

"What brought you over?"

Nina answered this time. "We saw the guy, Mike Waters, leaving this morning with his car packed full of boxes and furniture. It looked like he was moving out, but we still heard his dog crying. We thought he'd left her behind, so we came over to rescue her."

Michelle piped up, "Except this time, she didn't just howl. She said, 'Help!'"

"How long ago did he leave?"

Nina looked at her watch. They were already late for work. "About forty-five minutes ago."

The first officer looked at the second. "Put an APB out on Mike Waters. He couldn't have gotten very far in that old jalopy he drives."

Michelle interrupted, "Wait, you know him?"

Officer #2 finally spoke, "He's got a criminal record. Since it's public knowledge, I'll just tell you. He's been arrested for domestic abuse. Not surprising, I'm sure. But this? This is a whole new level. If we catch him this time, he's not getting out."

The officers dismissed the two women. Once they'd gotten out of earshot, Michelle turned to Nina. "I can't believe Alice didn't tell us! I feel betrayed."

"There's a chance she didn't know. I mean, she hasn't lived here in a while. She wouldn't have seen the police cars in his driveway and Mike being carted away in handcuffs. Unless she pays attention to local news, she could have missed it altogether."

"I hope you're right." Michelle walked the rest of the way with her arms crossed over her chest. When they reached their backyard, a door slamming caused them to look up. Barry walked quickly around the corner of the house.

"Are you guys okay? I got worried when you didn't show." His concern-filled eyes took in the cop cars across the pond.

"We're fine. But that wasn't a hound in the shed. It was a woman." The tears that had lurked just beneath the strong exterior Michelle had been determined to keep broke through the dam of her resolve and flooded her cheeks.

Nina's eyes watered, but she didn't want to cry in front of Barry. So she took Michelle into her embrace and hid her face that way. She spoke to him without facing him. "Mike was keeping a woman chained in that shed. The ambulance picked her up. She's badly traumatized and dehydrated. The cops told us he has a record of domestic violence."

"I'm sorry you had to see that. Man. You don't hear about stuff like that in this town often."

Michelle recovered from her sobs and asked Barry, "Did you know him or about him?"

"No, I didn't. I only moved here six months ago, so I don't know very many people, and I don't watch the news much. I'm guessing Alice didn't know either."

Nina countered, "Oh, she knew him. She even called him Crazy Mike. I'm just hoping she didn't know about his arrest."

Barry's phone rang. "It's Leslie." He answered, "Hey Leslie, we've got a situation over here." He explained what was going on. When he hung up, he turned to Nina and said, "Leslie is relaying what happened to Alice. She's probably going to tell you to take the day off. You'll likely hear from her soon."

Nina objected, "I appreciate that, but I can't afford to take a day off. I'd really like to work if she'll let me."

Michelle wiped her face and agreed. "Me too. I know I'm a mess right now, but I can snap back into work mode. I just need to keep my mind off of it. Barry, you can help me with that." Addressing Nina, she explained, "He's a tyrant in the stockroom."

Nina looked at Barry and smiled. Shaking his head, he had to look away, because if he looked at her right now, she would see that she melted his insides. Changing the subject, he said, "I'd better get back to work. Wait till you hear from Alice about coming in. Leslie and I can handle it for one day. See you later." Not waiting for a response, he walked to his vehicle and drove away.

Nina stood staring after him. "Have you noticed that when Barry leaves, he practically runs away?"

Michelle shrugged. "I guess."

"Yeah, he manages a goodbye of some sort, but he never waits for a response. He just exits as fast as he can."

Michelle sniffed. "Some people just aren't good at goodbyes."

Nina laughed. "Well, it's not like he's leaving forever or even for a long while. We'll probably see him later today."

Not wanting to explain the reason for his awkward departures, Michelle stopped responding. She started to head up the steps to the back door, but Nina's phone rang. "It's Alice." She put it on speakerphone.

"Hey, girls. I'm so sorry about what you had to go through this morning. Don't feel like you have to come in today. I'm sure you're shaken up."

Michelle came closer to the phone. "Alice, did you know Mike Waters had been arrested for abuse before?"

Alice gasped. "No, I didn't." She remained silent a moment, processing that information. "If I had, I would've warned you."

Nina replied, "We figured you didn't know. Is that poor woman his wife?"

"He has a wife. Did she have long, curly blonde hair?"

"Yes," they said in unison.

"That's her. Gertrude."

Michelle and Nina shared a look of disgust. "That's what he told us his dog's name was. That lowlife!"

"Again, I'm so sorry for all this. Please stay home today, with pay. You've been through a lot."

Nina and Michelle nodded at each other. Nina answered, "Thank you so much, Alice."

"You're welcome. I'll see you tomorrow."

Chapter 21

Alice sat in her lawyer's office. The powder blue suit she wore reflected the peace she currently possessed. "I'm ready to make my final will and testament."

"Okay, we can do that," answered Lane Bergens. He had been her lawyer ever since she and Fred had become business owners. "I hope you're doing okay healthwise?"

She smiled that pearly Alice smile. "I've been better. But the reason I'm ready is that I finally know whom I want to leave my property to."

"That's good to hear. I'll pull up the paperwork for you." He clicked his mouse and stared at his screen a moment. "Okay, what are we leaving and to whom?"

Alice answered with certainty. "We are leaving ownership of Seahorse Treasures to three people: Nina Carter, Barry Sable, and Michelle Kingsley."

"How do you want ownership divided among them?"

"Equally," Alice ordered.

Lane typed a lot in a short amount of time. The legal terms flowed through his fingers like a melody through an expert pianist.

"Okay. What else?"

"I'm leaving my house and land to Nina Carter and Michelle Kingsley. Equal ownership."

Lane keyed in the information. "Anything else?" he asked with fingers poised for more action.

Alice held her hands up. "That's all I got. My apartment is just a rental, and Leslie has been instructed to give my belongings to Goodwill when I pass."

Lane shifted in his seat. "I'm curious. What about Leslie? She's been with you a long time. Why not leave the shop to her?"

Alice expected that question. "I would if I knew she wanted it. But she and her husband are going to move to Bonita Springs, Florida next year. He's a doctor, and he's planning to open up a clinic out there. They aren't hurting for money, if you know what I mean."

Understanding came over Lane's features. "I see. Okay, well, I'm sure you know what you're doing. These three are blessed to know you."

"You're so sweet."

With a click of the mouse, Lane announced, "Paperwork's printing." He pulled the sheets together and stapled them. "I'll leave you to read over everything. I'll go pull a couple of witnesses from the other room and get a notary public when you're ready. I'll be in the lobby. Just let me know."

Alone, Alice read through the document that would affect the lives of three people tremendously. She hoped they'd be happy with their inheritance. It did come with responsibility, but the blessing should outweigh the burden.

Everything seemed to be in order. Alice started to stand and make the journey to the lobby to fetch Lane, but she thought better of it. After all, she had to choose her energy expenditures wisely. She only had so many left.

She leaned forward until she could reach the phone on his desk She punched the button that called his secretary's office. Expecting Lane, the secretary answered, "Yes, Mr. Bergens?"

"Mr. Bergens is in the lobby. It's Alice Rowland. He asked me to come find him when I'd finished reading, but I'm having trouble getting up. Would you be willing to tell him I'm ready to sign?"

"Sure thing, Mrs. Rowland."

"Thank you, Susan." She hung up and waited patiently. Today was one of the best days she'd had since her diagnosis. If she didn't know from experience what would happen if she pushed herself to move around, she would have attempted it.

The door opened and Lane entered with another man and two young women. "Jane and Katie are going to be your witnesses today, and Stan is our notary public. If you're ready, we'll go ahead and get you to initial the bottom of each page and sign the last page. Your witnesses will sign right behind you."

All of these people looking over her shoulder would have made her nervous if she'd had any doubt about the decisions within the will. She had perfect peace about this. Her hand didn't even shake as it normally did when she wrote.

After the notarization, she shook hands with Lane and stood to go. Susan surprised her by entering with a wheelchair. "We want to make sure you get to your car safely," she explained.

This delighted Alice. "Oh, thank you. How thoughtful!"

Susan wheeled right up to her, so all Alice had to do was sit down. Lane approached and said to Susan, "I can take it from here. Thank you."

He wheeled her out of the door, down the hallway, and into the sunshine. He helped her get up and into her car. "Drive safe, Alice."

"Bless you, Lane." She thanked God for considerate people. Without them, life would surely be a lot harder.

Chapter 22

Too troubled to rest, Nina and Michelle crossed the street to the beach. They had tried lounging on the couch and watching TV, but neither of them could focus and both needed to work out their restlessness.

The day was overcast but bright. A steady wind ruffled the yellow flags in the sand that warned of a possible rip current. They walked barefoot along the edge, letting the foamy swash inundate their feet.

"Nina?"

"Yes?"

"I'm glad you're here."

Nina smiled to herself. "I'm glad you're here, too."

Michelle continued, "I don't think I could stay here now if you weren't. This is … this is a lot."

Nina simply nodded. She had to agree. Though she had seen more than Michelle during the fifteen extra years she'd had on this planet, she must admit that she had never witnessed cruelty to this degree.

"Can I ask you something? And if you don't want to talk about it, I understand."

"Go on," Nina urged.

"Did Donovan abuse you?"

She heaved a sigh. "Not physically. He played mind games. But he never resorted to violence."

Michelle remained quiet, prompting Nina to ask her, "Did Kevin abuse you?"

"No, but he mentally manipulated me." She kicked a seashell with a struggling creature inside back into the water. "We never had a healthy conversation, now that I think about it. I told myself he challenged me, like that was a good thing, and it would have been if it weren't just constant questioning of my every thought."

Nina advised, "Be glad you're out of that relationship. Use what you've learned to help you with future ones. You know the signs now. If you see them, run!"

"I will," Michelle said with absolute certainty. "What sort of mind games did Donovan play?"

Thinking back felt a bit like wading through mud. It wasn't pleasant territory, nor easy to traverse. But if she could help Michelle by providing her with more warning signs, she'd muck through all of it.

"He liked to keep me in my place. Underhanded compliments were his thing. But he also didn't shy away from outright cuts."

"Can you give me an example?" Michelle asked.

"Okay. I was a pretty good painter, or so I thought. During our first year of marriage, I painted this beach landscape that I was really proud of. It was probably my best work. I showed it to Donovan and asked if he thought I should set up a booth at our local arts festival, with this painting being forefront and tagged with the highest price. He told me it was definitely good enough to hang on our wall in the hallway, but he didn't want me embarrassing myself by putting it out at a public festival. He didn't think anyone would pay more than twenty bucks for it. My heart just sank. He was smart enough to make me think he was saying these things for my own protection, so I wouldn't face rejection from others, but the worst rejection I could have received had just come from him."

Michelle gasped. "That's so sad, and so sneaky! I'm sorry he was so awful to you. But now you've got me wanting to see this painting! Do you still have it?"

Nina shook her head sadly. "No. Unfortunately, everything I own is back at our house, except the few things I brought here."

"Well, what about taking a road trip to go get your stuff?"

"No, absolutely not. I need to stay away from him. Nothing I own is worth facing Donovan again."

Michelle thought a moment. "Then I guess you'll just have to make new paintings."

Nina laughed. "I haven't picked up a paintbrush since the day he killed my dream. I may have lost my skill by now."

"Well, there's only one way to find out. How about we take a short drive to Shelly's Arts and Crafts and get you stocked up on supplies?"

"I need to be saving money right now. Art supplies are expensive." Plus, Nina was uncomfortable with the idea of trying again. She felt certain that Donovan's voice would haunt her, making her question her every brushstroke.

"What about buying a new tube of paint every week until you have enough to do a painting? Then buy the canvas last, since it will probably be the most expensive thing you need."

Nina could see that this would be a losing battle for her. "Anyone ever tell you you'd make a great car salesperson?"

"What?" asked an amused and confused Michelle.

"Or any kind of salesperson, really. You don't give up. You just keep throwing out new options."

Michelle took that as a compliment. "Thanks. I've been told I'm persistent to a fault." Movement to her right caught her eye. A great blue heron, possibly the one from her back yard, moved subtly to one side as it honed in on a small fish in the shallows. "So, about that paint? You ready to take a ride?"

Chapter 23

A lone tube of deep green acrylic paint rested on Nina's nightstand, with a half-inch brush as its sole companion. These were the only two purchases she had allowed herself. At this rate, it would take a couple of months for her to be able to start her first painting of her third life, as she referred to the post-Donovan phase. Her first life was with her parents, her second with Donovan, and her third and hopefully best life had just begun.

Night had fallen and morning had come without any sign of Gertrude or Mike next door. If he was as smart as he was creepy, he would stay away. His past run-in with law enforcement only added to the reasons he shouldn't return to the address they had on file for him.

Nina brushed her hair while sitting in front of her mirrored dresser. Though the brush didn't have far to go, she made each stroke slowly and deliberately. Somehow it calmed her. Her mother had brushed her hair this way. It always made her sleepy, which surely meant she was content. She didn't feel sleepy now, but perhaps she was a tiny bit less jittery.

A glance at the clock told her it was time to walk to work. She stood and straightened her neon orange tank dress. It accented her golden tan, making her look worthy of working in a beach souvenir shop.

Michelle walked into the room at that moment. "Are you ready … hey, hottie! Look at you!"

Nina smirked and grabbed her purse from the bed. "I'm ready."

"Seriously, do you have a date after work I don't know about?"

"Nope. I just like this dress."

"You'll probably have one lined up by tonight."

Nina ignored her and opened the front door. A brilliant sun lit the world. The cloudless dome above allowed every single thing below to reflect its true colors. It would've been a perfect day to stay outdoors, but duty called. And what a duty it was. Nina and Michelle had the task of providing other beachgoers with things to help them enjoy their vacation to the fullest. And once their shifts were done, they had the freedom to walk across the street and indulge every day in what most only got to experience for a week or so out of the year.

Michelle unlocked the back door to the shop. She veered off into the stockroom, where Barry was already unloading a new shipment. Nina walked to the front of the store and flipped the Closed sign to Open. She unlocked the door and took her place behind the register. There were no cars in the parking lot. Everyone was likely at the beach, enjoying the morning sun before it heated to unbearable degrees. Store traffic always increased around noon.

Barry came through the door with a couple of boxes stacked in his arms. He put them down, ripped them open, and began stocking the racks with shell jewelry. A flash of orange in the corner of his vision caused him to turn and look toward the front of the store. When he saw Nina, he dropped the fistful of necklaces he was holding. She moved from behind the counter to a nearby shelf like an exotic fish well aware of its beauty, waving its elegant fins for all the undersea to admire.

He caught himself before she noticed him staring. He stooped to pick up the jewelry and find his missing heartbeat. As he concentrated on his breathing, a voice directly behind him said, "Hey there."

He turned to find this vision in orange standing two feet away. His mind must be fooling him, because he was sure she exuded a glow not of this world. Barely enough of him remained in his control, but what little did allowed him to stand and say, "Hey."

"I don't have any customers. Need some help?" This was the first time she had approached him at work. Though he didn't need assistance, he wasn't about to turn her away.

"Sure. I'm just hanging these on this rack." He made the mistake of looking at her again. "You look great, by the way." There. He'd said it. He had to say something, because standing before her silent was like walking up to the edge of the Grand Canyon for the first time and not speaking of its glory.

"Thanks. You look good, too. I really like that color on you."

Had he heard her correctly? It took him a moment to respond. "Thanks. I woke up, looked outside, and said, 'I think I'll match the sky today.'"

The light blue t-shirt indeed reminded Nina of her view on the way to work. It also cast Barry in a new light. She had only seen him wear dark colors, mostly gray or black. This was a nice change.

Nina grabbed a handful of jewelry. She watched as Barry unwrapped the plastic from each piece before hanging it on a hook, so she did the same. They filled one rack and moved onto the next. Neither of them spoke, yet Nina found working next to him comforting. He possessed a calming presence. From time to time, she would glance at his face, and all she saw there was a content focus.

Finally, he must have noticed her looking, because he asked, "Is my face doing that weird twisty thing it does when I concentrate too hard?"

She laughed. "No, not at all. You seem focused, but not in a twisted way."

This got a good laugh from him. He looked at her as he said, "Good to know." His eyes smiled along with him.

This was the first time Nina really noticed his eyes. They contained so many colors. Green, brown, and blue tendrils swirled around his pupils, seemingly in competition for dominance. The result was nothing short of beautiful.

The urgent opening of the front door broke the spell Barry's eyes had cast on Nina. She and Barry turned to find a breathless Leslie standing there with tears streaming down her face. "Guys, it's Alice. She's gone."

Chapter 24

"What?! No! What happened?" Nina knew of Alice's health problems, but she had seemed just fine yesterday when they spoke on the phone.

"Her heart stopped. I found her this morning when I went to pick her up for work. She didn't answer the door, so I let myself in. She was still in bed, not breathing. But she looked so peaceful! She had a little smile on her face. I think she probably saw Fred as she was leaving her body."

A sob choked Nina. She raised a hand to her mouth. Barry instinctively put his hand on her back, and she turned to him. He brought his other arm around her and held her, sorry that the first time he touched her had to be under these circumstances.

Nina cried as if she'd known Alice all her life. In what little time she had, Alice had shown greater kindness to Nina than anyone. The knowledge of her precarious health situation did little to soften the blow of this news. What a great woman, and what a great loss to everyone in her life!

Michelle emerged from the back. She stopped in her tracks when she saw everyone crying. "What's going on?"

Leslie told her, and she reacted in much the same way as Nina. Michelle accepted Leslie's offer of an embrace, and the two of them cried on each other's shoulders.

Nina's sobs dwindled as Barry rubbed her back gently. She knew she should pull away, but instead, she pressed her head into his chest, and he held on more tightly. She wasn't ready to leave the comfort of his warm embrace just yet.

He didn't mind. Barry was the type of person who took comfort in giving comfort. So the longer they held on, the better off the both of them would be.

He couldn't believe Alice was gone. He should have expected it, but the woman seemed to defy every odd. She possessed such strength in the face of her physical weakness that she almost made everyone forget her mortality.

Leslie let go of Michelle and turned to face the group. "Do you guys want to close up shop for the rest of the day?"

Everyone nodded in agreement. Leslie locked the door that Nina had unlocked less than an hour ago. She flipped the sign back to Closed. Rejoining the group, she announced, "Alice wanted to be cremated. I'm taking care of arrangements. I'll let you know as soon as we have a date for the memorial."

Nina lifted her head and Barry slowly released her. Her eyes darted up to meet his as she whispered, "Thank you." Tears glistened on her long lashes.

He still held her elbows as he replied, "You're welcome."

She slowly stepped away from him. Everyone walked toward the private exit at the back. Michelle locked up behind them. Leslie got in her car, but everyone else just stood around. No one really wanted to go home, but they couldn't concentrate on work like this. "Can we all just go sit under a palm tree or something? I don't want to sit inside the house and think. It's depressing." Nina needed air and scenery. Staring at the wall would only make her crazy.

Michelle offered, "I'll go grab some lawn chairs, and we can sit out front in the shade of the big palms. Barry, you coming?"

Barry looked at Nina, who surprised him by taking his hand. "Please come." Her eyes pleaded with him.

"Yes," he answered, and she surprised him even further by holding his hand the entire walk to their yard.

Michelle had walked on ahead and didn't even notice this exchange. When she returned from the storage area under the house carrying a stack of three chairs, she saw their entwined hands and stopped nearly five feet from them. Her eyes widened in shock. Trying to recover, she stuttered, "I – uh – here you go. Chairs." She busied herself with setting them up.

Nina let go of his hand. "Here, let me help you."

Barry grabbed the third chair. They arranged themselves in a triangle under the shade of some tall palms and thick flowering bushes. "I'll go get us some drinks," Michelle offered.

Nina leaned forward. Sighing, she asked, "What happens now? Does someone come in and close the shop, or do we just keep working?"

Barry answered, "We just keep working. At least until someone tells us not to. I'm sure Alice made arrangements for the business to continue. She wouldn't just leave us hanging like that, especially since she knew the time was coming."

The door banged shut behind Michelle. She carried three bottles of cold coconut pineapple juice. Her hands shook as she passed them out.

When she finally allowed herself to sit down, she drank half the bottle at once. Then she placed it on a nearby tree trunk. "Crying makes me thirsty."

Barry noticed a vehicle with a flashing light on top in the Seahorse Treasures parking lot. "Mail's here."

Nina and Michelle's mailbox was right beside the store's. "I'll go get it for you," Barry offered. Before they could tell him not to worry with it, he had disappeared.

"See? He's the master of rapid exits."

Michelle smiled at Nina's description of him. Unlike her usual chatty self, she didn't have anything to say. Always the one to quote something uplifting and perfect for the moment, she suddenly found herself all out of words. With her head tilted back, she stared up at the palm fronds and wondered what their future held now that their boss and landlady was gone.

Barry returned with an important looking document for Nina. "For you," he said as he passed her the envelope. She tore into it, pulled out the papers, and gasped as she read the words she didn't expect to see for months.

"What is it?" asked Michelle.

"My divorce is final."

She looked up at Michelle, whose grin grew larger by the second, and then at Barry, whose eyes were shining as he said, "Congratulations."

Michelle jumped up and ran over to hug her. "That was quick!"

"I can't believe it. Donovan must've paid extra to get this finalized A.S.A.P." She held the papers in her hand and read through them one more time, fearing she'd missed something, some exception that would ruin this moment. But everything seemed to be in order. She was legally a free woman. "I'm going to go put this inside."

After the door shut behind Nina, Michelle looked at Barry and smiled a big goofy grin. He returned the expression.

"Well," she said.

"Well," he replied.

Given the heaviness of the day, Michelle didn't urge him further. It seemed inappropriate to play matchmaker at a time like this. But she could see happiness emanating from him. If she took a step back now, he and Nina would probably gravitate toward each other without a push.

Michelle reached for her drink. "I'm just gonna sip my pineapple juice."

Barry laughed. "You do that."

She held up her bottle. "A toast," she said, waiting for him to lift his in kind. "To the future."

"To the future." They clinked glass and drank to wash away the past.

Nina saw them toasting as she walked back down the steps. She took her seat and grabbed her bottle. "Are we toasting to Alice?"

Michelle and Barry exchanged a look. Thinking quickly, Michelle lifted her glass toward the center of the triangle. "To Alice."

"To Alice," Barry and Nina echoed. As they drank, Michelle winked at Barry from the far side of her bottle. He just kept right on sipping his pineapple juice.

Chapter 25

The three of them sat around talking about Alice for the next hour. Since none of them had known her very long, they ran out of things to say. Then the conversation shifted.

Barry looked at Nina and wondered if he should ask what he so desperately wanted to ask. Michelle hadn't told him much about what was going on with Nina out of respect for her privacy. He simply knew she had been going through a divorce. Up to this point, he had been afraid that asking about it would cause her to shut down and tell him to mind his own business, but the three of them had been spending a lot of time together recently, and they seemed headed in the direction of becoming lifelong friends.

A lull in the conversation gave him a chance. He decided to go about it very gently, giving her an out. "Nina, I want to ask you something. If you don't want to tell me, I understand."

Curiosity filled her eyes. "Go on."

Softly, he asked, "What happened with you and Donovan?"

Nina smiled and looked down at the sand. "He dumped me."

Barry's jaw dropped. He couldn't imagine someone lucky enough to call her his wife ever letting her go. "Why?"

The question was so saturated with amazement that Nina couldn't help but take it as a compliment. Her face softened further as she looked up at Barry and said, "He found a younger version."

Barry just shook his head. His eyes held both disdain and adoration as he declared, "He's crazy."

She smiled once more, then cast her eyes downward. "I appreciate that. Looking back, I can see it was for the best. He controlled everything about our relationship. I just made the mistake of letting him. I haven't been able to be myself in fifteen years. I tried during our first year of marriage, but he found ways to break every part of me down without me even realizing he was doing it on purpose. I just thought I needed reshaping, that I'd been broken all along and didn't know it."

Barry looked at Michelle, then he reached over and took her hand. With his other hand, he reached for Nina's. Michelle surmised that she should take Nina's left hand. When they were all linked, he said,

"We are here to support you. No one is going to cut you down and get inside your head as long as we're around. We're gonna help you heal and find yourself again. Okay?"

The love in this circle overwhelmed Nina. She had never had this kind of support, and it made her heart burst with happiness. The tears broke through so suddenly that all she could do was nod. Her friends squeezed her hands, and she tried to pull it together.

She took a double breath and said through tears, "I've never had so many different emotions in one day. I'm sorry, guys."

"Don't ever be sorry for feeling. Or for crying. Like fire therapy, it helps you work things out. You should have good dreams tonight."

"Thank you," she said as they released her hands. She wiped her cheeks. She wanted to lighten the mood to roll aside the heaviness of the morning. A subject change might help. "Now. Who's hungry?"

"I could eat," said Michelle.

"I can always eat," agreed Barry.

Nina stood. "I'll go make lunch. Does sautéed shrimp, tomatoes, and grapes sound good?"

Barry and Michelle were impressed. "I didn't know my roommate was a fancy chef! Were you hiding this as a surprise?" Michelle teased.

Nina laughed. "I don't know about fancy, but I do like fresh cooked food. That will be something you get living with me."

"Alright! Any time you wanna make something, I'll help you eat it, girl."

They left their chairs but grabbed their bottles. In the kitchen, Nina heated some olive oil in a skillet and thawed shrimp in a colander under cold running water. She chopped the grapes and tomatoes as Barry and Michelle sat on the living room couch and talked about daily, insignificant things. Nina enjoyed their conversation as background music. What they talked about was irrelevant; what mattered was the happy noise of life in the house. It felt like something she hadn't had in a long time: family.

The sense of peace that overtook her medicated her frazzled soul. If three weeks ago, she could've seen into the future to this moment, she wouldn't have believed it. As she turned off the cold water, she breathed a simple prayer, "Thank you, God."

The hot olive oil ran smoothly and quickly from side to side when she lifted the skillet, so she could tell it was ready for the food. She put the tomatoes and grapes in for three minutes before adding the shrimp. Grabbing the dried basil, she sprinkled everything generously.

Then she added just a touch of salt and a good dash of black pepper. Seven minutes later, she announced, "Lunch is ready."

They sat around the dining room table with full plates and glasses of water. Michelle bit into hers first. "Oh, girl, this is good. Really good."

Barry took the next bite. "Mmm. Wow. Good job."

Nina glowed. She hadn't felt like she'd had much to give to her friends since they'd met. It seemed like she was perpetually on the receiving end of kindness, and in her emotionally dehydrated state, she had soaked it up like a sponge. Maybe this could be her way of giving back. She could show her love through food.

After the meal, Michelle and Barry insisted on cleaning up. "You go sit down. You did the important part," Michelle demanded.

Nina leaned back on the couch and shut her eyes for a moment. When she opened them, they'd already finished the dishes and were heading to join her on the sofa.

"It's too hot to sit outside. Wanna play a game?" Michelle asked.

Nina wasn't sure she had it in her to play any games right now, but what else could they do? It seemed like as good an idea as any, so she said, "Okay. What'd you have in mind?"

Michelle's eyes lit up as she ran to the entertainment center. She pulled a boxed board game out of the cabinet and announced with joy, "Balderdash!"

Barry spoke up, "I love that game. Nina, have you ever played it?"

Nina shook her head. "No, I never really played board games."

Michelle gasped. "What?! Why not?"

She shrugged. "No one would play with me."

Barry and Michelle both said, "Aw!" but not in a mocking way. That confession really broke their hearts. As he pictured a young Nina sitting alone in tears in front of a game that required four players, he wanted to reach over and hug her. He didn't, though. He was still trying to choose the right moments to show affection.

Michelle scooted closer to the coffee table and sat down on the floor. "Well, we'll show you how. It's a lot of fun, I promise. I've got lots of board games, and now that I know you're new to all this, I can't wait to show you all of them!"

Nina wondered if she were dreaming. She wished she could zip back in time and show this moment to her childhood self. Sitting up straight, she readied herself to pay attention to Michelle's instructions.

She explained that the object of the game was to make your answer so believable that others would guess it was the true answer, which was also mixed into the pot. Nina had no idea what most of the words, people, and dates in the categories were, but she had a knack for writing, so she turned out to be pretty good at this game.

They played for two hours before switching over to Scattergories, another word-based game at which Nina excelled, prompting Michelle to say, "Dang, Nina! For someone who's never played, you're unbelievably awesome."

She smiled at the compliment. "I never knew how fun this could be. I always told myself that games were probably too hard and boring, just to make myself feel better about not getting to play them. I eventually came to believe it."

Several hours later, the evening sun cast orange rays through the living room window. Michelle looked up. "This is my favorite time of day. Do you mind if we take a break and walk over to the ocean?"

"I think that sounds wonderful." Nina loved watching the colors change in the sky, sand, and water as the sun trekked westward through the atmosphere. She looked at Barry, who was already headed toward the door.

The women followed. When he reached the base of the stairs, he waited for them, and they walked side by side through the sand that had cooled a few degrees since the morning. As they walked past the parking lot of work, they noticed a man in a suit getting out of a car.

"Are you Nina, Michelle, and Barry?" he asked.

"Yes?" Barry answered with a question in his voice.

The man approached, holding a big envelope. "I'm Lane Bergens, Alice's lawyer." He paused to shake their hands. "We normally wait at least a few days to do this, but given the circumstances, Alice wanted me to go ahead and share this news with you. Is there somewhere we can talk?"

Barry offered, "There's a picnic table across the street on the beach. We can sit there."

Nina was grateful that he didn't suggest going inside. She needed fresh air, especially if this news turned out to be bad.

Lane agreed, so they crossed the street and sat around the wooden table. Before he began, Lane took a look at each of their faces and smiled to put them at ease. "Nina Carter, Michelle Kingsley, and Barry Sable, you are the new owners of Seahorse Treasures."

Nina gasped. Michelle said, "What?!" and Barry's eyes opened wider than Nina imagined possible.

"That's right. She dictated that ownership should be divided evenly among you three. Leslie is moving to south Florida next year, so that's why she isn't included. And there's more," he announced, waiting for them to prepare themselves.

They all looked at him with raised eyebrows, so he continued, "Nina and Michelle are now owners of the house in which they currently reside."

Michelle and Nina squealed with joy. Two weeks ago, they were homeless. Now, they owned beach property.

Recovering their senses, a touch of panic worked its way into their minds. Nina gave it voice, "But we know nothing about being business owners. What do we do?"

Lane anticipated this question. "Don't worry. Alice arranged for her accountant to help you. You have her assistance for the first two months prepaid. After that, you can decide if you want to keep her on and pay her out of your business account or if you've learned enough to move forward on your own."

Nina let out a relieved warble. She, Michelle, and Barry just looked back and forth at each other, still in shock and not knowing what to do next. Barry caught Nina's gaze and reminded her, "See? I told you Alice wouldn't leave us hanging."

Lane reached into the envelope and pulled out three copies of Alice's will. "Each of you take one and keep it somewhere safe. Once we get a copy of Alice's death certificate filed, everything will be 100% official."

They each took their copy. Lane stood to leave. Shaking their hands once more, he said, "Congratulations. I'm sorry for your loss, but I'm also happy for your gain."

They thanked him and watched him walk away. Finally, Barry spoke, "I'm going to put this in my vehicle for now." He stood, and the others followed.

"I have a fireproof metal lockbox in my room. We can put ours there if you like," Michelle offered.

"Yes, thank you." Nina was glad that Michelle had brought most of her belongings with her, because she had nowhere to store such an important document.

They all met back up on the beach and wordlessly walked together into the edge of the surf. The golden light dancing across the foam reminded Nina of the beautiful painting in her bedroom. If so many things she thought impossible could come to be, then maybe she could rekindle her creativity and paint again. She looked into the red edge of the setting sun and gave herself permission to hope.

Chapter 26

As the sun dipped out of sight, weariness overcame Michelle. "I think I'm gonna turn in for the night. See you tomorrow morning, regular time?"

"Oh yeah, we didn't discuss that. Do we want to open tomorrow at normal time and just go about business as usual?" Nina planned to call Alice's accountant in the morning and see what she needed to keep track of on the business end of things.

Barry said, "I think that's best. Do you, Michelle?"

Michelle's mouth had already opened in a giant yawn. When she could speak, she answered, "Yes. We should keep it going. I'm sure we'll need to meet and discuss things soon, but I don't see any reason not to go ahead and do our jobs." She turned to go. "Goodnight, guys."

Nina said, "Wait, I'll go with you."

Michelle stopped her. "No, don't feel like you need to go home just because I am. Stay here. Enjoy the night."

In truth, Nina wasn't ready to go home. She knew her mind wouldn't let her sleep. So she was relieved when Barry offered, "I can build a fire if you like. I've got blankets in the trunk."

"Yes, that sounds like just what I need."

They walked together to the parking lot to retrieve the blankets. Barry still had some wood from the other night to use as kindling. In no time, they were seated on a blanket next to the flames. The night air had cooled considerably. Still wearing the sleeveless orange dress, Nina shivered as the breeze chilled her arms. Barry reached behind them and pulled forth another blanket. He unfolded it and draped it across Nina's shoulders.

This unrequested kind act surprised Nina. "Thank you," she said with authentic appreciation in her voice.

"You're welcome." He faced the fire to avoid staring at her. He struggled to keep his actions and words toward her platonic. Inevitably, his admiration would seep through in little ways from time to time, but he seemed to be doing an okay job of hiding it so far. She hadn't run away, had she?

Together they stared into the blaze wordlessly for what seemed like a long time. Nina finally broke the silence. "So, what's your story?"

"What do you mean?"

"You know, your situation. You said you're a dude who lives alone. What brought you here? Who do you hang out with when you're not with us?"

Barry laughed lightly. "I don't have much of a story, I'm afraid. I got tired of living in a place far away from water, so I moved here. My old town had nothing but trees and humidity. Here, I don't mind the humidity because it comes with a tropical setting. I traded pines for palms. My grandparents lived here up until they died twelve years ago, so I have an emotional connection to the area. That's why I chose Orange Beach instead of somewhere in Florida, like typical beach seekers do. I haven't made any friends other than you and Michelle, because I'm kind of picky about who I hang out with. I'm an introvert, so I have to really like you to want to be around you."

Nina smiled at that comment. "I feel special. But I want to know more. What did you do before you came here?"

"I worked in a warehouse, so almost the same work I do now."

He didn't expound on that, so Nina prodded further. "Did you have friends there?"

Barry sighed. She wasn't going to stop until he opened up. He didn't like to talk about it, but telling her would only be fair, since she had told him about what had happened with Donovan. "I had a girlfriend."

"Had?" Nina was trying to be gentle in her quest for information. He seemed reluctant to talk for some reason, so she didn't want to spook him.

"Yes, had. We broke up before I moved here." He picked up another piece of wood and tossed it into the fire.

"Are you okay?" she asked in a quiet voice. If talking about it made him throw things into the fire, then she assumed he was not.

"Oh, yeah. I'm fine now. My anger got me through. Kept me from being sad."

Nina sat up straighter. Did he have anger issues? Should this be a sign she should stay away from him?

As if reading her mind, he said, "I don't have a temper. As a matter of fact, it's actually really hard to make me mad. But she managed to do that by cheating on me with my best friend."

"Oh, I'm sorry." Nina could relate to being the victim of a cheater. She chided herself for thinking even for a moment he might be dangerous.

"It's okay. I'm better off knowing. And overall, in life, I'm better off. I have a place near the ocean, good friends, and now, I'm a co-owner of a successful business." He smiled at Nina. "You and Michelle can say the same."

Nina nodded. "That, we can. It's hard to believe how much better off we both are. I've had such disappointment in life that I'm not accustomed to good things happening. I mean, yes, I had money for many years and all the opportunities that it brings, but I always felt empty. Now, I'm starting from scratch, but I wake up feeling happy and wondering what each day will hold. I actually look forward to life." She turned toward Barry, who had been gazing at her face without disguising his adoration. He didn't have time to pull the veil down before she asked, "Why are you looking at me like that?"

He played dumb. "Like what?"

"Like maybe you think I'm being cheesy?"

Good. She had misread his admiration. "Not at all. I was just admiring your zeal for life. It's great. I hope you never lose it."

"Oh. Good. Thanks." For a moment there, she'd been afraid he was about to make fun of her. But that fear was just an unfortunate side effect of living with Donovan all those years. She had forgotten that not everyone stood ready to ridicule her feelings.

They looked on in silence as the flames consumed the gray color of the firewood, turning it as black as the night around it. Barry eventually spoke, telling her of his old friends and things they liked to do together. He even told her a little about his childhood. She, in turn, opened up to him about how her parents had given her an ultimatum when it came to Donovan. He found it so sad that she truly had no one in this life before she met Alice, Michelle, and him. He determined within himself then and there that he would do everything in his power to be there for her. The need to be her person consumed him now, the fire of his devotion changing the very color of his being.

An hour later when he walked her home, he hugged her and held her long enough to let her know he cared for her a great deal. At least, he hoped that came across. When he let her go, he noticed tears in her eyes, so maybe it had. She smiled through them and said, "Thank you for tonight. I look forward to many more like it."

He had to fight the urge to say, "I love you," because his whole being wanted nothing more than to express his innermost truth. But he knew it was way too soon for this confession. She needed to know she had someone in her corner who would be there for her without ulterior motives. He would hold off on telling her for as long as he needed to in order to be that person she could feel comfortable with and rely on. He hoped the day would come when he could tell her everything, from how he had been smitten with her the moment he first laid eyes on her to how his feelings only deepened with each new truth she revealed about herself. For now, he would simply say, "Goodnight."

Chapter 27

Michelle felt more than just weary as she walked alone to the house. Loneliness had been boring a hole through her slowly all day long, and now that hole had become a chasm too big to ignore.

She really was happy for Nina and Barry. Though they weren't together yet, they were definitely growing closer. Michelle had forgotten that the unintended consequence of setting up your friends was becoming a third wheel. All day, she had felt like the front tire of a tricycle.

When the three of them hung out at the bonfire, Michelle had really felt like a part of one big friendship. Today when she had emerged from the stockroom and saw Barry holding Nina, she surprised herself by feeling a twinge of jealousy. That only intensified when she came out of the storage area later to find them holding hands.

This jealousy wasn't based on feelings for Barry, however. At least, she didn't think so. He was twelve years her senior, and she had always dated near her own age. They were definitely close, joking and teasing each other, but he was more like an older mentor to her than a crush. Oh, she'd noticed he was very handsome, but she didn't think of him as a potential love interest.

It had more to do with the slow morphing of the friend triangle into a straight line, with Barry and Nina as close points at one end and her all the way at the other. She had found the friendships she had sorely needed in the wake of her breakup. She sensed their impending withdrawal like a slow leak that had already begun, and to suffer another loss so soon after Kevin would be devastating. Just facing the possibility gave her a migraine.

She rubbed tiger balm on her forehead to stave it off and got under the covers. She wouldn't let the tears come, because they would just make the headache worse. Instead, she shut her eyes and let the strain of the day claim her body. It responded by falling fast asleep.

Chapter 28

The next morning, Nina got a phone call at 8:30 a.m. from Alice's accountant, Mary Marsden. She and Michelle were having coffee at the table, so she put Mary on speakerphone.

"I'd like to come by the shop and meet you as soon as possible. I know you open at 10. Is there any way I could sit down with you before you open for business to go over a few things? I could be there by 9 if that works for you."

Michelle looked at Nina and nodded. Nina responded, "Sure, we can be there by then."

"Okay. See you at 9." They hung up and rushed off to their respective rooms to get ready quickly.

Michelle finished first, so Nina asked her to call Barry and see if he could make it in early. He answered and said that he happened to already be at the beach across the street, so that worked out well. Nina finished her makeup and joined Michelle on the front porch.

They got to Seahorse Treasures just as Barry strolled up from the beach. Michelle glanced at Nina's face as she watched Barry draw closer. Something softened in her gaze. It was so subtle, it would have been imperceptible to anyone else, but Michelle noticed.

He walked up to them with a smile that was all for Nina. He didn't even notice Michelle standing there, or so it appeared. It seemed her separation from the group was happening ahead of her predicted schedule. As Nina and Barry gravitated increasingly toward each other, they inevitably travelled further from Michelle.

Mary arrived, so Michelle turned to unlock the front door. They all shook hands before going inside. Nina led Mary to the office that had belonged to Alice. Michelle and Barry followed, and everyone took a seat around Alice's old desk. The meeting lasted about forty minutes. Mary covered the basics, making sure to use words and analogies that normal people could understand.

As they stood to exit the room, Nina told Mary, "Well, I feel much better. I admit I was a little intimidated about becoming an overnight business owner. You've calmed my nerves a good bit today."

"Glad I could help. Call me anytime with questions. Alice was a wonderful woman, and I want to see her legacy thrive."

Mary got in her car and drove away. Michelle looked over to find Barry and Nina engrossed in conversation, so she disappeared to the stockroom. A few minutes later, Barry looked around. "Where did Michelle go?"

Nina turned in a circle. "I don't see her anywhere. I guess she went to work, though we still have fifteen minutes before we usually clock in. Since we don't really need to do that anymore, she may have just started working."

Barry backed up from the counter he had been leaning on and said, "I don't even think I said hello to her this morning. I'm going to go see what's she's up to." He walked into the stockroom and found Michelle pulling boxes onto a dolly. "Getting a head start?"

Her eyes never left the boxes as she answered, "No reason to wait until 10."

"I guess not. Hey, wait, you're not going to go all tyrant on me now that we are technically all each other's bosses, are you?"

She didn't laugh. She didn't even crack a smile. "How could I go tyrant when we're all in the same boat?"

Her lackluster comment told Barry something was wrong. Michelle always had spicy comebacks. She liked to spar. "Hey, are you okay?"

She continued stacking, so he put a hand on her arm. She stopped long enough to say, "I'm just steeling myself for what's to come."

"What does that mean?" he asked incredulously.

She had almost confided in him. She couldn't do that. Not when telling him the problem could potentially alter the progress of the very thing she had been trying to accomplish. So she searched for an excuse. "All the things that come with owning a business. I'm not sure I'm ready for them. I am only twenty-two, after all." She hated saying that. Not only was it untrue; she abhorred it when others doubted her abilities because of her age.

Barry stopped her by touching her elbow and saying, "Hey. You are one of the most capable people I know. Don't doubt yourself. Out of the three of us, you are the most likely to take charge and lead us to where we need to be. It doesn't matter that you're the youngest. You have the most prowess."

Michelle smiled at him in spite of herself. "Prowess, huh? I like that." She couldn't put a wall up between herself and Barry. He was too good at tearing them down.

Then a thought occurred to her. The stockroom was their lair. Nina never came in here. As long as Barry worked back here with her, she would never feel like a third wheel. This was her safe place.

She decided to insure this newfound security blanket. "Hey, Barry, I want to run an idea by you."

"What's that?" He carried over the box he had been holding and set it down, giving her his full attention.

"Do you think we should define our positions? I mean, things have been working great the way they are. If we hire new people, I'd like to know that you and I are still going to be heads of the stockroom, and Nina will still be in charge out front. Just so we don't go shifting spots and messing up a good thing."

Barry thought about it. "Well, since we are the ones in charge, we won't ever be forced to move ourselves around. Have you thought of some loophole that could get us kicked out of our own stockroom?"

Michelle hadn't thought it through before speaking. It didn't make much sense. Still, she was skilled at getting people to think she knew what she was talking about, so she continued, "There are exceptions. Legally speaking, it's better to define our titles now before we grow our business into something tougher to control." She had no idea what that meant, but she hoped Barry wouldn't see through it.

"Okay, I trust your judgment." Good, she had convinced him. She felt a bit deceptive, but it was for the good of their continued friendship. She loved spending time with Nina, but she could do that at home. Work belonged to her and Barry.

Leaving the stockroom under the guise of restocking a rack of t-shirts, Barry took the box straight to the counter. "We have a slight problem," he announced to Nina.

"What is it?"

"I think Michelle is starting to feel left out."

Nina seemed surprised. "Why do you think that?"

"I can tell by her demeanor. Remember how she left us alone on the beach last night? Well, earlier yesterday I noticed something. When she came out into the yard with the chairs and saw us holding hands, she acted strange, almost like she'd been slapped."

"Well, that's odd. I thought she wanted …" Nina trailed off. She caught herself just in time.

Or so she thought, but Barry knew what she meant. "I know, me too. I think she is starting to realize that bringing two closer means one is farther away."

That was the best way he could've worded it. He managed to acknowledge something between the two of them without giving it a name that would possibly scare her away. "So what do we do?" Nina asked.

"I'll give you two some space. I think I'm gonna spend some time on the beach alone after work. Why don't you see if Michelle wants to do something with just you?"

"Okay." The disappointment was evident in her voice. Nina had gotten used to having Barry around. She didn't want to distance herself from him, but she also didn't want Michelle left alone and hurting. "But how do we go about all coming back together as a group? I don't want to have to divide time between you guys forever. I like it when the three of us hang out."

"I don't know yet. We will figure something out, even if we have to confront Michelle and see what she needs from us. But just for tonight, I think the two of you need some time without me around."

Nina frowned. "Okay. You're probably right. But I don't like it."

His smile reached his eyes. "Are you saying you're gonna miss me?"

"Well, yeah." She felt her cheeks flush a little at her admission.

He was still smiling as he took the box and backed away. "May your heart grow fonder," he said as he pushed open the door with his backside.

Chapter 29

The minute Michelle walked through the door, Nina called out, "Hey, you. What are you doing tonight?"

Michelle looked at her with suspicion in her eyes. "I thought I'd just hang out at home. Why?"

"I thought we could do something. If you don't feel like going out, I could make us dinner."

"Okay. What did you have in mind?"

"Chicken cashew stir fry sound good?"

Michelle finally smiled. "That sounds delicious." Her expression changed as a thought occurred to her. "Will Barry be joining us?"

"No. He's having some 'me' time tonight." Nina saw Michelle's face relax subtly upon hearing this.

Michelle rolled her eyes. "He's so weird."

Nina laughed but said nothing in response.

As they walked to the house, Nina could already sense a change in Michelle. The dark cloud that had shaded her usually sunny disposition disintegrated, and the tension loosened its grip on her muscles. If all it took was some one on one time, then Nina felt bad for not offering this sooner.

Upon entering the kitchen, Michelle asked, "What can I do to help?"

"You can start the noodles and chop the cashews while I sliver the chicken and carrots."

"Teamwork makes cuisine work!" Michelle quipped.

Nina shook her head. She obviously felt so much better. Michelle hummed as she chopped, filling the air with good vibes.

Nina had just finished washing the raw chicken juice from her hands when someone knocked at the door. A glance out the stained glass window revealed the vague shape of a woman with blond hair. Nina pulled it open and gasped. "Gertrude!"

The woman shut her eyes. "Mike was the only one who called me that, and I hated it. Please, call me Geri." She reached out her hand, which Nina and then Michelle took in greeting.

"Please, come in," Nina invited, opening the door wider.

She stepped inside. "I can't stay long. My aunt is waiting in the car. I just wanted to come by and thank you. I had been in that shed for three long weeks when you found me. If not for you, I would have probably died in there."

Michelle put a hand on her arm. "I'm so sorry! Why did he do that to you?"

Geri smiled through the pain. "Why does Mike have a frog sanctuary in the backyard? Why does he talk to his stuffed raccoon? Why does Mike do anything he does? Oh, he'll probably be able to legitimately claim insanity, but at least he'll be institutionalized and not just in prison for a few years. I doubt I'll have to worry about him again ... that is, after they find him."

"They haven't found him yet?" The officers had seemed so certain that he wouldn't get far in his old vehicle. Nina had just assumed they'd arrested him by now.

"No. Unfortunately. He ditched his car about thirty miles from here. Which probably means he's trekking through a swamp, living off the land. He is a pretty skilled survivalist. And that worries me."

Michelle and Nina looked at each other with terror in their eyes. Michelle suddenly asked, "What about you, Geri? Do you have a place to stay? I assume you don't want to go back home, since he might return to look for you there. We have an extra room here. I know it isn't very far from your house, but you'd at least have two other people here to look out for you."

"Thank you, but I'm staying with my aunt. She came to pick me up from the hospital, and she's taking me back to her home in Savannah, which is plenty far away from here. Mike has never even met her and doesn't know where she lives, so I feel pretty safe there. So, I should go, but again, thank you. I'll never be able to repay you for what you did, but if I can ever do anything for you, here's my number." She handed Nina a business card with her name and number scribbled on the back.

"Sure. I'm glad you're okay. Stay safe out there."

Geri waved as she shut the door behind her. Michelle turned to Nina and said, "Should we be afraid?"

Nina sighed. "I don't think so. He doesn't know that we are the reason she is free. He probably doesn't even know that she's out of the shed, which is truly disturbing. He left her in there to die."

Michelle shuddered. She walked toward the hallway. "I'm double checking all the windows and doors, just to be safe."

"Good idea." Nina headed back into the kitchen to finish cooking. In spite of what she had just told Michelle, her hand shook as she picked up the pasta server.

She plated the food and sat at the table to eat. They tried to make lighthearted conversation to settle each other's nerves, but every little noise made both of them jump. Finally, Michelle put her fork down, looked Nina in the eye, and said, "Maybe you should call Barry."

"You want me to?" Nina clarified.

"It would make me feel better if someone else at least knew that Mike is still out there and may come back looking for Geri. And yes, it would help if that person were in our inner circle and cares what happens to us."

Nina scooted her chair back. She grabbed her phone from the kitchen counter and dialed Barry's number. He answered on the fourth ring, just as she was about to give up. "Hey, Nina. I didn't expect to hear from you tonight."

"Hey Barry. Some new information has come to light and we'd like to share it with you. Are you still at the beach?"

"Yeah. Do you want me to walk over?"

"Yes, if you don't mind. Michelle and I would like that," she threw her name in so he would understand that both of them wanted him there.

"I'll be right there. Oh, and Nina?"

"Yes?"

"I've missed you, too."

She heard the smile in his voice. He hung up without waiting for a response. She couldn't keep the smile from infiltrating her face.

"What did he say?" asked Michelle.

"He said he's on his way." Nina turned away to put the phone down, trying to hide her expression.

"You really like him, don't you?" There was an almost mournful sweetness in Michelle's question.

"I do. I can't help it."

"You don't need to help it! It's great." She put on a strong front to hide her own feelings of becoming an outcast.

"Are you okay with it, though? I know the three of us have become tight, and I don't want you to feel like you're an outsider if Barry and I become a thing." There, she said it. She didn't have much time before he arrived, and she wanted to clear the air.

"I am more than okay with it. I'll admit, I have been feeling a little lonely lately, but that just means I need to get out there and meet people. Maybe find a Barry of my own. Do not, I repeat, do NOT let my mopeyness get in the way of your happiness. I want this for you, more than I even want it for myself. For you and Barry both." She sealed that declaration with the biggest smile ever.

Nina believed her. Michelle had gone so far as to admit that she had been down about the two of them, but she seemed absolutely sincere in her encouragement for them to move forward. Finally, she said, "Okay. Thank you."

Michelle reached up and hugged her. Another knock at the door brought the two of them toward it. Since Nina stood at eye level with the window, she looked out to confirm it was Barry. Michelle opened the door for him. As he stepped inside, she surprised him with a big hug. "To what do I owe this?" he asked.

Michelle smiled at him. "You're just precious." She looked at Nina. "Both of you are." She cleared her throat. "Okay, now, down to business. Barry, take a seat. You may be here a while."

Chapter 30

Barry sat down on the sofa, but Michelle and Nina remained standing. They had too much nervous energy to sit still. He looked at them expectantly, so Michelle began to explain.

"We just had a visit from Geri, er, Gertrude, who likes to be called Geri, by the way. She informed us that Mike Waters is still on the loose."

Concern painted Barry's features. "They have no idea where he might be?" His voice took on a deeper, more serious tone than Nina had ever heard from him.

"All we know is that he ditched his car about thirty miles away. Geri thinks he is living in a swamp or the woods or something. She said he has survival skills, so he could potentially live out there for some time."

Barry ran his hands through his hair, clearly struggling with this new information. He had to protect them. He couldn't live with himself if something happened to either of them. "Okay, here's what I think we need to do. Either I stay here and sleep on your couch until Mike is found, or you two come to my house. I don't want to let you out of my sight until he's no longer a threat."

Though Nina loved both of those ideas, Michelle felt trapped. She had just decided she needed to get out more. How was she supposed to meet someone with Barry tagging along? Nevermind the compounded loneliness she would feel if she were stuck with the two of them even in her own home.

Barry and Nina both looked at Michelle. When it became clear she had nothing to say, Nina turned to Barry. "I think those are great ideas. I'm up for either of them. Michelle, what do you think?"

She couldn't tell them she needed space. Not right now, with real danger a factor. "I think it would be wise for us to stick together," she forced herself to admit. "Barry, it's up to you. Just know that if you stay here, you won't have to sleep on the couch. We have a third bedroom."

Barry leaned forward. Stress lines that were not there before appeared on his forehead and beside his mouth. "If you stay with me, you'll be further away from his house. On the other hand, if I stay here, we'll all be able to keep an eye on the place and notify the cops if he comes back."

He looked at Nina, who turned toward Michelle. She sighed. Why did everyone always look to her for big decisions? Then she remembered what Barry had said earlier that day. She had prowess, the trait of a leader. Accepting the compliment, she recommended, "Barry, I think you should stay here. It's best if we watch to see if he comes back, and we can't do that from your place."

He nodded in agreement. "Nina, are you okay with that?"

"Yeah. I think that's best."

He was happy to hear that. He stood and said, "Okay. I'll go pack a bag. You guys come with me."

No one argued. They followed him to his vehicle and got inside. He lived only five minutes away in a very nice neighborhood. It wasn't right on the beach, but it was close enough to walk to it.

Barry's house had a white brick exterior. The size of it surprised Nina. "This place is big. You live here alone?"

He smiled sideways at her. "You mean, how can someone on my salary afford a place like this?"

She tried to backtrack. "I, uh, no, I just mean …" she trailed off when she noticed his laughter.

"I'm just messing with you. The truth is I can't. Just wait till you see the inside." Offering no further explanation, he opened the door and got out.

They followed him inside. Michelle and Nina both gasped at the spacious interior. The open floor plan let them see the living room, dining area, and kitchen all at once. The walls were painted white, making the space look even more open than it actually was. Past the living room, where the kitchen began, floor to ceiling windows framed the rest of the wall on the north side and wrapped around the corner to form the west wall. Walking into the kitchen, Nina noticed that part of the north window wall contained a sliding glass door that led to …

"An indoor pool?!"

Michelle ran forward and opened the door. She whipped around and said, "Barry, you've been holding out on us!"

He laughed and walked through the door. Nina joined them in the screened in pool room. Tropical heat hit her face as she stepped through, so she shut the door behind her to keep it out of the air-conditioned house. A long rectangular pool stretched across the concrete space that spanned the length of the living room and kitchen combined. Lounge chairs and potted palms lined the sides and corners.

"This is an impressive bachelor pad. I bet you have a lot of friends hitting you up to come over," Michelle observed.

"Actually, none. I don't know anyone in town but you two. I had to make sure you were the real deal before I let you in."

They both looked at him in shock. "I'm just joking. But not about not knowing anyone but you. You guys are my only two friends, and you are welcome to come swim here anytime."

Michelle turned to Nina. "Well if I'd known that, I would've brought my swimsuit. And I would've said we should stay here. This place is much nicer than ours."

"We can split our time between our houses, if you like. I do like the idea of sleeping at your place, though. Mike is more likely to sneak home in the night than in broad daylight."

"Um, yes," answered Michelle, who had kicked off her shoes and was already two steps down into the pool. "Oh, this water is perfect."

"Feel free to sit on the edge and dangle while I pack a bag. I'll be back in a few." He turned to go inside, and Nina joined Michelle poolside.

Michelle made sure Barry had shut the door before she said, "I don't know what the story is with this place, but if we find out he owns it, and you two get married one day, this could be yours." She pointed down at the pool as her eyes widened.

Nina giggled but changed the subject quickly. "So, can you swim?"

Michelle looked at Nina like she'd just admitted she ate starfish for breakfast. "Can I swim? Only backwards, forwards, and all day long. Girl, I was born in water, and I never forgot what to do."

"Wait, your mom did a water birth? For real?"

"Yes. I seriously think it's why I'm basically a mermaid. No joke." She tossed her long hair and sang out her best Ariel impression.

Nina applauded. "Now sing the dinglehopper song!"

She only got as far as, "Wouldn't you think my collection's complete?" before Barry slid the door back open. She cut her song short and smiled at him. "Hey, pool boy. I was just showing Nina here that I belong to the fish people."

"Yeah. Okay. The chlorine can get to you sometimes. Let's get you some fresh air." Barry reached out his hand.

Michelle grabbed it and pulled herself up, but she protested, "Are you kidding me? This is the best air there is right here. The smell of chlorine takes me back to summer days at the city pool, tanning with my friends on floats, flirting with boys." She inhaled deeply as she said, "I could breathe this all day long," in a nasally, airy tone.

Nina put an arm around her and led her forward. "Maybe later. Right now, we need to show Barry to his room."

Michelle moaned as if gasping for air when she stepped through the door. Barry slid it shut and asked, "Were you by any chance in the drama club at school?"

"Now, how did you know that? Have you been looking at my old yearbooks?" Michelle batted her lashes.

He just shook his head and walked to the carport door. They piled into his vehicle. As he backed out the driveway, the ever curious Michelle mentioned, "So, you never did tell us the story with this house. What gives? Are you a squatter?"

That got a laugh out of him. "No, I'm not a squatter. I really do own this house."

He stopped there, so Michelle prodded, "So you're secretly rich, and you just like working in a stockroom for fun?"

"No, I'm not rich." He got quiet again, and Michelle sighed. He liked toying with her, because she was so easy to annoy. But when she surprised him by staying silent, he admitted, "The house was in foreclosure. I got it at auction super cheap. It took everything I had in savings, but I bought it outright. Now I just have to come up with enough to pay taxes and insurance every year."

"This gorgeous place came super cheap? Do you know how rare that is, Barry? Also, do you need two roommates?" Michelle joked, but she just might have taken him up on it if he offered.

He replied, "Do you know how blessed you are to live right across the street from the beach? If I lived that close, I'd be there all the time. It's better than having a pool."

Michelle argued, "I don't know, Barry. A pool doesn't have sharks and jellyfish scooting around in it. Not to mention there's no riptide or little kids wearing poopy diapers upstream."

Nina and Barry both gagged and cackled at that. "I have to admit that's true. Okay, a pool is better for swimming. But you can't beat the beach for the soft sand, the view, the breeze off the water. And I can't have a fire out here at night. The houses are too close together, so it's frowned upon, and maybe even illegal."

"Who needs fire when you have water, Barry? I'm gonna call you Barry Bonfire, because you're obsessed."

Nina just listened to the two of them going back and forth. They could easily be mistaken for brother and sister. Their friendship thrived on a mixture of teasing and arguing, but in a healthy manner. That was the type of personality they seemed to share. Nina would imagine both came from big families where this kind of behavior was prevalent. Since she had been an only child, she never learned how to hassle someone in a friendly way. Were she even able to dish it out, she probably couldn't take it in return.

In no time, they were ambling across the sand toward home. Michelle and Barry were still going at it. Nina was happy to take a backseat and listen. It seemed like Michelle had returned to full form, not feeling left out at all.

Chapter 31

As the first rays of the morning sun filtered through the space between two curtains, Nina awakened. She stretched her long limbs and settled on her back, relaxed and suddenly aware of Barry's presence somewhere in the house.

The knowledge that he was here warmed and comforted her. She couldn't deny even to herself that she had come to look forward to work because she would, at some point in the day, see him, talk to him. Though she felt obligated by her extremely recent divorce to go through some sort of love avoiding phase, a sabbatical from men, she couldn't control her drawing toward him.

She arose and put on a rainbow pastel linen dress, another sleeveless with a drawstring at the top and a hem that fell about three inches above her knees. In the bathroom, she washed and moisturized her face. Nina had been blessed with a smooth, golden complexion enhanced by her time in the sun. She didn't need makeup. She did, however, apply a pale green shimmer shadow to her lids to give them a touch of color similar to the dress's background. Her platinum blond hair fell an inch above her shoulders and required little maintenance. She brushed it and slid a silver and gold headband into her crown.

Nina was aware of her beauty without being consumed by it. She never used her looks to get her way, and she didn't flaunt herself in public. She could walk down the street fully understanding why men stopped to stare at her without needing them to or wondering why when they didn't. Her only serious relationship had been with Donovan, so she had very little experience with flirtation. She had not needed to attract a date since she was twenty-two.

She applied a touch of pale pink frosty lip gloss, which her coffee cup would soon claim. Just knowing Barry was in the house made her want to look good, even if only for the few minutes before she ate breakfast. One last glance in the mirror showed her she would likely take his breath away. She backed out of the room and shut off the light.

Sure enough, as soon as Barry looked up from his coffee, he took on the expression of someone who had just seen a thing of incomparable beauty. "Hi," he uttered slowly and in more syllables than the word should ever possess. He tried to keep cool, but like a tourist viewing the seventh natural wonder of the world for the first time, he could not contain his awe. "You look stunning," he declared rather breathlessly.

With more charm than any canyon or waterfall, her smile portrayed an inner glow, as if she'd made peace with the effect she had on men. "Thank you," she crooned.

She continued to look at Barry with that smile, and he found the corners of his own mouth had edged up without his permission. Feeling suddenly awkward, he searched the near barren shelves of his brain for something to say. All he came up with was, "Coffee?"

"Yes, always coffee." She turned toward the Keurig. Scouring the cabinet above the appliance, she found a hazelnut K-cup and inserted it. She put one spoonful of sugar in a mug and placed it beneath the spout.

Barry watched her fluid motions and wondered how any human could be so perfect. Given that she was human, a flaw of some sort would be inevitable, but he had yet to see it. He didn't mind being blinded by her light to any darkness she might harbor.

Jarring him from his reverie, Michelle bounded into the room in an olive green jumper. "Good morning!" she sung as if the sunshine that had awakened her had seeped into her body and now shot forth from her pores.

Finding some semblance of control, he replied, "Morning yourself. You're happy."

"I'm just looking forward to swimming in someone's awesome pool later today." She wagged her eyebrows at him and held up a small beach bag. "I packed my suit."

"Hey, why don't you come swim in my pool today after work? I can even give you a ride."

She threw the soft bag at him and hit his shoulder. "If you don't, I know where you live."

Nina sat down beside Michelle with her steaming mug of coffee. "I need to grab my swimsuit before we leave. Don't let me forget."

In that instant, a loud crash outdoors brought all three of them to the kitchen window. "Get the binoculars!" Michelle yelled to Nina, who stood closest to them. She passed them to Michelle's waiting hand. After about ten seconds of observation, she announced with disappointment, "Raccoons."

She handed the binoculars to Nina, who aimed them next door in time to see the back end of a raccoon hanging out of Mike's garbage bin. His buddy scampered across the frame, taking his trashy prize to the pond. "Guys, he's washing his garbage before he eats it! Ha!"

Barry stood directly behind Nina and looked over her shoulder at the animal. "Actually, he's not washing his food. He's wetting his hands so he can more easily feel what he is about to eat."

Nina and Michelle turned to look at him. "Say what?" Michelle asked flatly.

"When they get their hands wet, it stimulates the nerves in their paws, so they can sense the texture and shape of their food better." The women just looked at him without comment, so he confessed, "I like watching nature shows, okay?"

Nina just smiled, but Michelle found it hilarious. "So not only are you Barry Bonfire; you're also Barry Biology." A fresh round of laughter cascaded from her mouth as she amused herself with alliteration.

"Okay, Mermaid Michelle. Eat your breakfast. You're gonna burn off your morning energy before you even get to work if you continue to entertain yourself at that rate."

She gasped with delight. "Mermaid Michelle! I love it." As she filled a bowl with Lucky Charms, Nina was struck by her childlike energy. Maybe Michelle was so precious in her eyes because she embodied the traits that a well-raised and loved child would manifest. Maybe Nina envied her a little.

Though Nina had been given a decent childhood, growing up alone had taken its toll on her. She never wanted for food, shelter, or basic human rights, but when it came time to play, she was told to go out in the yard by herself or go to her room and do a puzzle. That in itself was sad, but what really tore her apart was being cut off from the family upon marrying Donovan. How could parents who really loved her do that?

A tear crept up and coated her eye. Barry reached across the table and put his hand over hers. "Hey. You okay?"

The sudden warmth of his touch brought her back from the painful place. She turned to look at him and laughed nervously. "You caught me reminiscing."

"About Donovan?" he asked gently.

"No, no. I have no tears left for him. I was thinking about my family."

"Missing them?"

"Kind of. But more hurt by them than anything else." He still held her hand. He wished he could take her pain away.

Michelle joined them, blissfully unaware of their serious conversation. "Can I bust up in this lovefest and eat my Lucky Charms?" She didn't even look up as she took a seat and spooned the colorful marshmallows into her mouth.

Nina looked at Barry. "It's all good," she said without a hint of sadness. He squeezed her hand before releasing it. She wiped the moisture from under her eyes.

They put their dishes in the sink and stepped out into the ocean air. Nina could taste the salt today. Heavy, humid air pressed down upon them. A steady hot breeze whipped the palm fronds toward the house. "A storm is coming," she announced cryptically.

"Ooh, Nina. That gave me chills!" Michelle rubbed her own arms to calm the goosebumps.

Barry lent validity to her statement. "We are supposed to get severe thunderstorms tonight." He looked over his shoulder at the house on stilts, then looked forward to his vehicle. "Would you guys rather spend this stormy night in a brick house closer to the ground?"

"Yay! Pool party!" whooped Michelle.

He looked to Nina for confirmation. "Just let me go back in and grab a few things." Michelle followed her inside while Barry waited in the yard. Something red caught his eye at the base of the bushes. He stooped to get a closer look. A long pair of hedge shears jutted out from the branches at the base of a plant. A large pair of men's gardening gloves rested on top of them.

Quickly, he stood and surveyed the area. No one lingered in sight. Whoever had left these was long gone now.

He heard the women coming out of the door. He made a snap decision not to tell them about his discovery just yet. He didn't want to worry them, and honestly, there were much scarier items to find in your yard than a pair of trimmers and gloves.

Just to eliminate the possibility, once they were in his vehicle, he casually asked, "Have either of you ladies done any yard work since you moved in?"

"No. Alice never got around to telling us what we needed to do, so we haven't touched anything. With my luck, I'd kill all the plants," Nina answered.

Michelle asked, "Why? Does it look like we need to do some maintenance?"

"No. Just curious." Barry set his jaw as he pulled onto the open sand. He would have to remain vigilant.

Chapter 32

Barry handed the delivery man a tip as he took the bag of Japanese food from his hand. The smell of teriyaki wafted up from the containers, reminding him that he was quite hungry. He tapped on the glass to get his guests' attention. They were lounging poolside, not yet in their suits but anticipating a swim after dinner. They hopped up and raced to the door upon seeing the food. Today had been a long one, so no one had eaten much. Being business owners who had not yet met all of their employees, Michelle and Nina had sat down with each of them throughout the day to get to know a little bit about them and what shifts they generally preferred to work. Barry also attended the meetings, though he had already met everyone over the past six months.

Toward the end of the day, the three of them went over the shift schedule and realized that they could have the following day off. Michelle raised her hands and said, "What what! We should look at this thing more often. Who knows how many days we could potentially be off if enough people are working?" She high-fived Nina. "I say we hit the beach, all day." Then she surprised them both by asking, "Barry? You in?"

He dropped his pen on the table and shut his notebook. "I go where you go for now, remember? But yes, I'll be happy to join you on the beach."

Now, they were side by side on barstools pulled up to Barry's kitchen island, dining on hibachi shrimp. Nina sat in the middle. She stole a glance at Barry as he pushed his zucchini off to the side. "You're not going to eat that?" she asked.

"No. Real men don't eat zucchini." Noting her look of surprise at his aversion, he offered, "You can have it if you want it."

She speared a piece of teriyaki soaked green goodness and put it in her mouth. "How can you not like zucchini?"

"It's green and slightly squishy. Like the giant booger of the vegetable world. It's not that hard!" His bewildered expression matched hers.

Michelle distracted them by singing, "I. Like. Green. Boogers and I cannot lie!" then biting a forkful of zucchini.

"I'm done." Barry announced, shutting his styrofoam container.

"Hey, wait. Let me scoop the rest of that zucchini into mine if you're gonna put it away," Nina requested.

He set it back down next to hers and flipped the lid up. "Gladly."

She took her fork and pulled the wedges toward her pile of rice. "Thank you."

As they continued eating, Barry moved to the living room to watch the weather report. A sudden gust of wind shook the west wall, prompting Nina to ask, "What are they saying about the storms?"

"Looks like the worst of it will be here in about forty-five minutes."

Michelle grabbed Nina by the arm. "We'd better get our swim on now."

"Isn't it unsafe to swim indoors during a thunderstorm?" She turned to Barry. "Is the risk the same as if you're showering or doing dishes with lightning nearby?"

"Technically, the pool room is bonded and grounded, so if lightning strikes, it should travel down the rod. However, I guess there is still a slight risk of electrocution."

Michelle and Nina gasped. A low rumble sounded in the distance, causing Nina to suggest, "Maybe we should wait until after the storm to swim."

"I'm down with that." Michelle picked up their empty containers and tossed them in the trash.

Nina moved to the living room to join Barry on the sofa. He was all the way at the right end, so she sat in the middle, leaving enough space for Michelle on the left. Together, they watched the band of red on the radar in fast forward animation. It wouldn't be long now.

Barry noticed Nina fidgeting. "Are you scared of storms?" he asked.

In a small voice, she admitted, "A little." Then lightning cracked the sky, sending down a tremor of thunder so powerful it shook the ground. Nina instinctively curled toward Barry, hiding her face in his chest. "Okay, a lot."

He brought his arms up to hold her. She relaxed her tense position and settled into a snuggle. She stretched one lovely arm across his abdomen and held on, sure to squeeze his kidney when surprised by the next sudden boom. He didn't mind.

They listened to the weatherman's projection of timing for all the small towns between the center of the cell and their current location. Just as he read off Orange Beach's time as five minutes away, the power went off. The thickness of the cloud cover, combined with the time of the evening, thrust them into complete darkness.

Michelle yawned, a sound so out of place in the midst of the anxiety Nina felt. "I'm going to bed," she announced through a second yawn.

"How can you sleep at a time like this?" Nina whispered, as if she feared the darkness might hear.

"Storms make me sleepy," she replied, still yawning. "Night."

"Goodnight," Nina and Barry echoed in surprise. A little bit of cloud-filtered dusk light came through the windowed sides of the house, allowing Nina's eyes to adjust enough to see Barry's face. "I wish thunder had that effect on me."

"I find it exhilarating." His announcement caused her to pull out of the snuggle and look at him like he was crazy.

"So Michelle is sleepy, I'm a nervous wreck, and you're thrilled? Aren't we a tripolar trio?"

"That we are. And to explain myself, I like the energy in the air, the feeling of not knowing what's going to happen next. I watch storm chaser videos for fun. I would never get in a car and intentionally drive into a tornado like they do, but I appreciate the closeup view they give us people at home."

Nina looked at him and blinked deliberately before saying, "I turn those videos off as fast as I can. They add to my nightmares."

Barry pulled the arm that had been behind Nina toward himself. Leaning forward to reach the cabinet under the coffee table surface, he said, "Speaking of nightmares, I've got something for you." He opened the little door and pulled out a tray topped with three fat candles and a lighter. "How have your dreams been lately?"

She thought back to the last few nights. Since Barry had introduced her to fire therapy, she could not remember one single tornado dream. Suddenly recalling the dream she had the previous night when Barry was in the house, she was thankful for the cover of near darkness to hide her blush. In her dream, the two of them slow-danced on the beach at night. She had found herself completely captivated by him, unable or unwilling to look away from those eyes.

"Nina?" He brought her back to reality, but only halfway, since whether in one dimension or the other, she stared into the same eyes.

"Yes, dreams," she recovered. "They've been good."

He lit the first candle. "No funnel clouds?"

"None at all."

The wheel of the lighter flicked. The second candle sprang to life. "What have you dreamed about instead?"

She hesitated. "The beach."

Holding the button in position, he fed the third candle with the remaining fire from the second strike. "Day or night?"

"Night."

Still looking at the fiery display, he asked, "Was I there?"

Was he some kind of mind reader? A fire hypnotist, maybe?

Nina sat in stunned silence. He raised his eyebrows in a teasing manner. "I was, wasn't I?"

Now he was just trying to make her squirm. She looked about the room as if the words she needed might be just floating by, ready for her to snatch out of the air and use like they were her own. Well, the only thing floating in the air right now was the fire, so she said, "Candles, huh. Do you use those on rainy nights when you can't build a bonfire?"

He smiled and blinked away his previous attempt to extract private information from her. "I do. Fire is fire, no matter how small. What about you? Do you own any candles?"

"No. Unfortunately, the only thing I own right now is clothing. Oh, and a business. And a house." She smiled at her realization that she could no longer say all she had were the clothes in her closet.

"Well. Maybe it's time you went shopping for some candles."

"Maybe." Her eyes never left his.

"Or maybe I could share," he offered.

The gaze between them never faltered, as if locked in place by the electricity in the atmosphere. She didn't feel intimidated like she did when Donovan would stare her down until she caved to his point of view. Rather, she felt bound by something otherworldly. Something wonderful, of almost tangible purity.

He reached for her hand, and they interlocked fingers in midair. Looking down, he brought their joined hands to rest upon his knee. His eyes swept back up to rejoin the current upon which they were previously connected. With contact reestablished, he said softly, "I don't want to say or do anything to make you feel uncomfortable. I know that your life has been turned upside-down in the past two weeks, and I want to be a source of healing and solace for you. Please tell me if I'm anything but that, and I promise you, I will stop whatever it is I'm doing that bothers you."

"Wow," she whispered. "I've never heard anything like that. Thank you. No one's ever seemed to care how their actions made me feel."

He took her other hand. "You deserve so much more." His words held such authenticity of emotion, they broke her heart, but rather than in the past when it had shattered into a million irreparable shards, this time it fractured along clean, thin lines that could be easily resealed with the balm of love.

A long, steady rumble of thunder surrounded the house, building in intensity as it neared the structure. Nina didn't jump, but Barry felt her hands tense up inside his own. He opened his mouth to say, "It's okay," but the words were lost in a drowning wave of hail. It assaulted the roof like a hundred weighted ping-pong balls bouncing at once. The white stones painted the yard like a scene from a Christmas movie.

The noise was enough to disturb a sleeping Michelle. "What is going on out there?" she asked as she emerged from the hallway.

The three of them moved closer to the windows. They watched in awe as the sky spit the cold clusters like an angry icemaker. Barry kept one arm around Nina's shoulder. She looked as if she might run for shelter, but there was no storm cellar here. "Let's go into the hallway," Barry suggested. They filed into the windowless corridor. Barry opened a door on the left and punched a battery-powered touch light to reveal a big closet. "In here," he ordered.

They each took a seat on the floor. Nina gained a small amount of comfort in knowing she was in the most interior room of the house with no vulnerable openings. They sat there for the duration of the hailstorm, which lasted maybe five minutes. An eerie calm followed, prompting Michelle to say, "Hey, isn't this the part where the …"

Barry cut her off. "Storm moves on and we're all clear? Yes, should be. Let's just sit here a few more minutes to make sure." He shot her a death glare.

She caught the drift. "Yeah, we should be able to swim soon."

Nina rattled out a moan. "My nerves have given me enough of a workout for one night. I think I just want to lie down."

Michelle yawned again. "Good, because I was sleeping hard. I might pass out in the water."

They listened for remnants of the storm for another minute. Then Barry declared, "I think it's safe to come out now."

He opened the closet door. Nina and Michelle followed closely behind him to keep from bumping into anything in the unfamiliar territory. The kitchen window revealed a shiny white blanket over the ground. Michelle exclaimed, "Whoa! I wonder if we could skate on it."

"It would be more like gliding across a roller rink full of marbles than an icy pond," said Barry.

Michelle stared bleary eyed at the slick chunks. She finally shrugged. "Okay. Goodnight." Then she turned and disappeared down the dark hallway.

The electricity whirred to life. In the glare of sudden light, Barry turned to face Nina. She blinked as if in pain and said, "I think I'm gonna turn in, too."

"Okay, I'll show you to your room." He led her to the end of the hallway and opened the last door on the left. "This is yours." He flipped on the light and let her walk inside by herself. Standing with one arm resting on the doorframe, he smiled and gently said, "Goodnight, Nina."

She turned suddenly, as if surprised that he hadn't followed her inside. Upon seeing he had stopped in the doorway, she felt a surge of gratitude for his understanding of the strange yet happy mess her life had become and of her need for time and space to untangle it. She hoped the smile in her eyes relayed the appreciation in her heart as she answered sweetly, "Goodnight, Barry."

Chapter 33

The first thing Barry said to Nina in the kitchen the next morning was, "How did you dream?"

"In short bursts," she answered, taking the full coffee cup he offered. "I remember being surrounded by a ring of fire on the sand." She took a long sip to stir her senses. "The ocean washed a gap in the ring so I could escape."

"Uhoh. Did I overdo it with the fire therapy?"

"No. I'm not sure I even wanted to escape. I just turned in a circle, taking in the fact that I was surrounded by flames; but it was like a protective barrier."

"So instead of trapping you in, the fire was keeping something else out?"

"Yes. I suppose so, though I didn't sense any danger. When the ocean put a section of it out, I just walked through because it seemed like the thing to do."

Barry sipped. "Mmm. Okay, I think I can interpret that. Maybe I'm the ring of fire, since I talk so much about it and how it can help, and Mike Waters is the ocean trying to put me out. But if he does come around and knock me unconscious, don't go with him. It isn't the thing to do."

"Interesting take." She didn't think it was correct, but she enjoyed the creativity of his theory.

He observed her with quiet awe. In her natural state, with no makeup, wearing a white V-neck t-shirt with black fish bones on the front and gray drawstring shorts, she was every bit as enchanting as when she actually intended to be. She possessed sophistication in spades.

Michelle sprang forth from the hallway like a gumball from a machine. Though not at all like Nina, she definitely stood out from the crowd. Her exuberance surpassed that of anyone Barry had ever met. In a happy voice not designed for mornings before coffee, she announced, "Happy 1st Annual Owners Day Off!"

The edges of Nina's lips upturned just a touch as she asked, "Oh, are we making it a yearly holiday?"

Grabbing a banana from Barry's fruit basket, she replied, "Naw, girl. I hope it's more like a monthly thing." She looked toward the window as she peeled the fruit. "Woo, it's bright out there. And I forgot my shades. Barry, can we stop by the house and get them on our way to the beach?"

"Sure. I'd like to check the area anyway." He had lain awake puzzling over the gardening tool last night. The fact that someone had left it in the bushes seemed to suggest they were there to do some actual yardwork, but if that were the case, why hadn't anything been trimmed? Had Barry's presence in the house spooked someone who wanted to secretly do a good deed, or did they intend to use the sharp shears as a deadly weapon later when he wasn't around?

Michelle and Nina talked and laughed on the ride across the sand, but Barry remained on high alert. His eyes scanned the area, watching for any sign of movement. He didn't notice anything out of place until the bushes came into view.

Nina caught it right away. "Someone trimmed our hedges!"

Michelle added, "They cut like three feet off the top!"

Before, the tall greenery had given the yard some degree of privacy. Now, the plants stood only about a foot high.

Turning to Barry, Michelle asked, "Did Alice hire someone to do this? I thought she wanted us to take care of the yard as part of our agreement."

Barry murmured, "I don't know," while jogging over for a close inspection. The hedge shears were gone, as well as the gloves. Evidently, whoever had brought them here had used them for their intended purpose, after all. That made him feel a bit better, but still troubling was the fact that the yard was now more exposed, making it easier for someone to observe Nina and Michelle.

Nina held her phone to her ear. "I'm calling Mary to see if Alice had paid someone to do this." Mary answered, and Nina stepped off to the side to talk.

"I'm going to check the rest of the yard," Barry told Michelle.

"I'll come with you."

They walked around back. Michelle pointed to the base of the palm trees. "Look! That's fresh mulch. It's a different color than yesterday."

Reddish-brown chips surrounded the trunks. Everything appeared freshly watered. Barry walked over to the garden hose reel and saw a droplet slowly descending from the mouth of the hose. This had been done very recently, probably right before they arrived.

Nina approached them. "Mary said Alice hasn't paid anyone to do yardwork in eight years."

Michelle wrung her hands. "Maybe we should call the police."

"And tell them what? We'd like to report some unauthorized plant care?" Nina didn't mean to make light of the situation, but it didn't seem like something the cops would be willing to invest time and energy in solving.

Barry shook his head. "You're right. They'll probably laugh at us. We may have to figure this one out on our own."

"How do we do that? We can't just stay home all the time and wait for him to come back. Even if he plans to continue this, it could be weeks before he returns." Michelle was getting frustrated. It seemed that forces were aligning to keep her confined.

"Security cameras," said Barry. "We'll put them up on all sides of the house. Ones that record in high definition. We'll hook them up to the TV. If we notice anything different about the yard, we can just rewind to the time we left the house and watch what happened while we were gone."

"That sounds expensive," Nina pointed out.

"I've got some at my place that I never hooked up. They came with the house. I'll just bring them over here." Barry hadn't felt the need to use them at home. The crime rate in his neighborhood was pretty low.

Michelle asked, "But even if we record a stranger in our yard when we're not home, what good will that do? We still won't know who he is and why he's here if he's gone by the time we get home."

"At least we'll know if it's Mike Waters," Barry countered.

"Ah. I didn't even think of that. Okay, good point." Michelle considered the possibility. She looked over at Mike's barren front yard. Tufts of mostly dead grass littered the sand in odd spots. "I doubt it's Mike. He doesn't even have a lawn to maintain, just a backyard frog swamp. He might not even know how."

Barry had to agree. "Still, we need to rule out that chance. Also, a camera in the back pointed toward his house could watch for him when we're not here."

Nina spoke up, "I think it's a great idea. We should do it now, before anything else happens."

Michelle inwardly pouted. Her swimming plans had now been disrupted two days in a row. "How long will it take to get set up?"

"I don't know. I've never done it before. I'll have to read the manual."

She wanted to scream. Of the many good traits Michelle possessed, patience was not one. She managed to hold her tongue. Barry was doing them a favor, one he didn't owe. She must keep that at the forefront of her mind.

Nina suggested, "Well, let's get to it." They walked back to the vehicle without bothering to go inside for Michelle's sunglasses. Fate's determination of how they would spend their day off had them all let down. They rode in silence. Barry went inside his house alone to get the cameras, which had never even been taken out of the box. The previous owner had bought them right before he had lost his job and subsequently his home.

Back at the beach house, Michelle retired to her room to read. Nina assisted Barry with hooking up wires. Three hours later, the system was operational. Nina called for Michelle, and they looked at the four split screens on the television.

"It's so colorful! I expected it to be kind of blurry with a bit of static. This is like looking out a window!" Michelle exclaimed. Seeing the image quality made her feel like perhaps the outcome had been worth one ruined morning.

Barry showed them how to rewind and how to switch between regular TV and the security monitor. As they watched some birds near the pond and the breeze through the trees out front simultaneously, Nina said, "I must admit, I'm impressed that you did all this without previous experience, Barry."

He glowed at the compliment. "Thanks. I have a basic understanding of how stuff like this works. I hear having a lovely assistant helps."

Michelle fell over making a gagging sound. "Can we please go to the beach before I throw up?"

Barry scooted away from her. "Maybe we should walk. I just cleaned my vehicle."

Glancing at the clock, Michelle suggested, "Actually, I take that back. It's not nausea; it's hunger pains. Why don't we drive over to The Jellyfish? I've got a hankering for some fish tacos."

"Oh, I love that place. They have good sushi." Nina hadn't eaten there since she had become a resident of Orange Beach, but she and Donovan had been there many times in vacations past.

"Okay. I know where that is. Let's go."

They headed toward nearby Perdido Key. On the way, they passed through a state park. Nina looked at all the beautiful white sand surrounded by only sea oats and peppered with just a few pavilions and rest areas, unlike the majority of the boulevard leading up to this point. "I'd like to come out here sometime. It would be nice to see the beach away from all the condos and businesses, just get back to nature."

"It is a beautiful area. There's also Johnson Beach further down. I've been there several times. I'll take you whenever you want to go."

"Thanks." Nina realized they had access to a perfectly good beach across the street from home, but the undisturbed beauty here drew here in, made her eager to explore what lay beyond the dunes.

The Jellyfish came into view on the left side of the street. It sat above a souvenir shop. Michelle was the first to reach the stairs leading up to the restaurant, and she raced up them like the place was down to its last taco. She waited impatiently for Nina and Barry to climb on up. She already had her hand on the door when they got there.

The waiter seated them next to an aquarium. Barry was the only one at the table who had never been inside. He peered at the tropical fish behind the glass and joked, "Is this a super fresh sushi situation? Do we get to pick our own?"

Michelle hit him with the menu before opening it. "Ah, good. They still have my fish tacos."

Barry gagged slightly. "Two words that should not exist next to each other, especially on a menu. I do like sushi, though. What's good?"

"I like the shrimp tempura. I get it every time I'm here," suggested Nina.

"Hmm, oh, this looks interesting. BBQ eel. Ever tried the Unagi roll?"

Nina made a face. "No. I like eel sauce, but I can't get past the texture of actual eel."

Barry slammed his menu shut. "I'm getting that. I feel adventurous."

Michelle held her finger up to the aquarium, trying to get the attention of an impressive looking blowfish. It seemed fascinated by her, following her movements as if she were prey. "I'm going to call you 'Bob'."

Barry laughed and looked at Nina, who was staring at the artwork on the walls. Someone had painted a swordfish on a long piece of old wood with organic edges. Nina pointed and said, "I love it when people paint on natural surfaces rather than white canvas."

"So you're an art aficionado?" he asked.

"I used to paint."

Michelle chimed in, "And she is going to take it up again, now that her worst and only critic is out of her life for good."

"Is that so?" Barry wouldn't be surprised if Nina were a superb artist. It stood to reason that someone that beautiful could easily create a thing to be admired.

"Once I get enough money to buy all my art supplies, I'm going to try."

"You know, our monthly distributions will be ready next week. I don't know how much they'll be, but I would imagine you'll be able to buy everything you need with them and more." Michelle had been talking to Mary via email, trying to get an idea of what her financial future looked like. She, Barry, and Nina had agreed to reasonable and equal salaries, but on top of that, they'd get monthly distributions for being business owners. Mary hadn't been able to give her an exact figure, but based on numbers of the past, Seahorse Treasures appeared pretty profitable.

"Oh, I didn't realize we'd be getting them this soon. That's good news." Nina felt secret anxiety over daring to pick up a brush again. She had been relieved to use her lack of funds as an excuse to put it off, but it appeared she couldn't do that much longer.

"I'd love to see some of your work," Barry commented.

Nina smiled nervously. "I don't have any here."

The waiter appeared, relieving Nina from an uncomfortable conversation. He took their orders and disappeared. They talked shop until their food arrived. Michelle bit into her tacos as soon as the plate touched the table, causing the astonished waiter to snatch his hand away. Barry apologetically said, "She hasn't eaten anything but seaweed in two days. She chewed on my arm on the way up here. You're right to be afraid."

His eyes opened wide. "I'm just going to back away slowly." With his gaze on Michelle, he took several steps toward the kitchen.

Barry looked in the direction he had vanished and said, "We need to leave him a good tip."

Michelle didn't even put down her taco before slapping his arm with her free hand.

"Ow! Why are you so abusive?"

"I don't know. Maybe it's the salt from all the seaweed, or maybe I'm allergic to your flesh!" she said sarcastically.

"You're definitely salty, I'll give you that."

Michelle held up her hand as if to block him out. "Let me enjoy my tacos in peace."

Barry leaned forward and took a bite of his sushi. "Oh. Wow. This is great."

The sight of eel chunks going into his mouth sickened Nina. She looked away. She was grateful that the super crunchy texture of her shrimp tempura felt like the opposite of eel on her tongue.

They had the waiter split the check individually. Nina paid for hers first, then walked over to examine the art while Barry and Michelle took care of their checks. She was lost in admiration of exquisite photorealism when she felt a hand on her back and heard a low voice say, "You ready to go?"

She turned to find Barry standing closer than she had expected. She almost apologized, feeling like she had bumped into his aura. She regained her composure, though her heart raced independently of her calm exterior. "Yes," she answered in as normal a voice as she could manage.

They finally made it to the beach around 2 p.m. Michelle stretched out in a lounge chair to soak up some sun, while Nina and Barry headed into the waves. Though no flags flew on the beach, Nina could feel the tug of a moderately strong current beneath the long reaching wash of the waves breaking offshore. Clusters of bubbles partially hid the creatures swimming below, making her cautious about walking out very far.

Barry turned to look back at her. "Come on out a little further. I'll protect you." He reached out a hand, but she stood still, looking at the water as if it harbored piranhas. She lifted one foot to step forward, and the suction of a receding wave pulled her forcefully toward Barry. He reached out and caught her as the sea dumped her into his arms, and he held on protectively until the current passed. "Are you okay?" he asked with his hands still gently holding onto the sides of her waist.

Before she could answer, a big wave hit her from behind, pushing her further into his arms. She remained there for a few magical seconds, staring up at him, spellbound by nature's matchmaking efforts. His eyes sparkled as he observed, "I think the ocean wants us to dance."

Nina and Barry both heard the four-wheeler driving on the beach, but neither of them wanted to break eye contact. Only the sound of Michelle's voice calling out to them loosened the magnetism enough that they could turn and listen.

"Guys!" Michelle pointed to the yellow flags newly placed by the man on the ATV. "There's a strong current. Be careful out there!"

Nina thought to herself, *"You have no idea how strong."*

Barry's eyes reflected the swirling blue and gray tones of the sea as he said reluctantly, "I guess we should get out of the water."

"Maybe we could walk along the edge," Nina suggested, not wanting to break contact with either Barry or the sea that encouraged their proximity.

Without hesitation, Barry turned to yell to Michelle, "We're going for a walk."

She waved them on with a shooing motion. "She seems happy to just lie there in the sun." When they emerged from the powerful water, Barry took Nina's hand. Slowly, they walked where the waves reclaimed the shells they had just deposited seconds earlier.

Barry suddenly spoke, "Did you know 'perdido' means 'lost' in Spanish?"

Nina replied, "I think I'd heard that once. So, Perdido Key means 'Lost Key'?"

"Yes. I always think of that word when I see these shells tumbling back toward the ocean. The waves bring them onto the sand for just a moment, and you have just seconds to grab the treasure. If you fail, the ocean steals them away, and they're forever 'perdido'."

"That's beautiful. Very poetic."

Barry stopped walking and faced Nina. "I think today the ocean tossed me a treasure unlike any I've ever seen. I don't want to give it the chance to take it away."

Nina stepped closer. "Unlike the Key down the street, I'm not 'Perdido'. I'm not being tossed about with no sense of direction. I know exactly where I want to be, and that is right here."

A sincere smile spread across Barry's face. "That's good to know. Because I don't think I could let you go."

His words filled her with happiness. They also made her more certain than ever that she was ready to put down permanent roots in Orange Beach soil. She tugged Barry's hand, and they continued on their aimless journey across the line where water and sand remain in constant flux, giving of themselves so fully that one cannot be distinguished from the other.

Chapter 34

The dull dagger of loneliness persisted, slowly carving a hole in Michelle's heart. She watched the interaction between Nina and Barry, and it filled her with conflicting emotions.

On one level, seeing them connect felt like reaching the pivotal moment of a romantic movie, wherein you'd been rooting for the two main characters to get together for the first whole hour of the film, but something held them back, until finally ... magic.

On another level, she longed for what they had. She was supposed to have been married by now. Although she was glad she had dodged the bullet with Kevin, the void her sudden single status had opened up in her heart was at times too much to bear. In this moment, the pain in her chest stabbed so deep, she could barely breathe.

Nina and Barry were too wrapped up in their chemistry to notice the tears streaming down Michelle's face. She tried to wipe them away covertly, just in case either of the two should glance in her direction. The hurt became so intense that if she weren't twenty-two, she would think she was having a heart attack.

She whispered under her breath, "God, help me." It had been a while since she had prayed. Back home in Georgia, she and Kevin had attended a big church. She had listened to the sermons, sung the songs, and believed the Word. But something had been missing.

She never felt connected to the other church members. Sure, they shook hands or nodded stiffly in passing, but the interactions had felt cold. She had grown up in that church, however, so she just assumed that was the way all churches worked.

Michelle thought maybe God had forgotten about her. She had not viewed Kevin's dumping of her as punishment for any sin she had committed. Rather, she figured she had slipped through the cracks in the vessel of God's people. She hadn't been adamant in seeking Him, so why should he come find her now?

For some reason, that verse about leaving the ninety-nine to find the one lost sheep came into her head. She began to pray, "God, it's me, Michelle Kingsley, not Shumpert, like I was scheduled to be by now. I know it's been a while, and I don't deserve your help, but I'm going to ask anyway. I'm hurting, so much that it feels like I might be dying. I've never felt this much pain before. I'm a happy, positive person, but I've been hit, and I'm down, so down I can't see a way up. Can you help me? Can you show me a way out of this? Because if there isn't one, then I don't want to live." A sob racked her body with those last words.

A sudden gust of wind whipped toward her from the left. She shut her eyes to the storm of tiny sand grains pummeling her body. She cried harder. Was this God's response to her prayer? More pain?

Something sharp and substantial hit her leg. There in her lap, blown through the gap between the arm rest and the seat, lay a flyer with the heading, "In Jesus' Name Ministry" at the top. Michelle's heart leapt. She couldn't believe her eyes.

Bringing the flyer closer to her face and removing her shades, she read aloud, "We are a group of Christians committed to community outreach. We deliver meals to the hungry, visit the sick and bedridden, and do volunteer lawn maintenance for those who are physically disabled. Join our group and make a difference." The phone number listed below was local. Michelle glanced skyward and said, "If this isn't a sign, I don't know what could ever be. Thank you." Then she dialed the number and offered to give what little of herself remained to a worthy cause.

Chapter 35

When they returned from their walk, Michelle announced to Nina and Barry, "I'm going somewhere later, but you don't need to worry about me, because I'll be with these people." She handed them the miracle flyer.

They read it together. Then Barry looked down at her from where he stood. "Where exactly are you going to meet them?"

"At Christian Calling Church. The address is on the flyer."

Barry crossed his arms over his chest. "I'll drive you so I know you get there safely."

"No offense, Barry, but I really need to do this alone. I've got to have a thing that I do separately from you two. I love you, but I've got to get a life, literally. This fell into my lap, no joke, from the sky. I know it's what I'm supposed to be doing."

Barry started to protest, but Nina touched his arm. "I understand," she said.

"You do?" Michelle figured she'd have more trouble than this convincing them that she needed to go alone.

"Yes, I do. I set out on the same journey as you a few weeks ago. I get the need to find your place and build something from the ground up. You and I have had virtually everything we thought was ours taken away in an instant. If you feel that volunteering with this ministry is the next step in your journey toward becoming whole again, then by all means, do it."

"Thank you, Nina. I appreciate your understanding." She turned to address Barry. "I'll be careful. I'll be on the lookout for Mike Waters, though the only time I'll be alone is while I'm driving in my car. I think I'll be safe in there."

Barry could tell he was outnumbered. He looked at the sand for a moment, then he lifted his eyes to hers. "Okay. But call us the minute you get back in your car to come home."

"Yes, Dad," she teased. His stare bore a hole into her, so she continued, "Okay. I will. I promise."

A few hours later, she stood in the bathroom doing her hair and makeup. Excitement pulsed through her veins, and nervousness cramped her stomach. Nina had made flounder for dinner, but

Michelle couldn't eat. Instead, she drank a ginger ale while she got ready, a poor substitute for fish and steamed veggies, but at the moment, it was the best she could put in her body.

She drove to the church with the AC blasting to prevent nervous sweating. She pulled into the parking lot to find nine people milling around a white table outside. A poster board taped to the edge of the table read, "Sign Up Here." She put on her best Michelle smile and approached the man sitting in front of the clipboard.

"Hello there," he said before she could speak. As he stood, his long dreads fell across his shoulder. His smile glowed bright white against his ebony skin. Already his demeanor outshone that of anyone Michelle had ever encountered in church.

He reached out for a handshake. She clasped his hand and said, "Hello. I'm Michelle."

"Michelle, nice to meet you. I'm Damien."

"Nice to meet you, Damien."

He released her hand and asked, "Are you here to sign up?"

She smiled brightly. "I am."

"Great." He handed her a pen. "Just put your name and phone number here." She wrote down her information, then gave him back the pen. "If I may ask, how did you find out about us?"

Michelle sighed. She gathered the courage to confide in a stranger, but it wasn't too hard. Damien had a way of putting a person at ease. Looking him in the eye, she confessed, "I hit rock bottom emotionally today. I was praying on the beach, telling God I needed a way out of this depression. Then your flyer literally fell into my lap. The wind blew it down the beach, directly to the spot where I was sitting. I knew it had to be God."

Damien's head shrank back from his neck in amazement. "Wow. That's awesome. You definitely heard from God today. And I've got good news for you. There is nothing better to get you out of a slump than helping someone else. It's proven true for me many times. The best way to get over your own sadness is to brighten someone else's day."

Michelle believed him. He possessed a very sincere, convincing smile. "I'm looking forward to it."

Damien nodded. "Alright, here we go." Then he clapped his hands to get everyone's attention. "Okay, everyone. If you would please divide up into three groups. We have nine meals to deliver tonight, so each group will be assigned three."

It seemed everyone here already knew each other. They sectioned themselves off quickly, leaving Michelle standing by the table looking from group to group.

"Over here," someone in the trio on the far right said. "We could use one more." A woman with long, wavy red hair held her hand up, so Michelle walked to join her group. "Hi, I'm Alicia."

"Michelle." They shook hands, then turned to listen as Damien continued his instructions.

"You're new," Alicia observed.

They walked together toward the cooler to grab the meals. "Yes. This is my first day." Alicia handed one meal to her, one to a thirty-something blond man behind her, and one to a teenage girl.

"You can ride with me in Ryan's van. This is Ryan, by the way."

Michelle turned to greet the man holding the meal. Then she piled into the van with the three of them. She took the seat next to Alicia. "Ryan's one of our three volunteer drivers. We have two others who own vans and are nice enough to give us all rides."

They reached their first destination in less than a minute. Alicia explained to the newbie, "This is Mrs. Betty's place. She lost her husband last year, and she's had a variety of health problems since then. It's hard for her to get around in the kitchen, so we bring her an entire casserole once a week."

"Oh, that's so good she has you guys," Michelle replied with obvious emotion in her voice.

"You mean, she has *us*," Alicia reminded her.

Michelle smiled at the thought. She had already become a part of something better than her own attempt at building a new life for herself. Her heart filled with joy as she watched Mrs. Betty accept the casserole with a hug and a few tears. "She cries every time," Alicia whispered.

Mrs. Betty's eyes fell upon Michelle. "You there. I haven't seen you before. What's your name?"

"I'm Michelle. I'm new."

"Well, Michelle, come over here and get your hug."

She held back her own tears as she walked up to embrace the woman she'd just met. The old woman hugged her as if she were her own grandmother. She kissed the top of Michelle's head and said, "Welcome to the family." Michelle hugged her back, savoring the comfort reminiscent of home.

As she joined the others on the walk back to the van, her heart soared like a flyer aimed at someone in fervent prayer. Even if her current purpose was only to deliver two more meals to two more people in need, it was purpose aplenty for the night. She had no doubt that tomorrow would hold more needs to be met, and she would gladly accept whatever mission might be revealed.

Chapter 36

As promised, Michelle called Barry the moment she got into her car. With doors locked, she buckled up. He answered after one and a half rings.

"Hey Michelle. Everything okay?"

"Yes. It's all good. I'm leaving now, but I'm starving. I'm going to stop by the Shrimp Basket. Do you guys want anything?"

He mumbled something to Nina, then answered, "No, we're not hungry. Thank you, though. Be careful."

"I will. I'm bringing it home to eat it. Any new developments there?"

"No. Even though nothing seemed out of place, we watched today's security footage in fast forward just to check. Other than plants being blown by the wind, nothing moved."

"Good deal. Okay, see you in a bit." She hung up and made her way to the restaurant. About halfway into the meal deliveries, her nerves had calmed enough to allow her hunger to surface. All she could think about right now was eating.

She walked in and ordered the blackened redfish in seafood cream sauce. Fifteen minutes later, she had the bagged container in her hand. She put it on the passenger side floor and cranked the car. The heavenly smell caused her to consider eating it right there in the parking lot. Her eyes canvassed the area to see if anyone was watching. No one looked in her direction, but something familiar struck her about a man in a suit standing with two others in front of the far east side of the building. He had his back to her, but when he turned to face the door, she caught his profile. Was that – Kevin?!

It was Kevin. It was definitely Kevin. She had to get out of there. Frantically checking her mirrors, she backed out of the spot as quickly as she could without drawing attention to herself. She made it to the street. Casting one last glance in her rearview, she saw that he had never even noticed her car. He once told her she drove a very generic vehicle. He had meant it as an insult, but she had purposely picked a grayish blue older sedan. It wouldn't attract car thieves, and if she ever needed to be sneaky, she would be able to easily blend into a crowded parking lot, like right now.

She was so relieved she had looked around before digging into her food. If he had seen her doing that, he would have believed she had been reduced to dining alone in her car. He might have even assumed she was living in her car.

On the short drive home, she reflected on how seeing him made her feel. There was no longing, no brokenhearted nostalgia. All she felt was a rush of adrenaline and the need to flee the scene. That was a good sign.

When she arrived at home, Barry and Nina were waiting for her on the front porch. She approached them, and they were all smiles. "Glad to see you made it safely," Barry said as she stepped onto the deck.

An overwhelming sense of gratitude rushed through her. Kevin had never worried about her when she went out alone. He barely even noticed when she entered a room. This care and concern from friends was the light she needed to chase away the darkness of the past. She set her food down on the floor and hugged both of them.

"What was that for?" asked Barry, sensing there was more behind the gesture than just a greeting.

"For being true friends. Thank you." She beamed at them before retrieving her food. Not wanting to wait another minute, she sat down at the outdoor table, opened the container, picked up the plastic fork, and dug in.

"How did tonight go?" Nina asked.

Michelle chewed blissfully, holding up a finger. She swallowed, then said, "Amazing. I feel a renewed sense of purpose. I made new friends. I'm going to be a regular volunteer there. Also, I saw Kevin outside the restaurant. He didn't see me, and I drove away fast. I've never been so happy to put distance between myself and him. I just feel … refreshed. Alive. New."

"Wow." Though Michelle was generally a happy person, Nina had never seen her with this much of a glow. She radiated regeneration. "I'm happy for you."

"Thanks. I'm happy for me, too." Michelle relished the food and the company. The night breeze carried the essence of the ocean to her nose as she dined on the fruit of the sea. She was, in this moment, one hundred percent in her element.

Chapter 37

The next week, Mary called to let Nina, Barry, and Michelle know that their monthly distributions had been deposited into each of their bank accounts.

As Nina hung up the phone, trepidation set in. Now she had no excuse not to paint. Michelle would be on her about it. She had no doubt that if she tried to put it off, Michelle would drag her down to Shelly's and fill up her shopping cart for her.

She had to go tell the others. No customers were currently in the store, so she headed for the stockroom. She got their attention by knocking on the open door. "Distributions have been deposited," she announced.

Michelle squealed. She grabbed her phone. "I'm checking my account now. The suspense has been killing me." A few clicks and scrolls later, she attempted to scream but shock intervened, injecting air into the high-pitched sound. She looked at Nina with eyes as round and big as quarters. "It's over a thousand dollars!"

"What?!" Nina stood frozen in place. She had expected maybe a couple hundred, but a thousand? "Is that normal?"

"According to Mary, it is for the summer months. I didn't tell you, because I didn't want it to be a letdown if we didn't hit that mark."

"That will go a long way toward helping with property taxes and insurance on my house," Barry thought aloud.

Without ever looking up from her phone, Michelle told Nina, "You know we're going paint shopping tonight, right?"

Nina smiled to herself. "I know." Nina had made some space in her room for art supplies last night. Reluctantly, she had even moved that beautiful painting back to its previous perch in the hallway to make room for new canvases. She preferred to hang her works in progress on the wall, where she could see them from a different perspective while not actively working on them. It helped to get her out of her head, see them how someone walking into a room might view them.

She went back out front. Several customers had come into the store in that short time. The day flew by, probably because Nina didn't care about getting out of there. Ordinarily, she did. She usually looked so forward to the end of the day, because it meant spending time with Barry on the beach.

Right at 6:00, the stockroom door swung open. Michelle chirped, "Ready to go get stocked?"

"Yeah," Nina replied as she counted up the day's money. "In just a second."

Barry stepped into the room. "Am I driving, or are we taking your car?" he asked Michelle.

Nina felt a sudden surge of joy. She didn't know why she had assumed he wouldn't be coming with them. Maybe she'd forgotten that the new normal, while Mike was still on the loose and they had a secret gardener, was Barry being with them everywhere they went.

"I'll drive," offered Michelle. "I know where the place is."

Ten minutes later, they pulled up to an aptly named shell encrusted building. Nina grabbed a cart just inside the door and wasted no time. She remembered the names of all the basic hues she needed to mix a full spectrum of paint colors. Grabbing those and a few brushes, a palette knife, and some loose containers for storing the newly mixed shades, she headed toward the canvas section last. She chose several of medium size for practice and one large 24"x36" to hold her masterpiece. Then she spied an easel at the end of the row. She would definitely need one of those. Good thing her distribution had been so hefty.

Barry and Michelle just followed her around the store. She seemed to know exactly what she needed. Within fifteen minutes, she was ready to check out. Then they headed home.

On the car ride back, Michelle asked, "When are you going to start your first painting?"

"On our next day off." Nina didn't like jumping into anything requiring a lot of time after a full day of work. She needed to have an open schedule, freedom to explore and develop. Having a limited window of a couple of hours cramped her creativity.

Barry inquired, "Will you be setting up on the beach to do plein air? If so, can we watch?"

"I prefer to work from a photo. A live setup is subject to too many factors. Let's say you've got your eye on the perfect wave. By the time you dip your brush, it's already broken. You'll never be able to see the way the light shone through it again. Having a photo means being able to take your time, spread the process out over weeks or months. It's much less pressure."

"You're right about that," Barry agreed. "Do you have a photo in mind?"

"I need to take some. My life has been such a whirlwind, I haven't taken any since I got here. I'd like to get some around sunset, then tomorrow just after sunrise, and a few on my lunch break so I have plenty of lighting choices."

"I'll walk over with you." It was pretty much a given at this point. Nina didn't expect to be going anywhere alone for a while. She was surprised that Barry had been okay with Michelle going to the church meeting without him, but driving in a car and walking alone on a beach were at opposite ends of the stranger danger spectrum.

Back in the Seahorse Treasures parking lot, Nina grabbed her bags and started walking toward the house. A few steps in, she suddenly found them weightless and moving away from her. She turned to see Barry cradling their bulk with one hand while taking their handles with the other. "May I lighten your load?"

"Sure." She released her grip, sensing he needed to do this for her. She certainly didn't mind, though she was perfectly capable of carrying them. His Southern sense of duty would make him uncomfortable if she resisted.

Michelle unlocked the front door to the house and opened it for them. Nina stepped through first, followed by Barry. "Where do you want these bags?"

Pointing toward the hallway, Nina answered, "In my room on the bed. I'll find a place for them tonight."

As he walked into the corridor, the golden light of evening entering the window of his open bedroom reached through the doorway to illuminate the painting on the wall. He stopped without warning, and Nina bumped into him from behind. They both said, "Sorry," and she eased around him, expecting him to follow. When he didn't, she turned and found his countenance void of color.

"Barry? Are you okay?"

He still stared at the painting. Nina understood its mesmerizing effect, for she had been captured by it, too. But Barry's reaction held some other quality. He looked … haunted.

In a voice so quiet it seemed to come from far away, he asked, "Where did this come from?"

Puzzled, Nina approached him. "Alice said Fred bought it at an estate sale. It's been in my room." She put a hand on his arm, breaking the spell that bound his gaze to the art. "Do you recognize it?"

Barry opened his mouth, but before he could speak, Michelle yelled out, "Guys! I think Mike is back!"

Chapter 38

Desperately searching for the binoculars, Michelle pointed to the kitchen window. "Look!" She scrambled through some cabinets while Nina approached.

"That definitely looks like Mike." Nina watched a man with the same shaggy brown hair and short build as Mike walking toward the front of the house next door.

By the time Michelle found the binoculars, he was facing away from them. "I can't tell for sure, but who else could it be? Should we call the cops?"

Barry noticed one important detail. "This man came in a car. A nice one, at that. And look how he's dressed. Not like someone who has been living in a swamp for over a week."

The man opened the door and walked inside. Michelle panicked. "He could have broken in someone's house and taken a shower, stolen some clothes and a car. I don't want to take a chance on letting him get away again." She handed the binoculars to Nina. "I'm calling the police."

Michelle disappeared to the back of the house to make the call. Her phone was on the charger in her bedroom.

All Nina and Barry could hear as they kept an eye on the man who could be Mike was the rise and fall of Michelle's tone. From this distance, it sounded like excited humming. Just a few moments later, she came out of her room with an announcement, "It's just his brother."

"Wait, how do they know that?" Barry looked out the window again, expecting to see a police car lurking nearby.

"He got permission to come to the crime scene to see if Mike might be hiding somewhere on his own property. The police thought he could potentially have secret spots there where he could conceal himself from them, but if Mike saw his brother, he might just feel safe enough to come out."

Nina still stood at the window. "The door's opening."

Michelle rushed to her side. "Is he alone?"

"Yeah. He looks disappointed." His face bore the look of someone who had just wasted his time. He got into his car and drove away, leaving their adrenaline rush to fizzle like a long opened can of soda.

A phone rang at the other end of the house. "That's mine," Michelle said as she ran to grab it. She reached it on the third ring. "Hello?"

"Hi Michelle. It's Damien. How are you?"

"A little freaked out. How are you?"

He stuttered, taken aback by her answer. "Is everything okay?"

She sighed. "Do you have a minute?"

"Yeah, sure."

She told him everything that was going on with Mike. When she finished, he said, "Wow. That's a lot."

She let out a laugh. "Yeah, well, welcome to my life."

"I was calling to tell you about a project we're working on tomorrow, but you sound like you have your hands full. I totally understand if you don't feel up to participating."

"No, please. I want to help. I need to help. Please, get me out of here." She laughed nervously.

"Okay. Let me tell you first, then you decide if you want to come. There's a disabled widow in our neighborhood whose lawn is in desperate need of care. Ryan is bringing his mower, so that's covered, but there are flower beds completely full of weeds. We plan to empty them out and start over with fresh soil and new plants. How do you feel about that?"

"That's something I could definitely help with. I do have to work tomorrow, though. Are we going late in the day?"

"Ryan and Alicia actually wanted to do it early in the morning, starting around 6:00, before the day heats up too much. Would that work for you?"

"I don't have to be at work until 10, so yes. I'll do it. Just text me the address." She wasn't crazy about the idea of getting up that early, but the need both to belong to a group and to fulfill her new purpose trumped sleep. After Damien hung up, she immediately set an alarm for 5:15.

She headed toward the kitchen to see what everyone wanted to do for dinner, but she only found Nina. "Where's Barry?"

"He's in his room. He said he felt a headache coming on and wanted to lie down."

Barry was indeed in his room, but he wasn't lying down. He was sitting on his bed, staring into the late day light that moments ago had revealed a thing of his past, right here in his present. The enormity of it made his hands tremble. Nina had asked, but he wasn't ready to answer. He would tell her one day, but now would be too soon. Things were going so well between them. He had to keep this secret in its frame.

Chapter 39

Five-fifteen a.m. came quickly. Michelle wobbled bleary-eyed to the kitchen and made a strong cup of coffee. She sat at the table and sipped before attempting anything that might require vision.

Last night, she told Nina about her pre-work volunteering. She didn't see Barry before she went to bed. It was just as well. She didn't need a lecture on being careful. She was more freaked out than any of them.

With her coffee buzz beginning, she went to get ready. Sunscreen replaced makeup today. She French-braided her long hair, put on her coolest sleeveless tee and cotton shorts, and grabbed her gardening gloves before heading out the door.

The sun hadn't even crested the horizon yet, though enough light preceded its appearance to allow her to walk without a flashlight. The sand still held the coolness of the night air, feeling almost damp on her feet. She held her flip flops with one hand, preferring whenever possible to walk on the sand barefoot. The distant crash of the ocean beckoned to her. The desire to answer its call almost overpowered her need to be on time. Almost, but not quite.

"I'll see you tonight," she said to the sea. Once inside her car, she typed the address Damien had texted her into the GPS on her phone. Very few tourists were up at this hour, so driving was a dream. She had never seen so few cars on Perdido Beach Boulevard.

"You have reached your destination," her phone announced as she pulled into the driveway of a super small house. Two medium sized flower beds out front held weeds probably a couple of feet high. Ryan had brought a push mower. Michelle hadn't seen one of those in a long time. She had expected a much larger yard requiring hours of hard labor.

Alicia looked up from beside a stack of potting soil bags on the ground and waved. Damien stood at the door, talking to the owner of the house, Esmerelda Jones, who was all smiles. Michelle got out of her car, put on her gloves, and approached the flower beds.

"Hey girl," she greeted Alicia.

"Hey you. I'm glad you could make it. Not many people are willing to get out this early, as you can see. That means you and I are in charge of the flower beds 100%. Damien has weed-eater duty, and Ryan's on mowing."

"Fine by me. What are we planting today?" Michelle looked around for some potted flowers.

"It seems the owner would like us to start from seed. But this is not your typical store-bought collection. Her late husband had saved some zinnia seed from their previous garden before he died."

Michelle gasped. "That's precious!"

Alicia pointed to some damp paper towels on the windowsill. "The seeds are soaking over there. She prepared them for us last night. We can leave them in the wet towels while we strip and refill these beds."

Damien approached them. "How's it going? Michelle, I hope you didn't have any more excitement at your house last night."

Alicia looked between the two of them. "What went on at your house last night?"

Michelle sighed. "Long story. Let me tell you while we work."

She began relaying the Mike Waters saga to Alicia. To her surprise, upon hearing his name, Alicia interrupted, "Wait, I remember seeing him on the news! Wasn't he arrested for domestic violence a while back?"

"Yes! But he served his time and went right back to his wife." She continued, telling her of the horror poor Geri had endured. She concluded with Mike's brother's visit to the house last night.

"So he's still on the run? No wonder you're nervous at home!"

Michelle yanked small handfuls of weeds. It was easier to get a few at a time in her grip and pull with all her might than to tackle a big section. Large clumps of weeds worked together, strong in their united battle to remain rooted. Dividing and conquering accomplished more.

Ryan mowed far enough away from the women to avoid hitting them with debris. Damien used the weed-eater along the perimeter of the yard, which ended in a swampy looking forest. Alicia and Michelle couldn't talk over the noise of the lawn equipment, so they focused on the task at hand. In forty-five minutes, they had cleared the beds completely. Using gestures, they determined that Alicia would cut the bags of soil open and pass them to Michelle. She dumped three bags into each bed. Alicia retrieved the paper towels, which they carefully unfolded, knowing the irreplaceability of this particular seed collection. Following Alicia's lead, Michelle made indentations in the soil with her finger about six inches apart, then dropped a single seed into each. She covered them gently. Finally, Alicia grabbed a sprinkling can. With a gentle shower, the water moistened the soil, sealing the seeds into their little dirt wombs. Michelle hoped that each would come to term fully, providing Mrs. Esmerelda with bouquets from heaven.

All done, Alicia and Michelle stepped back to admire the transformation. Sure, they just looked like rectangular boxes of dirt now, but they both could see in their minds the beauty that would come to be. And for the time being, even plain boxes of dirt were better than boxes of giant weeds.

They noticed that the noise had ceased. They looked around to find Ryan standing next to Damien at the edge of the woods. Damien was pointing into the forest. "Someone's out there," he said.

Michelle looked at Alicia, and both rushed toward the men. "Where?" asked Michelle frantically.

Damien stood directly behind her, looked over her shoulder, and pointed so he would be even with her line of vision. "There, next to that pond. Do you see?"

She could barely tell if what she saw was human. It was covered in mud and squatting in front of the small body of water. Then she heard a loud, "Ribbet!" as what must surely be a frog leaped through the air toward the center of the pond. The human, revealing himself to be such by his size, surprised them all by leaping in after it.

"Call 911," Michelle said firmly. "I know who he is."

Chapter 40

She didn't want Mike to see her face, because then he would likely blame her for his arrest. She stood behind Damien, still wearing her shades, her long, braided hair now also in a bun to hide its length. Peering around his arm, she caught a good enough glimpse to confirm that the man in handcuffs was definitely Mike Waters.

Michelle waited until the police car pulled out of the driveway to step around in front of her friends. Alicia noticed her trembling and asked, "Are you okay?"

She nodded. "Great now. I can finally relax. Well, once this adrenaline rush fades, that is."

"Do you need us to drive you home?" Alicia offered.

Michelle shook her head. "I'll be fine once my nerves settle. I might go sit in my car for a few minutes before heading back." Then she thought about the homeowner. "What does Esmerelda think about all this excitement in her yard?"

Damien answered, "She takes a midmorning nap every day. I don't think she even knew the police were here. I don't want to wake her, but I would like to let her know about it before she sees her home on the evening news. I'll give her a call this afternoon."

They all said goodbye. Michelle turned the air on full blast in her car. She shut her eyes and let the cool air calm her with the steady sound of rushing wind. She was safe now. Geri no longer had to worry about being found. Nina could feel secure at home without Barry around.

Michelle's eyes popped open. She wondered how Nina would feel about Barry going back home. Probably pretty bummed. Though Michelle loved Barry, she was ready for him to go back to his house. Even with her newfound purpose helping to fill the void in her heart, she would rather not feel like the third wheel in her own home.

The sound of her stomach grumbling reminded her she still hadn't eaten breakfast. Mojo's Coffee Shop was on her way home, so she stopped in for an espresso and a giant cinnamon roll. She still had an hour before she had to be at work, so she took her treats to the beach. In the shade of a big pavilion, she ate the massive roll, flicking globs of sugary sweet glaze into her espresso to sweeten it to her liking. When she had finished eating, she took her drink down to the water's edge for a caffeinated stroll.

Coaxed by the clear, cool waves teasing her ankles, she waded out knee deep. She wanted to go further, to let the swaying saltwater wash away the heat, sweat, and soil of the morning. Looking at the cup in her hand, she turned around and jogged over to the nearest trash can to dispose of it. Then she bounded into the waves, lunging with a breaststroke across the most gentle of breakers. She turned and swam parallel with the shore, taking care to stay where her feet could still touch bottom. Cool currents below mixed with sun-warmed surface water, giving her the feeling of being inside a hot fudge ice cream sundae. Flipping over mid-stroke, she floated on her back, rising and falling with the motion of the water, surrendering to the whims of the waves.

She stayed like that, moving her arms and legs only enough to keep her face above water, until a family with loud children set up camp nearby. She could hear the kids splashing toward her, so she flipped forward and began swimming to shore. Only when she started walking across the sand toward home did she realize she didn't have a towel.

She squeezed as much water as possible from her shirt and shorts with her hands. Ah, well. She had to go home and shower, anyway. The warm breeze clashed with her cold, soaking wet clothes, giving her chill bumps. The heat of the sun kept her from growing truly cold, the contrast utterly confusing to her inner temperature regulator. She welcomed it, though, for it was the epitome of a summer swim.

At the bottom of the steps, Michelle turned on the faucet and rinsed the sand from her feet and ankles. She opened the door and stuck just her head in to find Nina and Barry drinking coffee at the table. "Would one of you mind handing me a towel?"

Nina stood. "I'll go get one. What happened? Did they hose you down?"

"No, I jumped in the ocean just because I wanted to. You should try it sometime. It's exhilarating!"

Unable to tell if she was being sarcastic or not, Nina handed her the towel with a serious face. When she had soaked up at least the dripping portion of ocean water from her clothing, she tossed the towel over the deck railing and went inside. "I'm hitting the shower."

As her skin traded saltwater for fresh, she thought about her spontaneous plunge. It had been the best swim of her life. Why? Because it wasn't planned. She wasn't dressed for it. Hadn't even intended to go to the beach until after work. The only thing she had really done differently was to do exactly what she wanted to do without worrying about reasons not to. She had to be at work in an hour, she didn't have her swimsuit, but she did it anyway. Maybe this should be her new normal.

She got ready for work quickly, since they had to leave in ten minutes. It wasn't until they had descended the steps and their feet hit the sand that she remembered she had big news to share. "Oh, guys! Mike Waters is in police custody."

Barry and Nina stopped walking, turned around, and said, "What?!" at the same time.

"Sorry, I forgot to tell you. Our gardening crew spotted someone in the woods. Once I saw him jump into a pond after a frog, I knew it could be no one else. They called the police. I watched them take him away in handcuffs."

Barry's face grew concerned. "Did he see you?"

"No. I hid behind Damien. Also, my hair was up and I had on dark shades. He didn't even look in my direction."

Barry and Nina shared a sigh of relief.

Taking care not to sound too excited about it, Michelle mentioned, "Barry, I guess this means you don't have to stay here and watch out for us anymore." She made her voice sound a little sad.

He ran a hand through his hair as he thought about that. "I guess. There still is the matter of a stranger coming into your yard with sharp lawn tools, though. I know we have the security cameras going, but how do you feel about it? Would you feel safe if someone wielding hedge shears was just outside your door?"

"I mean, I'd call the cops if that happened," Michelle reasoned.

Nina spoke up, "I wouldn't feel safe. What if in the ten or fifteen minutes it took for them to get here, he broke down the door and hacked us to death?"

Michelle could see she was losing the argument. She hadn't wanted it to come to this, but now, she had no choice. "I have a gun in my car. I can bring it in the house. Just in case, of course. I don't plan on shooting whoever shows up if they stay outside the door, but if the cops didn't make it to us in time, we'd have an option."

Nina's eyes grew wide. "That makes me nervous."

"Don't worry. I know how to use it. I can even take you to a shooting range and give you a few lessons. It's just for backup. It never hurts to know how to defend yourself in an emergency."

Barry surprised Michelle by agreeing with her. "It's not a bad idea, Nina. You really should learn how to shoot a gun, even if you never put the knowledge to use."

Nina looked from Barry to Michelle. She could see she was outnumbered. "Okay."

"I can look up shooting ranges online and find the one closest to here. We can go tonight if you like." Michelle hoped the sooner she could get Nina comfortable with a gun, the sooner Barry could go back home.

Nina looked at Barry. "We were going to take beach photos tonight."

Barry shook his head. "This is more important. We can take photos tomorrow night. If you've never handled a gun before, you need to get familiar with one as soon as possible. I can hang out at your house until you get back, just to keep watch."

"Thank you. I appreciate it." Nina turned to Michelle. "Okay, let's do it."

On her lunch break, Michelle found the website of nearby Pensacola Indoor Shooting Range. Even though they didn't close until 7:00, they wanted customers to already be shooting by 6 p.m. She texted Nina to make sure they could leave work by 5:00. Leslie had come back to work today, so it was fine.

They had a successful session. Nina turned out to be a pretty good shot, hitting the target more often than not. Though put off at first by the noise and recoil, she quickly adjusted her expectations and learned how to aim effectively. Michelle was already comfortable with her gun, having been trained thoroughly by her dad before moving away. By the time they left the range, both felt confident in each other's ability.

As they neared home, the sunset pierced the sky with laserlike orange beams. What remained of the blue received a purple cast from the puffy clouds. Michelle felt bad that Nina was missing out on capturing this. "Want to walk over for a few shots?" she asked as they pulled into Seahorse Treasures.

Nina started to say yes but hesitated. "Let me text Barry."

Michelle reminded her, "We don't need him anymore." She pointed to the gun. "We have Felicia."

"You named your gun Felicia?"

"You got a better name?"

Nina shook her head. "Let's go. I don't want to miss this."

Michelle grabbed Felicia and stuck her in her purse. Nina had her phone's camera set to its highest resolution capability as she snapped photo after photo, varying angles and focusing on every thing of beauty kissed by the departing sun. On the walk home, neither of them felt vulnerable or afraid. Nina commented, "I hope Barry doesn't feel unnecessary now."

"I'm sure he'll get over it if he does. Whether or not you need him for security, you still want him around. Just because he goes back to staying in his own house doesn't mean you won't be spending a lot of time together."

"I know. I'll just miss him always being there." Nina sounded so sad, Michelle almost felt bad for empowering her. Then Nina said, "But it will make the time we do spend together worth even more. I do feel better after the lesson. And I feel, given the similar circumstances that brought you and I to where we are now, there was no one better to show me. Thank you."

Michelle got the warm and fuzzies. "You're welcome. We gotta look out for each other. I have no doubt that God brought you and me together. It's just too coincidental to be a coincidence, you know what I mean?"

"I do. I don't believe in coincidences. I think uncanny occurrences are God's way of showing us He's here, and He cares."

Even after they arrived at home and Nina bounded up the steps to give Barry a hug, Michelle didn't feel alone. Nina's words stayed with her, warming her from the inside. She believed the same. Hearing someone else say it just lent validation to her theory.

Chapter 41

Barry waited on the back deck, grill tongs in hand. The previous night, he had stayed up later than the others and made a chicken marinade. He wanted to grill for them, giving Nina the night off from cooking. Then, Michelle surprised him by basically telling him he could go home now.

He understood how she must feel. He and Nina were undeniably wrapped up in each other, so much so that it surely must seem they overlooked Michelle at times. They had made an extra effort to include her, but when you're busy falling in love, it's hard to care about anything else.

At least he hoped they were falling in love. He knew he was, without a doubt. He didn't dare tell Nina that, though. He wanted to show her through his actions. She had to be able to trust that he wasn't going to be another Donovan. In everything he did and said, he needed to be the opposite of that man. It shouldn't be too hard. From what Nina had told him, he already was.

Barry hadn't had a chance to process what had happened the night before. Finding that painting here in Nina's house, of all places ... well, it floored him. Although the former owner was no longer living, he never dreamed he'd see one of her possessions in the home of someone who had never even met her.

That painting had belonged to his grandmother. When she died twelve years earlier, Barry was in the hospital with pneumonia and couldn't come to the funeral. He hurt over that on a level that made his own recovery even more difficult. His family tried to console him, saying Grandma would've understood, but the feeling of powerlessness it caused, in addition to grief, earned him another week on oxygen.

Now that Nina mentioned an estate sale, he did recall hearing that most of his grandmother's belongings were being sold and the money split between her children. He had thought surely she would've arranged for the painting to go to him. Perhaps if he had made it down to Orange Beach for the funeral, Aunt Patricia would have set it aside and given it to him. After hearing about the sale, he thought he would never see it again.

He still couldn't believe it. While he was home alone this afternoon, he had stood before it, just staring in awe. Barry might believe in small coincidences, but this … this was an outright miracle. It gave him faith in something he already felt with all his heart. Well, two things: that God was real, and Nina was the one.

Female voices reached his ears, bringing him back to the present. Nina and Michelle came out the back door. "Something smells like something I hope you'll share," said Michelle.

Barry lifted the lid off the grill to reveal three perfectly cooked chicken breasts. "I planned on it." Using the tongs, he moved the chicken to a plate. "There's also some potatoes and pineapple that I grilled earlier wrapped in foil in the kitchen."

"I didn't know you could do all this." Nina seemed pleasantly surprised.

"I like to harbor some secrets to reveal when you least expect them. Keeps things interesting." He gave her a mischievous smile.

"Well, let's see what secrets your chicken will tell. I'm starving." Nina took the plated fowl from him and headed for the kitchen. She opened the potato and pineapple foil packets. Trapped steam shot forth, causing her to jerk her hand back.

Barry grabbed the edge of the foil with the tongs. "I got it." Nina stepped away and let him serve the sides safely. He would miss being around to do little things like this for her.

When they were all seated at the table, Michelle raised her glass of water. "A toast," she declared, "to the nonexistence of coincidences."

Nina clinked her glass with Michelle's, repeating after her.

Barry nearly dropped his water. "What?"

Michelle and Nina giggled. "Oh, just a reference to a conversation we had earlier."

"Oh," he said, attempting to steady his shaking hand as he joined the toast. His own clink sounded distant to his ears, as if he were immersed in an eerie alternate reality, viewing his life through an underwater chamber. He pinched his leg to do the dream check, but he felt it. He wondered what sort of test he could perform to see if he were in a coma? Then he looked at lovely Nina and decided that even if he were unconscious, this was the reality in which he wanted to be.

Chapter 42

Nina scrolled through the photos from last night at sunset. She looked out the window and sighed. The sun would rise soon, but she had no one to accompany her to the beach.

Barry left last night. She hadn't wanted to agree to Michelle's plan of protection, but once he got on board with it, there was no point in resisting. If he had one iota of doubt that everyone in the house wanted him to stay, he'd be gone, and she was sure Michelle's suggestion placed that seed in his mind.

Nina considered taking the gun with her to the beach, but what if someone came up to the house while she was gone and Michelle needed it? She couldn't risk that. So, she'd just wait.

One photo leapt out at her. The sharpness of the individual colors reminded her of the painting in the hall. She didn't hope to match the beauty of that artist's expertise, but the more magnificent the photo she worked from, the better her painting could be.

Michelle, being a graphic designer, had her own computer and color printer. She had offered to let Nina use them to print her reference photo. Of the dozens of shots she had taken yesterday, this was the one she kept coming back to, so there wasn't a need for her to return to the beach this morning.

She went into the living room, where Michelle kept her equipment. She plugged her phone into the computer, downloaded the photo, and sent it to the printer. Michelle had already shown her how to choose the highest quality setting and photo paper option. She kept matte photo paper in the tray, since she used it almost exclusively.

Nina made coffee while she waited. The printer slowly eked out the ink, taking its time creating its very own masterpiece. She hoped the sound wouldn't wake Michelle. She usually slept until 9, so she was due another three hours.

It wasn't like Nina to be up this early. A sadness pervaded her sleep, and dreams eluded her. She awoke at 5:30 with a sense of loss. She knew it was silly, because she hadn't lost Barry. Not in the least. But losing even the little time she had gotten used to spending with him before work, along with the comfort of his presence in the house at night, created a black hole in her heart that sucked her joy and sense of wellbeing down into its abyss.

Since sleep wasn't an option, and drowning in self-pity for four hours didn't appeal to her, she determined to start on her first painting in fifteen years right then and there. As soon as the printer presented its artwork, she picked it up and headed to her room to transform it into her own. She began by choosing a pencil with soft lead to lightly draw on the canvas. With the scene sketched out before her, she put base colors down. Starting with the underlying blue background of the sky, she temporarily ignored the oranges and purples that played upon its surface. She just needed to get a solid framework. Next, she mixed up a cream color for the sand. The ocean at that time of day possessed a blue-gray tone underneath the gold and pink frosted breakers. One solid sea was all she currently needed, so she generously swiped the porpoise shade across the white space between sand and sky.

She stopped midstroke when she realized she had forgotten to use the smaller canvas as practice. Oh, well. She would just have to make this one good.

With one layer of paint per large subject area down, she started again with the sky, adding a second layer to hide any white streaks of canvas trying to peek through. She was covering up the last section of single coat sea when the sound of Michelle's alarm travelled through the wall. Nina could hardly believe she had been working that long. Hastily, she finished the section and left the painting on the easel to dry.

She washed her brushes and put the lids on the containers of paints she had mixed that morning. Laying them on a rag to dry, she moved on to getting ready for work. With a minimal amount of makeup applied and a blue and purple tie-dyed dress on, she left the room to join Michelle in the kitchen.

Nina hadn't had an appetite earlier, but now, as she watched Michelle fill a cereal bowl, her stomach growled. She grabbed a bowl for herself. Then she sliced a banana and washed a handful of blueberries. On top of the fruit, she poured Multigrain Cheerios and milk. Since she'd had a long morning, she figured another cup of coffee couldn't hurt.

At the table, Michelle asked, "So, how did you sleep?"

"Not that well. You?"

"I crashed hard. Slept through the night. Were you worried that if someone broke in, we might not be able to take him?"

Nina chewed and swallowed before answering. "No. I'm not too worried about that. Now that Mike's been captured, I'm convinced that whoever worked on our yard was trying to do a nice thing. Any other explanation just doesn't make sense."

Michelle nodded. "I have to agree with you. I think Barry overreacted out of caution. But I think we're going to be just fine."

She didn't pry to find the source of Nina's lack of sleep. She had a feeling it had to do with missing a certain someone's presence in the house.

Nina neared the bottom of her bowl. She checked her watch. "Wow, 9:35 already." With the last spoonful, she rose to put the bowl in the sink. She stood at the kitchen window, staring out at the pond while sipping her second coffee.

Michelle joined her. "Wonder what will happen to Mike's place."

"Don't know. Hopefully Geri can keep it. Unless it isn't paid off yet and she can't afford payments. Then, the bank will repossess it. They could sell it cheap, and some lucky buyer will wind up with a frog sanctuary for a backyard."

Laughing, Michelle said, "That could make it harder to sell."

Nina shrugged. "All most people around here care about is proximity to the beach. If a house just across the street from the ocean comes cheap, they won't mind what's in the backyard. They'll likely be spending their time out front – as in *way* out front, across the road."

"True." Michelle rinsed out her cup and bowl. "I'm going to brush my teeth. Be ready in just a few."

Nina headed to her own bathroom to do the same. As she walked through her doorway, she jumped when she saw her painting, having already forgotten it was there. Standing at this distance, she could imagine the many layers that would come in time. The prospect of having, in the near future, her own completed beach painting hanging on her wall after this long artistic hiatus thrilled her. Shivers of anticipation ran through her, making her long for more time to develop the scene. "Soon," she promised herself. Now that the desire was present, holding herself to it would be easy.

Chapter 43

Barry waited for them by the back door to work. As they approached, he stood. "How did last night go? Any incidents? Strange noises?"

"Nope, not a one," Michelle answered proudly.

"That's good to hear," replied Barry as he stared at Nina with that smile that indicated he was barely aware of anyone else nearby.

Michelle took the cue to go on in alone. Once she had shut the door behind her, Nina said with earnest, "I missed you."

Her blue eyes did, in fact, appear bluer than yesterday. "I missed you, too." He took her hand and squeezed it. "What are you doing tonight?"

"I have no plans. What do you have in mind?"

"Want to take a dolphin cruise?"

He smiled with such enthusiasm that she didn't dare tell him she thought those were for children. She just wanted to spend time with him. She supposed she could be happy on a boat if he were there.

"Sure," she answered.

"And we can invite Michelle. There will be a ton of people there, so maybe she won't feel like as much of a tagalong as she does when it's just the three of us."

"That's a good idea. You go ahead and invite her when you get to the stockroom."

"Okay," he said as he released her hand. They went inside, each to their separate areas. Nina set about readying the register and opening for business. She was relieved that Michelle's dismissal of Barry from his personal security post hadn't caused him to distance himself from either of them. Her fear had been that he would wall himself in emotionally. Him pulling back from her in that way would have yanked her heart right out. She was thankful to still have it in her chest where it belonged.

At lunch time, Nina sat in the break room, her spinach and strawberry salad laid out before her. The raspberry vinaigrette oozed down into the leaves from the bottle she held above. She had just taken a forkful of food into her mouth when Barry entered and announced, "She said yes."

All Nina could say was, "Mmm," as she chewed and dabbed the errant dressing from the sides of her mouth with a napkin.

"I'll drive. Leslie is closing up tonight, so we can leave early enough to make the 6:00 departure time. I bought tickets online, so all we have to do is board."

Nina was impressed. "You've thought of everything."

"I tend to do that." He smiled at her, and she was certain the color swirls in his eyes moved. She really wanted to paint those eyes one day.

They left work at 5:15. "The marina is just on the other side of town," Barry explained as they got into his vehicle.

Michelle spoke up from the backseat, "I'm glad you thought of this, Barry. I love dolphins. I haven't been on a dolphin cruise since I was thirteen. Kevin never wanted to go on one when we were vacationing here with our church's youth group. He thought they were childish." She rolled her eyes.

So Nina hadn't been the only one to think that. To be fair, Nina had never been on any such cruise. It wasn't Donovan's style to sail cheap with large groups of people. Rather, he preferred to rent an entire boat, along with a private captain, for a day's voyage with just the three of them. It had always felt excessive.

They parked in a lot next to the dock. After a short walk up a wooden ramp to the ship's entrance, Barry presented the three tickets to a worker who tore them in half, gave him the stubs, and said, "Enjoy the ride."

Once on the ship, they had the option of choosing either the air-conditioned interior or two exposed outer decks with a better view. "Where do you want to sit?" asked Barry.

Michelle and Nina both said, "Outside." Michelle always opted to be front and center for the action, and Nina wanted to get the full experience with her maiden voyage. They found an unclaimed area on some bench seats on the first deck.

"Look at all these people," Nina said as she glanced around at other areas of the vessel. "I don't see a lot of kids."

Michelle did the eye roll again. "See? Kevin didn't know what he was talking about. Grownups like dolphins, too!"

"I just enjoy moving across the water. It's a good feeling. Very relaxing," Barry said.

Nina jumped as the captain's voice came through a speaker on the wall beside her head. Michelle and Barry laughed.

"I'd like to welcome everyone. Please keep your hands and feet inside the railing at all times. Should the need arise, life vests are located under the bench seats along the outer deck. Don't let children climb on the railing. Food and drinks are available at the concession stand indoors. Stay safe and enjoy the ride."

The engine roared to life, and the boat began moving away from the dock. Nina smelled gas. The odor made her cough. Barry leaned over and softly said, "It'll get better once we pick up speed." There was something so intimate in the way he leaned in, the tone of his voice, the reassurance that things would soon improve. It caught her off guard, but pleasantly so. Her heart skipped a beat, freezing the moment in time. She stared at him, her eyes revealing that something had affected her.

Then the captain's voice jolted her once more, interrupting the moment. "I've just gotten word from our sister ship of the location of a playful pod of dolphins. Folks, hold on. We're going to zoom out to them before they swim away."

The sudden increase in speed pushed Nina into Barry's shoulder. "Sorry," she apologized.

"Don't be," he replied in that same soft tone as he put his arm around her.

She smiled and settled against him. Michelle had joined a few other people standing at the railing, hoping to be the first to catch a glimpse. Another ship came into view just beyond the canal, and their own speed dropped drastically.

"Folks, look up here on the left. You should see a dolphin soon." People aimed cameras in that direction.

"Shall we stand?" Barry asked.

"By all means," Nina answered. She stood next to Michelle, who had her phone ready to take video. A cry rose up from the crowd as two dolphins arced out of the water side by side. Their shiny skin resembled the shade of paint Nina had spread across the ocean that morning. Everyone waited for them to resurface, but to their surprise, two new dolphins emerged right next to the ship. They swam the length of it, much to the delight and photo opportunity of everyone standing on that side. A moment later, the other side of the ship gasped. The dolphins had been considerate enough to make an appearance to everyone on board.

Once it became clear that the creatures had departed for the undersea, the ship began to move again. This time, when the captain spoke, Nina was ready for him. "The water is calm, so we are going to head on out into the Gulf. Keep your eyes peeled, and shout when you see another dolphin."

The ship approached Perdido Pass. The tall bridge loomed overhead. "Are we going under that?" Nina pointed.

"Yeah, probably. Don't worry, it's safe. Except maybe from bird droppings. But we've got a roof over our heads," Barry reassured her. Nina was thankful for the small awning that shielded them from whatever might fall. For reasons she didn't quite understand, she held her breath as they rode underneath the concrete structure.

They passed several islands dotted with people and smaller watercrafts. The captain told the names of each slice of land. He said that they were sanctuaries for several types of animals and plants in the area. When he mentioned seahorses, Nina and Michelle perked up. "Okay, we have to rent a jet ski and go," Michelle insisted.

On the placid waters of Perdido Bay, the vessel had remained level. Then they rounded the corner into the wide open waters of the Gulf of Mexico. Instantly, they felt the rise and fall of the ship with the motion of the waves. Barry said, "This is the best part. I could stay out here all day." He shut his eyes and soaked in the feeling.

Nina loved it, too. She had the odd thought that it felt like being back in the womb. How would she know that? She just imagined it as a place of absolute peace, a fluid environment of gentle motion.

The time to turn around came too soon. The return journey did at least come with narration. The captain revealed which celebrities owned which homes along the bay. He also told the cost of some of the fancier vessels they passed in their docks. Nina thought to herself, *"If I paid that much for a boat, I would just live on it."*

The sun had set and twilight appeared, bringing with it the glow of waterside lamps. Nina stared out at their reflections rippling on the surface. This experience had been more enjoyable than a day-long trip on a private boat with Donovan. It felt more like real life. A bunch of people gathered together for one purpose: to find a dolphin. Everyone seemed satisfied that they had achieved their collective goal. The trip into the Gulf was just an unexpected bonus, and the narration a nice touch. The joy on board was contagious, and Nina caught it.

Barry bumped her with his elbow. "What are you thinking?"

"That this is the best time I've ever had on a boat. And I've been on a lot of boats." She smiled at him, the glisten of emotion in her eyes as she said, "Thank you."

He returned the smile. "I'm glad you enjoyed it."

Filled with gratitude for all the wonderfulness that was Barry, Nina put her hand over his. All the hope he had brought into her life had kept this time of loss from seeming like too much of a bad thing. Though her world had flipped, she found she liked the upside-down version better. Or maybe *this* was the right-side up.

Because her specialty was bringing frivolity when things got too serious, Michelle added her hand to the stack. When they turned to look at her, she said, "I'm starving. Please tell me we are going to eat somewhere after this."

"As you wish," answered Barry. The boat pulled carefully up to the pier. They put a tip in the jar as they disembarked. "Where do you want to eat?"

Nina pointed to a brightly colored building nearby. "What is that?" she asked, thinking it must be a giant playground.

"Ooo, that's Tacky Jack's! I always wanted to eat there, but Kevin wouldn't go." Turning to Barry, Michelle pleaded, "Can we?"

"I don't see why not. Nina, you up for it?"

Nina secretly hoped they had salad but feared their menu might consist entirely of fried food. Not wanting to crush Michelle's dream, she answered, "Sure."

They waited about twenty minutes to be seated. Upon perusing the menu, Nina was relieved. They had several healthy options available. She chose the grilled seafood salad. Michelle and Barry wanted to try the fried green tomato fries, so they split the appetizer. Then they each ordered the Tacky Shrimp.

After the waiter walked away, Nina asked, "What's Tacky Shrimp?"

Michelle answered, "Apparently, it's awesome. My friends who've eaten here have told me it's the best thing on the menu. It's shrimp in this spicy seasoned broth, and it comes with bread so you can dunk it and eat it up.'

"Ah." Nina tried to avoid bread.

"You'll have to try a piece," Michelle said. Nina knew that to argue would be pointless.

"I'll try a bite," she offered. One bite couldn't hurt.

Their food arrived, and as expected, Michelle offered Nina some before trying it herself. "Try the shrimp and the bread both," she insisted.

Reluctantly, Nina dipped a chunk bread and placed one shrimp on top of it. She bit into it, and her eyes popped open. "Oh, wow."

Michelle took a bite immediately after Nina. "Wooo! This is awesome sauce," she exclaimed.

Barry nodded in agreement. In truth, Nina could have eaten a lot more of it, but she declined when Barry offered to share his. She wanted to stay in the habit of eating healthy, so she stuck to her salad.

When they had finished dinner, Michelle said, "Well, we have to try the peanut butter pie."

"Have to," Barry agreed.

"I'll pass," said Nina.

"Do you hate yourself?" asked Michelle.

"On the contrary. I love myself enough to control what I put into my body."

Barry laughed. "Oh, snap."

Michelle replied, "Well, excuuuuse me." She put her hands up in surrender.

Nina feared she'd protested too heavily. "Sorry. I didn't mean that to sound rude. It's just that I've made a lifestyle decision, and I like to stick to it. If I make exceptions, before long, those allowances will turn into five extra pounds. I've been there before. Not going back."

"Mmkay. Mmkay. I got you. I won't peer pressure you." Michelle didn't seem offended. Good.

As Michelle and Barry received their desserts, they exclaimed over how wonderful they were. But neither of them offered a bite to Nina. She appreciated their acceptance of her dietary choice.

All during their meal, Michelle had been watching a guy at a table diagonal to theirs. Barry finally noticed as he caught her looking. He asked teasingly, "Whatcha staring at?"

Lowering her voice, she said, "Yes, Barry, I'm looking at that guy over there. He cute. He real cute."

Nina cast a glance in his direction. Then, though it was something she herself would never dare to do, she suggested, "You should go talk to him."

"What? No. I don't do that."

"What, talk? I beg to differ," scoffed Barry.

"No, approach strangers because I think they're cute. I prefer to stare until they pick up on the hint that I'm interested."

"That's not creepy at all," Barry said with a completely straight face.

Rolling her eyes, she looked to Nina for support. "Nina, you know what I mean. Don't you?"

Nina had to agree. "Yeah, I wouldn't do it either. Sorry, I know I suggested it, but I was just throwing that out there on the off chance that you were feeling brave."

Michelle turned her gaze back to the cute guy. He had just laughed at something his friends said. "Oh, man. He has dimples. Dang it."

The door to the deck opened and a tan, blond beauty walked in. She looked around the room, eventually locking eyes with the object of Michelle's interest. She sauntered over to him, leaned down, and planted a kiss on his lips. Then he slid over so she could sit down.

"I guess those two know each other," Michelle said with a nervous laugh as her heart sank. She should've known better than to hope. Of course a man that good looking would be taken.

"I'm sorry, Michelle." Barry sincerely wanted her to find love. He was tired of feeling guilty about how well things were going with Nina whenever Michelle hung out with them. But he also had a heart for those who were lonely.

Michelle threw her napkin down on her pie plate. "Ah, well. There's more fish in the sea, right? And we live in the perfect place to find fish." Her optimism was fabricated. She couldn't stand for them to feel sorry for her. She didn't have much hope that she would find anyone as good to her as Barry was to Nina, but she had to make them believe she did.

They split the check three ways and paid the server at their table. Michelle didn't look over at the man again. In her mind, he symbolized the long, lonely road ahead. Against her best mental efforts, she settled into a funk. The ride home was quiet without her enthusiastic chatter. When they reached the door of their house, she simply said, "Goodnight," and left them to whatever they wanted to do next. She let the tears flow down her face with the shower water. It washed away their salt, but their sting remained.

Chapter 44

The three of them took the next day off. Barry planned to meet Nina at the beach that afternoon, but she had reserved the morning for painting.

With a cup of coffee in her hands, she stared at the three basic elements on her canvas. She envisioned the details forming one by one, planning her strategy to layer from bottom to top. She started with the purple cast in the sky. Over that, she formed the clouds with a white base, working the pastel reflections across their surface from darkest to lightest. Then she brushed white across the waves to form breakers. She decided to leave the kiss of gold and pink upon their bubbles for last. It seemed most special.

She worked on the shading in the sand. Chunky sections of gray variations with white heads became seagulls. The fine detail would come later. Today, her focus was the second level of development.

The sound of Michelle's door opening and her shuffling slowly up the hallway caused Nina to pause. She wanted to check on her friend. She put down the brush and closed the paint containers. Michelle had tried to play off last night like it was no big deal, but her hurt had been evident in her silence on the ride home.

Nina entered the kitchen as Michelle was making coffee. Not wanting to push, especially before caffeination, Nina simply said, "Hi."

"Hey," she murmured sadly. The light seemed to have seeped out of her overnight. She took a seat at the table. Sipping her coffee, she stared straight ahead at the wall.

Wanting to avoid the obvious subject yet get her engaged in conversation, Nina asked, "What are you going to do today?"

Michelle let her head fall into her hand. She covered her face as she replied, "Sit here and stare at the wall."

Nina put a hand on the arm that propped Michelle's face up. "Surely not. Want to go to the beach?"

Michelle stared at Nina, but her eyes seemed out of focus. She appeared to be looking through her. "I don't even want to do that."

Now Nina was worried. Mermaid Michelle had lost her need for the sea. Nina had no clue how to help her. She might have to call Barry for backup.

Before she could come up with other suggestions, Michelle's phone rang. "Excuse me." She walked back to her room to answer it.

She didn't recognize the number. "Hello?"

"Hi, Michelle. It's Alicia. Damien gave me your number. I hope you don't mind."

"Not at all. What's up, Alicia?"

"My cousin is in town, and we were thinking about playing some miniature golf at Adventure Island. Would you like to join us?"

Michelle stood speechless. She had expected Alicia to say they had another volunteer project and needed her help. Being invited to something purely for fun threw her off guard.

Finally, she found her words. "Yes. That would be great. What time?"

"About 1:30 work for you?"

Michelle glanced at the clock on her wall. It was 10:45 now. "That works. Meet you there?"

"See you there. Bye!"

She let her phone drop to her bed. A rush of excitement flooded her veins. She had a thing to do, a fun thing to do, that didn't involve Nina and Barry. She had an outing with a friend. This was her first since moving here. What should she wear?

Her mind jumped tracks like a rickety old roller coaster. She stopped looking through her closet as she realized she wanted to tell Nina. Running into the kitchen, she yelled, "I have a thing!"

Nina looked alarmed. "What sort of thing? Are you in pain?"

Michelle laughed at her concern. "No. I have a thing to do today! With people!"

A smile spread over Nina's face. "That's good! More volunteer work?"

Still out of breath from running from the closet up the hall to the kitchen, Michelle inhaled deeply before saying, "No. Golf! Of all things. Miniature golf with Alicia and her cousin."

Nina put a hand on Michelle's shoulder. "That's great! You're gonna have fun. Mini golf is the best."

That confused Michelle. "You've played before? I figured Donovan to be more the actual golf type."

Nina smirked. "He was. But I played in high school with friends, before I met him."

"Ah, ok. Well. Maybe you can help. What does one wear to a miniature golf course?"

"Shorts. Dress casually, because everyone else will."

Michelle thanked her for the advice and rushed back to her room. She pulled out a pair of denim shorts. A flowy periwinkle sleeveless top complemented the blue tones in the faded denim. "Shoes," she said aloud. Sorting through her summer collection, she chose a pair of denim wedges with a heel not so tall as to pose a danger should she twist her ankle yet tall enough to add an inch or so to her stature.

Back to her old self, Michelle chatted happily with Nina over an early lunch. They remained at the table until someone knocked at the door at 1:00. Nina stood, but Michelle said, "Wait! Let's put the security camera to use. Turn on the TV."

They waited for the black screen to change to the four-panel display. When it appeared, it revealed that the person standing on their front porch was Barry. "That is so cool," Michelle whispered. Then she shouted in the direction of the door, "You're on TV, Barry!"

Nina unlocked and opened it for him. "Hey," she said with an involuntary bat of her lashes. She couldn't help it. He made her face flirt.

"Hey." He hugged her gently before stepping inside. Looking at the screen, he feigned shock. "Where'd I go?"

"Ha ha, nerd," Michelle said in a nasal tone.

"What are you all dressed up for?"

"This old thing?" She gestured at her outfit. "I'm off to smack some baby golf balls around." Her giddy smile made him grin.

"Alone?" he asked, playing the role of the protective older brother.

"No. I know people. One of my volunteer buds invited me." She looked at her phone. "And it's time for me to head that way. See ya." She hopped into her car and headed down the highway. Even without GPS, Adventure Island would be hard to miss with that tall fake volcano shooting forth orange "lava." That was the first thing Michelle saw as she pulled into a parking space. "Awesome," she sang out.

Alicia spotted her first. "Michelle!"

Michelle turned and found Alicia waving one arm up in the air. It reminded her of the first time they met, when Alicia had motioned her over to join her group. She smiled at the memory.

As Michelle approached Alicia's car, she noticed someone getting out of the passenger seat. "Michelle, this is my cousin Alfred. Alfred, Michelle."

A wiry man in a pastel argyle sweater (wasn't he burning up?!), thick, black-framed glasses, and oxfords walked up to her and extended his hand. "Pleased to meet you Michelle." He sounded stuffed up, and he sniffed loudly. After the handshake, he pointed toward his nose. "Allergies." Then he snort-laughed.

Michelle couldn't help but think, *"Wow. A real live Urkel."*

She forced down a laugh and transformed it into a smile.

Alicia took charge. "Okay, guys. This way." They followed her inside to get what they needed for the game. Then they headed onto the green.

Fake rock hills, manmade waterfalls, and tropical plants surrounded them. "Cool scenery," Michelle commented.

"I would say it's actually quite hot," Alfred corrected, pointing with a goofy grin toward the volcano as it shot forth another blast of fire. Then he snort laughed himself silly.

Michelle gave him a sideways grin. She hoped her face didn't seem rude. People laughing at their own unfunny jokes was one of her pet peeves. Sure, she laughed at herself a lot, but that was different. She was the funniest person she knew.

Evidently Alicia had played before. She was a pro. Michelle came in second, better than she thought she could do. Poor Alfred kept hitting the ball way far away from the hole. He claimed, "Arm spasm," after his worst shot.

When the game ended, Alfred headed toward the restroom. Once he was out of earshot, Alicia turned to Michelle and asked, "So, what do you think?"

"About mini golf? I like it. I'm actually better at it than I thought I'd be."

Alicia shook her head. "No, about Alfred. He's single, you know."

Michelle tried to hide her shock. "This was a setup?" She honestly had not picked up on that. It seemed like Alicia simply taking her weird cousin out on the town for some fun.

Alicia admitted, "I hoped you guys might hit it off. Alfred's a funny guy, and you have a great sense of humor."

"Thanks, but no, I'm sorry. I just don't feel the chemistry there." Michelle let her down in the nicest tone possible.

Her shoulders slumped. "It's okay. You can't force it if it isn't there. Alfred has trouble meeting women. He's just too shy."

They spotted him coming out of the restroom. "Ok, pretend I never told you anything. I promised him I wouldn't embarrass him by bringing it up in front of the two of you."

"No problem." They started walking toward the parking lot. When they reached the asphalt, Michelle said, "Well, that was fun, guys! Thanks for introducing me to mini golf."

"You're welcome. See you soon," Alicia replied.

"Nice to meet you!" Alfred called out. He waved goodbye and got into the car. Good thing he was shy. Michelle would have hated to upset him if he had asked her out.

As she drove back home, Michelle was thankful that she had not known ahead of time that Alicia had someone there for her to meet. She would've gotten her hopes up, and she could not handle another disappointment so soon after last night. It had really been nothing, just a fleeting moment of allowing herself to hope cut short by reality's slap. But it symbolized what she feared she'd have to face time and time again before she met the one that would stick, if she ever did.

Chapter 45

Nina held the card Geri had given her in her hand, turning it over and over. Should she call and tell her Mike had been captured? Surely she was the first person the police had notified after his arrest. She had the most at stake.

Michelle stood at the sink, washing the dishes from the blueberry pancakes she'd made for breakfast. Because she substituted applesauce for half of the butter, Nina had eaten some. More importantly, she had actually enjoyed them.

A loud clamor caused Nina to turn toward the kitchen. Michelle had dropped the skillet in the sink, and now she stood open-mouthed, staring out the window. "Geri's back!" she said in disbelief.

Nina joined her, catching a glimpse of Geri's curly blond hair as she disappeared inside. "I was just considering calling her to see if she knew about Mike's capture."

Michelle washed her hands off and dried them with the dishtowel. "Let's go over there."

"Oh, I don't want to bother her. She's got some memories to confront in that house. We might startle her if we go knock on the door. I'm sure she's pretty jumpy right now."

Thinking aloud, Michelle suggested, "We could go sit on the deck. That way she'd see us when she comes out. If not, we could yell hello and it wouldn't be an invasion of her private moment."

Nina nodded. "That's a good plan."

They each took what was left of their coffee and stretched out on the patio lounge chairs. "Lovely day," said Michelle.

In truth, it was overcast and incredibly windy. "Sarcasm?" asked Nina.

"No, I really like cloudy, breezy days at the beach. It's my jam," Michelle explained in all seriousness, punctuating that statement with a long sip of coffee.

"I guess I get that. It's less hot. But I prefer sunny days."

"There's an air of mystery about," Michelle observed, suddenly sounding very much like a narrator.

"Name that smell," replied Nina.

"What?!" Michelle laughed.

"You know, the scent on the breeze. Wind this strong is bound to carry a bunch of different smells."

"Is this a real game?" Michelle didn't really think it was, but Nina had spoken the words as if she were giving voice to a faraway memory.

"No. But it's probably something that dogs play. Telepathically, of course."

Michelle raised an eyebrow. "What did Barry put in your drink last night?"

Nina threw back her head and laughed. "Water, I think."

Michelle mumbled something into her coffee cup. Nina didn't ask her to repeat it.

The door to Mike and Geri's house slowly came open. Michelle swatted at Nina's arm. They both watched to see if she would look in their direction. To their relief, she did, and she shouted out, "Hello!" before heading into their yard.

They got up and met her halfway. "How are you?" Nina asked.

"I'm doing well. As you probably know, Mike's been arrested, so I don't have to hide anymore. But I don't want to live here. There are too many traumatic memories in this place. I'm going to sell. I just came back to pack up my things."

"Will you be moving to Savannah?" Michelle asked.

"Yes, that's the plan. I'm going to keep my stuff at my aunt's house until I find a place. Savannah's a beautiful town. It's near the ocean, so I won't be missing out on that. I might even move to nearby Tybee Island. I love that place. If I can find a job there that pays enough so I can live on my own, that would be the dream." Geri's face glowed as she talked. She couldn't stop smiling.

"I'm happy for you. I've been to Tybee. It's beautiful," Nina remarked. In truth, there weren't a whole lot of beach towns she hadn't visited. That was one good thing about having been married to Donovan; she had a rich portfolio of travel experiences.

"Well, I'm going to get back to it. I just wanted to let you know the news. Maybe I'll see you around." She waved as she turned to go.

Back up on the deck, Michelle said, "Well, that's awesome. Good for her."

"Yes, very good. I hope she finds a boss like Alice who can help her along the way."

Michelle tilted her head and looked at Nina. "There's no one like Alice."

"She was one of a kind."

"The best."

Chapter 46

Barry had peeked at Nina's painting yesterday. Even though it was in the beginning stages, he could tell she possessed skill. The way she had worked the colored layers of light through the clouds testified to that.

He knew a thing or two about painting. His grandmother had given him that knowledge. She used to take him to art museums, teaching him terms of the art world, showing him how to critique a piece. She even showed him her painting techniques.

Barry had a feeling that Nina's beach scene would turn out to be worthy of the journey through the beautiful hand that painted it. He looked forward to seeing the finished piece. Maybe she would hang it next to *the* painting.

They hadn't spoken of his reaction to *the* painting since the distraction that had so conveniently dropped the subject. That was perfect timing. He wanted to tell her, but the moment must be right or it could ruin everything.

He was so filled to the brim with love for her that he struggled every day against telling her. Though he could tell she had feelings for him, too, there was a reluctance about her, a hesitation most likely born of a recently tanked fifteen-year union. He was a patient man. If it took fifteen more years before he sensed she was ready to hear it, he could wait.

Now, he lingered outside the backdoor to Seahorse Treasures, just so he could talk to her for a moment before going inside. Once they were in the building, they felt the need to be professional and get straight to work. That brief meeting outside the door fueled him enough to get him through the day in the stockroom without her.

He stood from his squatting position as he saw her across the sand. The breeze tossed her blond hair over her face, and she raised one graceful arm to tuck it behind her ear. She was the picture of poise. Wherever she entered, she owned the room without even trying. He wondered if she knew of her special power. If she did, that would make her sweet humility even more astonishing.

The song, "She's So High," played in his head as she grew closer.

Jarring him from the spell, Michelle yelled out, "We were just playing a game of Name That Smell. Ever heard of it?"

He stared at Michelle a moment before her words registered. She never said anything he expected to hear. This was no exception. "Can't say that I have."

Instead of explaining, Nina laughed and reached out to hug him. "You don't want to know," she whispered as they embraced.

He wished that moment could last all day. She smelled like peaches and happiness.

Alas, they had to go make money. It was the responsible thing to do, and they were liable now for the very survival of their business and the gainful employment of their workers. So, inside they went.

In the stockroom, Michelle started the conversation. "So, I got unknowingly set up yesterday."

"What? Like scammed?"

"No, silly. Like for a date. It didn't pan out, though." She heaved a box off a shelf at eye level.

"So, no surprise love match?"

"No. I'm glad I didn't know about it in advance. I didn't have a reason to be upset. He just was totally not my type."

"I would say I'm sorry, but no heads up, no harm, right?" He checked the boxes off the sheet as she stacked.

"Right." She paused to wipe the dust from her hands. "So, how was your day with Nina? Are you two official yet?"

She meant well, but her question wilted him. "No. I'm giving her all the time and space she needs."

"Got a question for you Barry." She looked toward the ceiling. "How shall I phrase this? Ah, yes. How will you know when she has no more need for time and space?"

He set down the clipboard with a sigh. "I'm not sure. Maybe I'll see it in her eyes."

Michelle shook her head. "That can't be it. She already looks at you like you're her favorite person."

Barry crossed his arms. "Then maybe I'll hear it in her voice."

Michelle held out her arm like a lecturer before a podium. "Again, it's full of syrup when she talks to you."

He shrugged. "Maybe she'll tell me."

"Hmm. I doubt it."

He was growing frustrated. "Look, I don't think I'm in danger of losing her by being careful. She's not exactly looking to date around right now."

Michelle shrugged. "You're right. What do I know?"

Barry got back to work. He pushed the unpleasant feeling aside for several minutes. Then it occurred to him that her rhetorical question might not have been rhetorical at all.

"What *do* you know?" he suddenly asked, facing her with such intensity that she took a step back. When she didn't answer, he rephrased his question. "Do you know something I don't?"

He thought he detected a lower lip quiver as Michelle answered, "No. I was just agreeing with you. I don't know how you can read Nina."

He studied her eyes a moment before determining she was telling the truth. "Look, I'm sorry. It's just a touchy subject."

She turned to face the shelf. Nodding, she said, "Uh-huh," in a slightly shaky voice. Great. Now he felt like a jerk.

Before he could apologize further, Nina knocked at the door. "We need more aloe vera."

Michelle said, "I've got it." She grabbed the box and practically ran out of the room. For the rest of the day, she spoke to Barry only when necessary for work. Like he did with Nina, he gave Michelle her space. He let it drop, feeling certain that she would talk to him again once the sting passed.

Halfway through the afternoon, he heard another knock at the door. He turned and saw Leslie standing in the entryway. "Hey, Barry. I was wondering if I could get your help tonight."

"What do you need help with?"

"Alice left me a few pieces of furniture from her house. I haven't been able to get them because my husband's down in Bonita Springs this week, and they're too heavy for me to lift. Would you mind helping me load them into my vehicle and get them into my house?"

"Sure. No problem." Barry didn't mind lending a hand to Leslie. She had always been great about covering for him when he needed to leave work early. He was bummed that it would cut into his time with Nina, though he tried not to show it.

Leslie thanked him and walked away. Twenty minutes later, another knock caused him to look up, and this time, he faced Nina. "What are you doing after work?"

It pained him to tell her, "I told Leslie I'd help her move some of Alice's furniture to her house." His expression revealed his apology for having to turn down whatever offer she was planning to give.

"Oh. Ok." Her pretty eyes looked down at the floor, her thick lashes like the heavy drape of a stage curtain at performance's end.

"Maybe it won't take too long and I can still see you tonight." Barry would move that furniture faster than Leslie thought possible if Nina wanted to be with him.

"I was just going to go to the beach. No big deal. We can do it another time." Nina offered a smile, but disappointment laced its edges.

"I'm sorry. It's just that Leslie has always helped me out when I needed it, so I kind of owe her."

"You don't have to apologize. It's a good thing you're doing. I'll see you later." She dropped her hand from the doorframe and disappeared.

Michelle walked back into the room. With the first non-work-related question of the afternoon, he attempted to find a substitute for himself. "What are you doing tonight?"

She look at him with suspicion. "Going to deliver meals with the church. Why?"

"Oh. Nevermind. Nina wanted me to go to the beach with her, but I have to help Leslie, and she seemed disappointed, so I was hoping you could go with her."

Michelle's sympathetic eyes took him in. "That's sweet that you're trying to keep her from being sad about not going to the beach. But if she's disappointed, it's probably because she can't go with you."

He didn't know what to say. So he just half-smiled and said, "Thanks."

"Honestly, she'll probably just use this time to work on her painting. It'll be good for her," Michelle reassured him.

"You're right." She wouldn't paint if he were around. He understood that. Painting was a very private process that required concentration on angles, colors, and spatial relationships. She would find it hard to ever finish a piece if he didn't leave her alone now and then.

At the end of the day, Barry said goodbye to Michelle and Nina as he got into his 4Runner to follow Leslie. It was strange to see Michelle getting into her car instead of strolling beside Nina, who now made her way alone across the sand toward home. He yearned to go to her, to keep her from feeling lonely, but he had a task to accomplish.

Chapter 47

Michelle drove to the church parking lot, her mood a bit sodden. Barry frustrated her by perpetually refusing to dive all in with Nina. In snapping at her for trying to help, he had accomplished his goal, though he didn't know it yet. She was done playing matchmaker.

What irritated her further the more she thought about it was that he tried to get her to go hang out with Nina so she wouldn't be lonely. Didn't he realize that Michelle had far more reason to be lonely than Nina? They were supposed to be three amigos, but Michelle knew her place, and it was forever the backseat.

One other thing had her in the dumps today. A friend from back in Georgia had texted her to inform her she saw a photo on Kevin's Facebook of him getting cozy with a female lawyer. It was one of those relationship announcement photos. Michelle wondered if the woman knew about the seven million Kevin would get if they married. If she did, would that offend her or give her more reason to say yes?

Hopefully spending some time with other people tonight would take her mind off things. She pulled into the parking lot and saw a couple of women she didn't recognize handing over casseroles to Damien. The ladies immediately got back into their cars and left.

She walked over and greeted Damien. Then she asked, "Who were those people giving you food?"

"Those are some of our church members. They cook the casseroles that we deliver. We have a rotating schedule so that the same people don't wind up cooking every time."

"That's a good plan. I wondered last time where this food came from. I thought maybe you guys cooked it."

Damien laughed heartily. "Oh, no. I wouldn't do that to anyone." He smiled brightly at her. "But if you ever want to throw one in the mix, we'd be glad to take it."

"Ahhh, no you wouldn't. And neither would the people doing the eating," she joked.

He laughed again. Then another woman approached him to hand over food. Michelle spied Alicia by Ryan's van and went to say hello.

"Hi Alicia." Michelle hoped there were no hard feelings over her disinterest in Alfred.

Alicia's face lit up with that same friendly expression it always held, so evidently all was well. "Hi Michelle. Oh, hey, the coolest thing happened after we left Adventure Island yesterday. Alfred and I stopped for ice cream, and he met someone!"

"What?" She tried to sound more pleased than shocked, but she wasn't sure she'd caught herself in time.

"There was this sweet lady working behind the counter who reminded me a lot of Alfred, really. She wore the same kind of glasses and seemed to share his fashion sense. And when he made a corny joke, she laughed so hard. I guess that gave him the confidence to get her number. I've never known him to ask a girl out before."

Michelle hated that she felt jealous of them right now. "That's great," she forced herself to say. What she thought was, *"That's great that everyone but me is finding their soulmate."*

Alicia looked in Damien's direction. "I think they're ready for us." Michelle followed her to collect the casseroles and load them in the van. Tears threatened to form, but she forced them down into the lump in her throat that she couldn't dissolve with positive thoughts.

On the ride to the first meal delivery, she threw herself into the conversation between Ryan and Alicia. As hard as it was to care about anything but her hurt feelings right now, she had to try. Breaking down in tears in front of her new friends was not an option. She even hated losing control of her emotions in front of people she'd known for years, so showing her pain to those in the circle she had just entered would be mortifying.

They pulled up to the apartment of the sweet woman she had met on the route last week, Mrs. Betty. When they entered her house, she surprised Michelle by remembering her name. She reached out to hug her, and Michelle almost let the tears come. Almost, but not quite.

Mrs. Betty released Michelle and held her at arm's length. "Tell me, dear, do you have a boyfriend?"

The question cut to her heart. "No," she said through the pain.

The old woman smiled. "I'd love for you to meet my grandson. He's quite the catch, if I do say so myself."

Michelle thought, *"Probably another Alfred."*

"He gives kayak tours here in Orange Beach." She took a piece of paper from a small notebook and a pen from her lampstand. She wrote something on the paper, tore it off, and handed it to Michelle. "This is the address of the place. You should take a tour sometime. His name is Jason. I would have you two meet here at my place, but he refuses to be set up. He would never go for it. But if you show up there, he's bound to fall for you." She winked and smiled as if she were completely convinced of it.

This was the oddest attempt at a setup Michelle had ever experienced. "Thanks. I'll keep that in mind." Of course, she had no intention of going. What would she say to him if she did? *"Oh, hi, you don't know me, but your grandmother thinks we'd be good together."*

They departed for the next house. Michelle stuck the paper in her purse and forgot about it. She felt certain that Mrs. Betty's grandson must be about to meet the love of his life, since there had been an attempted setup with Michelle. She seemed to have the Midas touch. Maybe she should advertise, "Want to meet your future spouse? Just have one of your friends set you up on a date with Michelle Kingsley. You won't even have to show up. Sit back and watch your dreams come true."

Michelle was trying hard to stay involved in the spirit of giving, to add to the conversation instead of letting her problems distract her into depression. It became clear as the night progressed that she should have just stayed home. She was losing the battle to keep her head above the water fighting to rise within it.

By the time they were en route back to the church, all she could do was stare out the window and pinch her arm. The discomfort kept her from succumbing to sadness. She was thankful that darkness had fallen so no one could witness her self-torture.

They were almost back when Alicia announced, "Oh, I almost forgot. We've got another yardwork event lined up this week if you're interested. It'll be one of those early morning jobs."

Michelle hadn't been too thrilled with getting up before the sun last time, but why not? The sadness and supposed curse would be there whether she slept or actually made use of herself. Might as well get up and help someone out.

"I'm in. Where is it?"

"Damien has the address. He'll give it to us when we get back, along with the date. Then we'll sign up on the sheet so he can have an idea of how many backup volunteers he'll need to call in, if any."

"Backup volunteers? I thought we were it." Michelle assumed the four of them could handle one yard.

"We're usually enough, but if one of us has prior plans and can't make it that day, there are others willing to help. They just aren't signed up as regulars."

The van came to a stop. Alicia, Ryan, and Michelle approached Damien at the signup table. He read aloud the address of the next yardwork event. To clarify the location, he mentioned, "That's directly behind Seahorse Treasures."

Michelle's jaw dropped. "That's my house!"

Damien looked at her in confusion. "No, that's Alice Rowland's place. We've been doing her yard regularly for the last two months."

Michelle's heart pounded. "That was you?! Oh, then, I guess you don't know. Alice passed away."

A shocked murmur made its way through the group. "No, we had no idea. What happened?"

"Her heart stopped in her sleep. Did you know she had a heart condition?" Michelle felt bad for being the one to break the news.

Damien replied, "Yes, one of our members recommended her for our yard project. Her terminal heart condition was the reason we added her to the top of our list. She was so gracious. When she found out who we were and what we do, she donated to our mission."

Alicia spoke next, "She was my favorite. So full of life despite the fact that hers was fading. Her spirit was an inspiration to me."

Michelle teared up. Finally, a good reason to leak. "Alice gave me a job when I was on the verge of becoming homeless. Then she gave me a place to live. She needed someone to take care of her old house, so she allowed me and a coworker to live there rent-free. When she passed, we found out she had left the house and the business to us."

A round of gasps ensued. Then, Alicia asked, "Wait, so the last time we did the yard, you were living there?"

Michelle laughed. "Yes. And you gave us quite a scare. We even installed security cameras to figure out what was happening."

Everyone laughed. Damien said, "I guess the hedge trimmers and gloves I left there the night before we came must have really freaked you out, huh?"

"What? No, I didn't even see them. What freaked me out was coming home to find three feet of privacy hedge missing off the top."

Damien's eyes widened. "Oh no. Alice had mentioned last time we saw her that she would like them trimmed down low so she would have a better view. I'm so sorry! If you'd like us to put up a fence to restore your privacy, we'd be glad to."

Michelle shook her head adamantly. "No. I should be thanking you for the work you did. I feel bad that you guys spent your time and energy on two people who didn't need it. But I'm grateful. Maybe I could come to your houses and do some work to pay you back."

Everyone objected at once. Then Ryan spoke for the group, "That won't be necessary. We do what we do not expecting anything in return. Consider it a yard-warming gift. Welcome to the neighborhood!"

Everyone echoed that sentiment. Damien referred back to the list of yardwork needs and moved on to the next address. They all agreed to meet there Thursday.

Michelle could hardly wait to tell Nina and Barry that the mystery of the yard fairy had been solved. This was just one more thing to put them at ease about their safety in their own home. It would be nice not to feel alarm at every single sound. She was tired of being so tightly wound all the time. Maybe they could finally relax and enjoy their new home as it was meant to be appreciated: without fear.

Chapter 48

Nina needed to be outside. She knew she had just been given the perfect opportunity to paint, but her heart wasn't in it tonight. She craved the company of the ocean.

She passed by the table on which Michelle's gun rested. She briefly considered taking it and leaving a note in case Michelle came home early, but then again, if she got back to the house before Nina and found herself in an emergency with an intruder, Nina would be to blame for whatever happened to her. So she left it.

In her beach bag, she carried a towel, her phone, and her house key. She had applied sunscreen before stepping out, and at this late hour, she wouldn't need to reapply. She crossed the street wearing flip-flops, but once she hit the sandy beach, she removed them and let her feet sink in. The sand here was like warm snow. The way it conformed to new shapes under the weight of her arches and toes resembled how snow caves to pressure in the palm of your hands and fingers to form a snowball.

A group of college kids were playing in the water. An older man on a jet ski zoomed over the crests of the waves, putting on a show. Further down the beach, some teenagers sitting on a blanket snacked on chips. A group of seagulls hovered before them, screaming their displeasure at the teens for eating junk food on their beach. A quick toss of chips into the air revealed the birds to be hypocrites.

The jet ski rider parked his craft in the shallows and approached the group in the water. Nina couldn't hear what was being said at that distance, but she saw two of the girls shake their heads. A boy from among them nodded. The man turned to go, and the boy followed. Nina watched it all from behind dark shades.

Once the older man mounted the jet ski, the boy got on behind him. They took off, built up speed, and jumped the waves, the bottom of the craft skimming them before going airborne. The young man let out a joyful shout, and the girls applauded and whooped. Nina just shook her head. She was sure it was fun for some people, but with age came the desire for safety and lack of pain.

When the man returned to shallow water, the boy hopped off, waved to him in thanks, and ran/jumped back to his crew, who saw his antics and laughed. The man waded to shore, seemingly focused on the group of teens to Nina's right. He had long, stringy hair and a thick mustache. He wore banana yellow shorts and looked to be anywhere from 50 to 70. This time, he was within her earshot, and she heard him say, "Do any of you want to take a ride on my jet ski?"

One of the boys, wanting to show out, replied, "Only if I can drive it."

The man laughed. "No, no one can drive it but me. The insurance won't allow it."

Looking around at her friends, one of the girls stood. "I'll do it."

"Alright. Follow me." He walked toward the water.

Her friend grabbed her wrist as she took a step in his direction. "Katie, are you sure it's safe?"

"You saw that other guy take a ride. Nothing weird happened. It'll be okay." She tugged her wrist free of her well-meaning friend, who stared after her in disbelief.

Turned out Katie was right. She had a fun ride, much like the young man who preceded her, and nothing wayward happened. Maybe this man just wanted people on the beach to have a good time. He had a way to make that happen, so he did.

Once Katie returned, most of her friends were willing to go next. The girl who had tried to stop her still wasn't convinced this was a good idea. She refused to be talked into it.

Nina grew weary of watching the kids. She lay down on the towel and shut her eyes, focusing on the give and take of the waves. Falling into a trancelike state could be so pleasant here, the relaxation destination of many travelers.

When Nina opened her eyes again, she noticed how quiet the world around her had become. She glanced westward, where the sun readied itself for bed. Sitting up, she looked around. Everyone had left the beach. Everyone except the jet ski man.

He emerged from the ocean with a smile on his face. As he neared her, he said, "Looks like everyone's had their turn but you. Wanna ride?"

She politely returned his smile. "No, thank you. There's a lot of motion out there. I prefer to stay still."

"Aw, where's the fun in that?" The man looked at her with a twinkle in his eyes, and something else. Nina felt a stab of panic as she sensed danger beneath his gaze. How did she let herself fall asleep out here without Michelle or Barry?

"I guess I'm more of a 'sit on the beach' kind of person." Trying to think of an excuse to get out of there quickly, she looked toward the setting sun. "It looks like it's time to head home. Thanks for the offer." She stood and grabbed her things. Out of the corner of her eye, she saw him walk away and stoop to retrieve something.

When she looked back up, he was standing right beside her. He had a beach towel draped over his right arm, concealing all but two inches of the gun pointed in her direction. "You're right. It's time we go home. Don't try to run away, or I will shoot. Stay on my left side and walk toward that yellow car parked right over there."

Icy fear infiltrated Nina's veins. She had never been colder. No matter how tempted she was to run, she knew she would be an open target out here. She had no choice but to do what he said.

The aroma of cigarette smoke that clung to him overwhelmed her sinuses. Trench-like creases lined his face, probably carved from years of chain smoking and sun exposure. He coughed as they walked, and the sound resembled that of a hospitalized pneumonia patient. Deep in his lungs, a tightly woven web of carcinogenic nature made breathing a chore. Yet he held the gun steady.

They reached the passenger side of the car. "Okay, you're going to get in. Then I'm going to walk around the back to the driver's side, but I will keep this gun trained on you at all times. I am willing to shoot through the windshield of my own vehicle if you try to run."

Nina nodded and got inside. The nicotine smell in here was overpowering. The foreign, nauseating scent increased her fear. This car had to be an old model. Years of cigarette exposure had yellowed the ceiling, doors, and even the manual locks. Nina's eyes widened. Manual locks! He couldn't control them from his side. He hadn't even thought to make her push the lock down. This could work in her favor!

She didn't move at all as the man rounded the back of the car to the driver's side door. He got inside, never letting the gun point in any direction other than Nina's. He cleared his throat. "I haven't introduced myself. My name is Leonard. What's yours?"

Not wanting to give him her real name but worrying that he might already know it somehow and become angry if she lied to him, she said, "Nina."

"Nina. That's a pretty name for a pretty lady." Something about the way he crooned the words in his hoarse, smoke-laden voice sent chills of aversion down her spine. They joined with the ice in her veins to freeze her further.

"Well, Nina, here's what's going to happen. I'm going to drive down the highway here, so we are going to find ourselves in traffic. A lot of people will be able to see us at traffic lights and what not. I have the unique ability to drive with one eye and watch you with the other. If you so much as mouth the word 'help' to a passerby, you will make things much worse for yourself when we get where we're going. Understand?"

Nina swallowed hard. "I understand. May I ask where we are going?"

He let out a low, multi-layered laugh. "Well, my house, of course. It's time to go home, like you said. You're gonna come live with me."

Nina stared straight ahead as he laughed some more. He guffawed himself into a coughing spell, but the gun never wavered. They headed down Perdido Beach Boulevard, and this time, she felt quite perdido. Her mind flashed back to that day at the beach when Barry told her the meaning of the word, and she longed more than she had ever longed for anything to be back there with him in that moment.

Barry would have no idea where she had gone. Neither would Michelle. They would worry themselves sick. She had her phone in her bag, but she felt certain that Leonard would take it from her once they arrived. Her only shot at getting out alive was to escape before they arrived, somewhere other people could come to her rescue.

Through several stops at red lights, Leonard never loosened his grip on the gun aimed at Nina's side. A shot from this angle would likely take out a kidney. If she knew that were all it would do, she would gladly sacrifice that organ for a chance at a longer life.

They had been driving for a while when traffic finally came to a halt. Many beachgoers, freshly showered and dressed up, were driving around, looking for a place to eat dinner. The line of cars moved now and then, but at a snail's pace.

They were beside the Waffle House parking lot when a gurgling sound arose from Leonard's throat. It transformed into an involuntary cough, and within seconds, it had worked up to a coughing fit so intense, it doubled him over. With Leonard unable to care about anything but taking his next breath, the gun shook wildly from side to side.

Nina glanced at the parking lot. Two police cars were parked in front of the Waffle House. The moment Leonard lost absolute control over the gun, she bolted. Leaving the door open to save time, she ran like she had never run before toward the door of the restaurant. Behind her, a cough so severe it seemed sure to strangle him faded into the distance, letting her know she had not been followed.

She burst through the door gasping for breath. Everyone, including the two officers, turned to look at her. She found enough air in her lungs to say, "I've been abducted. The man is out there, in his car. He has a gun." She inhaled so deeply she almost passed out.

"Which car, ma'am?" one of the officers asked as he stood with his hand already on his own weapon, ready for action.

Pointing toward the street, she answered, "The yellow one on the road with the door open."

Both officers rushed out the door. Nina collapsed into an empty booth. Since windows made up the entire front wall, everyone in the place had rushed forward to see what was happening outside. Taking deep yet shaky breaths, Nina watched the scene play out through the window directly in front of her.

Apparently, Leonard had never stopped coughing. The police dragged him up from the driver's seat and cuffed him. As they led him to the police car, everyone inside the restaurant cheered and clapped. Nina leaned back against the seat, immensely relieved yet understandably shaken. She trembled all over with gratitude and the aftereffects of adrenaline.

One officer left to take Leonard to the station. The other came inside. He held up the beach bag he'd found in Leonard's car and asked, "This yours?"

"Yes, thank you." She put the bag on the seat next to her. Then the officer took her statement. Despite her condition, she was able to control her emotions and give a detailed description of everything that just occurred. The officer asked if she knew the names of any of the people at the beach that day who had encountered Leonard. When she told him no, he said, "Well, it's likely they'll come forward once this hits the media. Even though he did nothing to any of them, it's helpful to have witnesses that can place both of you at the scene. For the record, I believe you. It will just be helpful in court."

A waitress placed a glass of ice water in front of Nina. "You look like you could use it," she commented as she cast her a look of sympathy.

"Thank you." Nina drank the whole thing, coming up for air only once when it was half empty. *"Today, it's half full,"* she thought to herself.

Chapter 49

The officer offered to drive her home, so she took him up on it. She could have called Barry, but he might be in the middle of moving a piece of heavy furniture, and she didn't want to cause an injury.

When they neared her home, she told the officer, "You can pull into the parking lot of Seahorse Treasures. My house is behind it, but you'd have to drive through a lot of sand to get there."

He parked in front of the building. Motion to her right caught Nina's eye, and she saw Barry pulling in beside them. His face went pale with worry.

She turned to the cop and explained, "He's my ... well ... we're sort of dating. Anyway, it's safe to leave me with him. He can walk me home."

"You're sure about that?" he asked with a raised eyebrow. He seemed wary of her uncertain explanation of their relationship.

She smiled. "I'm sure. Our relationship may be complicated, but my belief in his goodness isn't. I feel completely safe with him."

He shook his head and grinned. "Okay. Hey, be careful out there. No more going to the beach alone, alright? It's a sad fact of the world we live in today, but it isn't safe."

She nodded. "Believe me, I have permanently lost all desire to go to the beach by myself. Thank you so much for saving me today. I might be dead if not for you and your coworker."

"You're welcome."

Nina closed the door and turned to find a distraught Barry waiting for an explanation. She fell into his arms without hesitation. Sensing she needed it, he held her tight instead of grilling her. Nina still shook all over. She inhaled the scent of him, so different from the smoke-choked aroma of her captor. Barry smelled clean with a hint of woodsy cologne, and something else. Natural goodness, she supposed. It set her at ease.

With her nerves slightly settled, she finally pulled away from him to talk. He looked at her expectantly but let her speak first. She inhaled, then said, "I was kidnapped at gunpoint from the beach."

His knees buckled slightly, and he gripped her arms as he asked, "What?!"

She told him everything. When she had finished, his eyes were filled with tears. She reached out to hug him again, and he pulled her in and held her like he hadn't seen her in months. "I almost lost you," he said in a haunted whisper.

"Never again," she said into his shoulder. He pulled back, and his eyes were full of love and hope. Then she said, "I'll never put myself in that position again. Even if it means never going to the beach alone."

Something disappeared from those lovely color swirls in his eyes after she explained her remark. It was as if an extra web of light present a moment before went out as she spoke. She wanted it back.

His voice had lost some of its passion as he said, "Yeah, it's not safe out there." He ran his hand through her hair. The look in his eyes changed to one of sad longing, as if she were a thing he wanted but knew he could never have.

She gently laid a hand on his arm. "Barry, what's wrong?"

He smiled sadly and shook his head. "Nothing. Nothing at all. You're alive and well, and that's all I could ask for."

Nina continued to study his eyes, her gaze questioning, the sadness having leapt from his to hers. He put an arm around her and led her in the direction of home. "Come on. Let's get you home."

"Will you stay with me a while?" she pleaded.

"Of course. I wouldn't leave you alone after all this. I'll stay with you until Michelle comes back." Something was off. His voice sounded guarded.

"You don't have to leave just because she comes home. You know you're welcome at our house any time, right?"

He laughed lightly. "I'm not so sure Michelle feels the same way. Especially after today."

"What happened?"

"Oh, it's no big deal. I just called her out on being pushy at work. Then she gave me the silent treatment for the rest of the day."

Nina moaned. "Sometimes she can be too sensitive. And too pushy. But sensitive when you point that out."

Barry agreed. "All I can do is just apologize and hope we move on. I'm learning what not to say."

Nina leaned into him and squeezed his side as they walked. His warmth melted the ice that lingered in her veins from earlier. She needed him to stay by her side until her internal temperature rose to normal, both mentally and physically.

They had just walked up to the front door when they saw Michelle's headlights enter the parking lot of work. Nina looked at Barry, whose gaze never left the car. With one hand, she unlocked the door, and with the other, she pulled him inside. Shutting the door with her eyes fixed on him, she entreated, "Please don't go."

As she stared at him, his eyes questioned her meaning. She took a step closer, with every intention of kissing him. He read her look. He leaned forward, the light of love returning to his eyes, about to realize a dream; but suddenly, like a man bent on destroying himself, he said, "We should go meet Michelle and walk her home. It isn't safe out there at night."

Feeling as if she had been shamed during her most private confession, she stepped back, the hurt evident all over her face. "Um, you go ahead. I need to sit down."

He put a hand on her arm. "Are you sure you feel safe here alone?" he asked with so much concern it squeezed her heart.

She stepped further away, unable to bear his touch right now. Not making eye contact, she answered, "Yeah, I'm fine. I have a gun, and you'll be right back with Michelle. I'm gonna go shower."

Though she was already heading toward the hallway, he called out, "Okay. Goodnight."

Somehow she'd known he wouldn't be coming back inside. What on earth had gone wrong? He had been so into her up until the moment when she'd said she'd never go to the beach alone again.

She didn't have the energy to analyze it right now. The new sadness she felt was quickly sapping what little life force she had left. She had to shower and lie down before she fainted from exhaustion.

Chapter 50

Barry was more conflicted than he had ever been in his life. For one brief, sweet moment, when he had told Nina he thought he'd lost her and she replied with, "Never again," he had believed she was about to profess her love for him. Then her next sentence shot his hope from the sky, punching a hole in its parachute.

Maybe the elevated emotions had worked his heart up to a place where he believed nothing could go wrong. Perhaps he thought she had been swept up in the river of love pouring out of him in that moment, that some of it had spilled into her heart and had a cupid's arrow effect. The disappointment he felt when he realized the feeling was all his could not be measured by any human instrument.

Then inside the house just now, her eyes had pleaded with him. Like the scene in all of his sweetest dreams, she was about to kiss him. She had made that move, but he couldn't let her follow through. She was riding high on the joy of being alive after the events of the day, and the decision to kiss him was likely due to her unstable emotions. He wanted her to make that choice psychologically sober.

He needed to get away for a while. Sort out his emotions without Nina around. Not have to worry about whether or not he would hurt Michelle's feelings every single day.

But there was still someone out there with a pair of hedge trimmers who knew where they lived. Security cameras could only reveal identity. They couldn't avert tragedy in the moment. He felt responsible for their protection.

Michelle met him in the sand a few feet from the parking lot. "Hey, Barry. You'll never guess what I learned today."

"I've got news for you, too, but I'll let Nina tell you. She had quite the eventful day. Okay, now, what did you learn?"

"You know the volunteer ministry I've been working with? They did our yardwork! They thought Alice still lived there, and they were trying to help her out because of her heart condition. Isn't that awesome?" Michelle sounded so animated. All hints of irritation with him were gone. That was one small relief.

"That is great. Wonderful news. Now we don't have to worry." Now Barry was free to leave town for a while.

"I know, right? I can't wait to tell Nina. Also, I'm curious about what she has to tell me."

"She's in the shower right now. She looked pretty tired. You'll probably have to catch her before she hits the bed."

Barry walked Michelle up the steps. When she put her key in the lock and turned the doorknob, he said goodnight and descended. He couldn't take another day of this frustration and pain. He would call Leslie in the morning before he left for his hometown to let her know he would be gone a few days. That way he wouldn't have to answer questions from Nina and Michelle, and they wouldn't worry when he didn't show up to work. He only hoped he could clear his head enough to find the strength to come back.

Chapter 51

When Nina stepped out of the bathroom, Michelle called to her. Nina had hoped to escape to her bedroom for the night, but no such luck.

She entered Michelle's room. Michelle immediately said, "So, I've solved the mystery of who trimmed our hedges and mulched our palm trees."

Despite her condition, Nina perked up and took an interest. "Who was it?"

"It was the ministry I've been volunteering with! Damien told us the address of our next job, and it was here! I had to tell them about Alice. They didn't know!" Michelle explained with such fascination that Nina couldn't help but share it.

"That's such a huge coinci – nevermind. We don't believe in those. And this is a good example of why."

"Amen. And Barry said you had some news. What's up?"

Nina shook her head. "He didn't tell you?"

"No, he said he'd let you tell me."

"I was kidnapped by a man with a gun. He cornered me on the beach when everyone else left for the night. I had to get into his car. If he hadn't been such a heavy smoker, I might not be here right now."

"Wait. What??" Michelle shrieked.

"He sounded like he had emphysema. He started coughing so hard that he bent over and couldn't hold the gun straight. That's when I made my move. We were going super slow in traffic anyway, so I bolted out the door and into the Waffle House, where two cops were eating. They arrested him and drove me home."

Michelle sat speechless, a rarity brought on by an even bigger rarity. She reached out and hugged Nina. Finally, she found her words. "I'm glad you're okay."

"Thanks. Me too."

Michelle studied her. "But you're not totally okay. Something's wrong. What is it?"

In addition to being a good talker, Michelle was also a keen observer. She listened really well, even when messages were conveyed silently through body language.

"Something's up with Barry. I hurt him somehow, and I don't know what I did." Nina's face scrunched up with worry.

"Hmm. He did seem a little distant when he walked me home. Well, what did you say and what did he say? Maybe I can help you figure it out."

"The thing that seemed to bring about a change in him was when I said I'd never go to the beach alone again. That doesn't make sense. If anything, that should make him happy, relieved. Why would that make him sad?"

Michelle thought back to how he had tried to get her to accompany Nina to the beach. "Maybe he's feeling guilty for not being there to protect you. If he hadn't been helping Leslie, he would have been with you, and none of this would have happened."

"Yeah, that thought crossed my mind, but I don't think that's it. This was like a complete shutdown. Like I pressed a button and forever deleted something precious."

Shifting to a more comfortable position on the bed, Michelle said, "Okay. Walk me up to that moment. What was said before that?"

Nina thought back. "I had just told him that I'd been kidnapped at gunpoint. He hugged me and said, 'I almost lost you.' Then I said, 'Never again.' He pulled back and looked at me, and his eyes were full of this beautiful light, overflowing with love. Then when I said, 'I'll never put myself in that position again. Even if it means never going to the beach alone,' that's when I saw the light leave his eyes."

Michelle sat up straight. "Well, there's your answer."

"Where?"

Michelle clarified, "He said, 'I almost lost you,' and your response was, 'Never again.' He obviously thought you were about to tell him how you felt about him. He probably was expecting, 'I love you, Barry,' instead of 'I'll never put myself in that position again.' Don't you see? It was an epic emotional letdown."

Nina put her head in her hands. "Oh, no. I hear it now. I had no clue." She agonized over the revelation. "But that doesn't explain his reaction a few minutes later when I tried to kiss him."

"You what now?" Michelle leaned in as if she hadn't heard Nina correctly.

"He was acting all sad. I couldn't get an answer out of him when I asked what was wrong, so when we got to the house, I leaned in to kiss him. He stopped me. Said we should walk over and meet you in the parking lot to get you home safely."

"He WHAT?!!! I'm gonna kill him. I am gonna kill Barry. When we see him tomorrow, you better say goodbye, because he is DEAD."

"Whoa. That's a bit of a strong reaction," Nina looked at Michelle with an eyebrow raised.

"You don't know how crazy he is for you. Or maybe you do. But if you do, it's not because he told you. I keep trying to coax him into telling you how he feels, but all I get is snapped at for pressuring him. And then he has the perfect chance, and he walks away?! No. This ain't happening."

Nina narrowed her eyes. "Are you sure there's anything for him to tell? I mean, I thought so, too, but after tonight, I'm not so sure."

Michelle was still fuming. "Is there anything to tell?" She hit Nina with a pillow. "Of course there's something to tell! It's so obvious. How can you not see that the man is absolutely crazy in love with you?"

That took Nina's breath away. Her voice grew quiet with the seriousness of the moment as she asked, "Did he say those words?"

Michelle growled in frustration. "He didn't have to!" Hitting the pillow against the bed in anger, she punctuated each word of her next sentence. "Barry loves you!"

Nina just stared at her.

Michelle couldn't contain her irritation with Barry. She stood and paced the room. "Where is my phone? I'm gonna call and give him a piece of my mind."

"No, don't do that. It was my fault. Just let it go."

In the grip of indignation, Michelle insisted, "No. He's not getting off the hook for this one. You don't understand how big of a moment he just missed out on." Despite Nina's argument, Michelle called and waited. His phone rang four times and went to voicemail. After the beep, she simply said, "Barry, what the heck," and hung up. He would know what she meant.

Nina stood. "I'm exhausted. I need to go to bed. See you in the morning."

"Goodnight." Michelle would probably stay awake fuming about this for hours. Nina felt bad for giving her this problem, but she had, in a way, solved it. At least Nina now realized what she had said to bring about a change in Barry. Hopefully she could get him alone tomorrow to talk about it. If she weren't so very worn out from the day's stress, she would likely stay up worrying over it all night. Upon the mattress, she closed her eyes, and sleep came as easily as it had on the beach earlier, when it hadn't been a good idea. Now, she had every reason to feel safe. Leonard was in prison. So was Mike Waters. Their mysterious gardener was a church group. All threats were neutralized. All except the one to her heart.

Chapter 52

When Nina and Michelle arrived at work the next day, Barry was not waiting by the back door where he usually stood. The sight of the empty spot where Barry should have been filled Nina with something bordering on despair.

"Did he ever call you back?" Nina asked worriedly.

"Nope. Not a call, not a text, nada. I'm not surprised. He knows he's in trouble." Michelle was still upset with him. If she confronted him before Nina could clear things up between them, it could make things messy.

"Let me talk to him first. Please? I need to try to undo the damage."

Michelle sighed. "Okay. But you didn't do anything wrong. He just chose to take what you said as discouragement. You fully made up for it when you tried to kiss him, just so you know. In my opinion."

"Okay. Thank you." Nina reached for the doorknob and turned. "It's locked," she said in shock. She had gotten used to Barry unlocking it before they got there. "Either he's still upset, or he's not here yet."

Michelle already had her key out. She unlocked it and held it open for Nina. They walked at a fast pace to the stockroom, both eager to see Barry. The room was empty.

They looked at each other and silently agreed to split up and check other rooms. Nina took the front of the store, while Michelle searched the office and breakroom. They met back up in the hallway a moment later.

"He's not here," Nina said with a lump in her throat.

"It's not 10:00 yet. Maybe since he's being standoffish, he's just waiting until opening time to arrive so we won't have time to confront him."

"You mean, so I won't have time to discuss this with him," Nina reminded Michelle.

"Yeah, you first. I know."

They heard the back door open again. Both of them were disappointed to see only Leslie.

"Hey girls," she called out.

"Hey. Have you heard from Barry?" Nina asked. She had a bad feeling he was going to be more than just later than usual.

"Yes, I have. He called me this morning and said he had to go out of town for a few days. He didn't want you to worry, so I said I'd pass the message along."

Nina and Michelle exchanged a look. Nina asked, "Did he say where he was going?"

"Back home for a visit. He hasn't seen his family since they helped move him down here, so he figured it was time." Leslie hadn't a clue that anything was odd about this.

Michelle grumbled under her breath and headed to the stockroom. Nina thanked Leslie for letting them know. Then she headed to the register, struggling not to cry.

On Nina's first break, she went straight to the stockroom. When she found Michelle, she calmly asked, "How do I fix this?"

With conviction, Michelle answered, "You wait for him to come back. Then when he comes to you, and he will, you talk. That's all you can do. He's not answering his phone. He's hundreds of miles away. So, you wait."

That answer hurt because it was true. Through soreness of heart, she summoned the strength to surrender. "Okay."

Chapter 53

His hometown hadn't changed a bit in the six months he'd been gone. Pine trees still swallowed the land, blanketing it with their straw, prohibiting most other plant life. Humidity choked the air with its suffocating hands. Narrow county roads intersected the one two-lane highway through town. Life moved on at a turtle's pace.

Barry felt unsettled about the way he had left Nina. He had seen the hurt in her eyes when he stopped the kiss from happening. His desperate attempt at self-preservation had ricocheted, injuring Nina instead.

He hoped the time apart would do them good. It was too late for regrets now. He was hundreds of miles away in northern Mississippi. He might as well stay a few days.

When he pulled into the driveway of his parents' home, he wasn't surprised to find his mother waiting on the porch swing. Since she'd retired, she spent most of her waking hours out there, either reading or sketching. She had inherited the art gene from her mother.

She stood when she saw him. They met each other on the walkway leading from the front porch to the driveway. His mom's age-freckled face and straight, shoulder-length white hair were a welcome sight. They hugged, and when she pulled away, she took his face in her hands and said, "It's so good to see you." She patted his cheek. Then she led him back to the swing. Indicating the space beside her, she said, "Sit. No one else is home right now to visit. So tell me all about life in Orange Beach."

Her ankle length denim skirt, long sleeve white shirt, and crocheted vest seemed so out of place in the sweltering summer heat. "Mom, aren't you burning up? I'm sweating just looking at you."

She gave him a knowing look. "Have you forgotten already how cold-natured I am? It feels perfect out here to me. I was too cold in the house. Your father keeps the thermostat on 72, regardless of how I shiver."

"So you're okay, then? You're not sick, not losing weight, no thyroid problems?"

She laughed. "Barry, no! I'm fine. Now I want to hear about you. Are you still working at Seahorse Treasures?"

"I am co-owner of the place now," he admitted without explanation.

His mother gasped. "That's wonderful! So you own it with that sweet lady, Alice?"

He sighed. He had a lot of explaining to do. He took a deep breath and told her everything. He even told her about Nina and how she seemed to have altered the very structure of his heart. He hadn't known it could hold so much love before she came along. Getting it all out made him realize how much he had needed someone to talk to about everything. Michelle wanted to be there for him, but her version of support was chiding him for not moving faster. It was nice to tell someone whom he knew would be on his side.

His mother let him talk without interruption. When he had finished with the reason he had left town to come for a visit, she still said nothing.

He couldn't interpret her silence. Finally, he had to ask, "What do you think I should do?"

She rocked in the swing with him, contemplating. She took her time answering. "I think you're doing the right thing by Nina."

"You mean giving her time to process her divorce and figure out what she wants from life now?"

"Absolutely," she didn't hesitate to reply. "If it were me, I'd want a friend more than anything. It would be a long while before I'd think about a relationship again."

That helped some. "But what about how I rejected her when she made a move? In hindsight, I wonder if that was an irreparable mistake."

"No, I don't think so. She's probably thankful for it. Whether she knows it or not, the girl's not ready. You did a good thing. I feel certain of it." His mother's smile could convince him of just about anything. He could have come home bearing a severed head, and she would have said, "That person probably didn't need that head anymore, anyway. You did a good thing." Still, it was nice to hear.

"I hope so. Anyway, I want to get my mind off of things back there for a few days. What's going on here? Any news?"

She laughed. "Same ole, same ole. That's the way of things. I'm not complaining, though. You know how I dislike change."

It was true. His grandmother had tried to get the whole family to move to Orange Beach on multiple occasions, but his mother wouldn't even consider it. She liked the comfort of knowing her surroundings. Barry had thrown her for a loop when he'd moved away, but by now, she had found her new normal. It might have a Barry-sized hole in it, but at least the rest of it stayed the same.

"How's dad?"

"Same as always. Down at the warehouse, making people behave."

"Of course he is." Barry's father owned the warehouse where Barry had worked before his girlfriend, Jane, had gotten together with his best friend, Tanner. After that, Barry knew the time had come to move far, far away. He couldn't very well stay in a place where memories of both of them lurked on every corner. Though his grandmother was gone, he knew she would be pleased if he came to live in the place that had brought her so much joy.

"Mom, I need to ask you something. You remember the painting of the beach at sunset at Grandma's house in Orange Beach?"

"Yes. The most beautiful painting I've ever seen."

He smiled briefly before his expression grew serious. "Why didn't Aunt Patricia save it for me?"

His mother's face showed concern. "She didn't?"

"No. It was sold at an estate sale."

She frowned again. "I asked her to keep it out for you. Mom would've wanted you to have it."

"Well, she didn't. And that's another amazing thing that happened to me. That painting wound up in Nina's house."

His mom gasped. "How on earth?"

"Alice's husband bought it at the estate sale twelve years ago. It hung on the wall in their house all that time. Nina recently inherited the house, and by default, the painting. I know I reacted as if I'd seen a ghost when I first saw it there."

Barry's mother grabbed his hand. "You know what this means."

One of the reasons he loved his mother so much was her tendency to remember all the important things. "I know."

"Well, that changes things."

"How so?" he asked.

She looked at him intently. "You have to tell her now."

"But you just said …"

"I know what I said, but that was before. Now …" she threw her hands up in the air. "Now it's out of our hands."

"You really think …"

With the ferocity of a rabid raccoon, she hissed, "I know."

Now it was Barry's turn to throw up his hands. "Okay."

She patted his leg. "It's settled then."
"Case closed," he agreed.
"Let's go get some sweet tea."

Chapter 54

Michelle tried to get Nina to go bowling with her and her church friends to keep her mind off of Barry, but she declined. Being around people might help Michelle in times of sadness, but it just made Nina restless and eager to escape. She wanted to throw her pain into her art. It was time to paint.

She ate some leftovers first so she wouldn't have to stop painting when hunger set in, and though she barely tasted it, the food filled her empty stomach. She dove into her project, determined to give herself over to it as long as she could stay awake. Hours passed, and with them, the canvas took on more beauty and light. She had no need to look at the clock, for her singular objective for the evening was to finish this first painting of her third life.

When she began feathering the gold and pink highlights upon the white foam, her hands grew shaky with the magnitude of the moment. She was almost finished! And it was beautiful. Not as beautiful as the painting that came with the house, but she couldn't aspire to that level of artistry without many more years of practice, if even then. However, she felt certain that most people, upon seeing her painting, would pause to appreciate it and maybe even feel compelled to comment on its beauty.

As she used a fine-tipped brush to stroke the last highlight across the final breaker, her arm began to shake. She used her left hand to support her right, and together, they made the last brushstroke. As she pulled the brush away from the canvas, it dropped onto the supply table below. Her arms jiggled like shaken gelatin.

Michelle came through the front door at that moment. "Hello! I'm home. I saw lights on, so I guess you're still up." She rounded the corner of the hallway. "I can't believe you're awake. You know it's nearly eleven, right?" As she approached Nina's room, she noticed that she was shaking all over. "Are you okay?"

She entered the room and grabbed Nina by the arms to steady her. "What is it?" Michelle asked, fearing that something had happened in her absence.

Nina simply gestured toward the painting. Michelle turned and gasped when her eyes took it in. She immediately said, "It's beautiful.

So lifelike. I feel like I'm looking out the window at sunset." She whirled around to face Nina. "Nina, this is really good. Like, pro-level good. I'm impressed."

"Thanks," said a still-trembling Nina. "Sorry I'm such a mess. I just put my soul into it, and now that it's finished, I guess I'm relieved? Used up? I'm not sure what's going on with me." Her face crinkled as the tears came without warning.

"Hey, it's okay. You did good." Michelle took her by the shoulders and led her to the bed. She eased her down to a sitting position. "Rest, just rest now. You accomplished a lot today."

Nina now had her face buried in her hands, sobbing uncontrollably. She tried to speak, but her words came out as indecipherable, high-pitched noises. She gave up and let herself wail.

Michelle sat next to her with her arm around Nina's back. After several rounds of body-jolting sobs, the weeping seemed to have run its course. Nina still cried, but now, the energy was confined to her face in the form of tears and sniffles.

"I'm going to go make us some chamomile tea, okay? That always helps me relax, makes me sleepy. It's easier to sleep after a good cry, too, and you've had one of the best. Will you be okay if I go to the kitchen?"

Nina nodded, the tears still falling. Michelle passed her a box of tissues, which she gladly accepted. Her eyes weren't the only thing flowing.

Waiting until Nina had blown her nose, Michelle asked, "Do you want to come with me to the kitchen, or would you rather wait here?"

Sniffing away enough of the drainage to allow words passage through her throat, Nina answered, "I'll come with you." The mysterious overtaking of her body had her not wanting to be alone right now. She still didn't understand what had set her off like that.

In the kitchen, Michelle boiled the water while Nina waited at the table with two mugs, each holding a chamomile tea bag. "Want to talk about it?" Michelle asked.

Nina had been resting on her elbows. She now sat up straight. "The only thing I can figure is I just had a culmination of opposing emotions."

Michelle looked at her out of the corner of her eye. "Okay. Have you had one of those before?"

"No. But I think the joy and sadness sandwich my life has become these past two days set off an explosion inside me. Just yesterday, I escaped a life or death situation. Joy. Then I hurt Barry, who in turn, hurt me. Sadness. Then I finished the first painting I've even attempted in fifteen years, and it's great. Joy. Boom," she flicked her fingers out and into the air, "I just short-circuited."

Michelle slowly nodded her head. "Makes sense. You have been through a lot in a short amount of time. It takes a while to process things like trauma, but you didn't even have time to do that before Barry went and broke your heart on top of it. I still want to kill him. But hey, let's try focusing on the positive. You're alive, and your painting looks great."

"Thanks." Nina picked up the paper tab on the end of the tea bag. She swirled it around in the cup absentmindedly.

An idea hit Michelle. "Hey, you should sell your art at Seahorse Treasures!"

The thought paralyzed Nina with fear. "I don't know about that."

"Why not?"

The chief reason was her lingering insecurity from Donovan's claim that no one would want to buy her art and that putting it up for sale would only result in embarrassment for her, but the excuse she offered Michelle was, "We don't sell stuff like that."

Michelle threw her hands up. "What's stopping us? We own the place now. We can sell whatever we want."

Nina felt a wave of weariness wash over her. She leaned back upon her elbows for support as she argued, "People come into our shop looking for cheap souvenirs, or beach towels, flip-flops, shades. The people with money to spend on paintings go to art galleries."

Michelle came closer, a sure sign she was about to ramp up her argument. "Not necessarily. I mean, we wouldn't just toss your painting on the shelf next to some $5 mugs. We could create an art corner. You could fill it with paintings over time. Do some smaller ones as well for the people who like your art but might not be able to afford a big piece like the one you just did. If people respond well to it, we could even offer space to other local artists for a small fee. It would be a great networking opportunity. Get your name out there in the local art community. Help out other new artists."

Michelle's smile indicated that she wasn't going to let this idea go. That was fine with Nina. It sounded like a good opportunity. She liked the thought of using her position as a storeowner to help other artists like herself who struggled with finding a place to sell paintings without first being judged in a competition or paying hefty fees. "I like that idea."

Michelle opened her mouth prepared to argue but caught herself as Nina's words registered. "You do?"

"I do. You've got business sense, Michelle. And a good heart for wanting to help."

Michelle could hardly believe her ears. "Aw, thanks." She grabbed the pot of boiling water and headed toward the mugs. "I really thought you'd fight me on that. I'm glad you can see the potential." She carefully filled each mug three-quarters full.

Back at the stove, she set a timer for four minutes. Nina watched the steam rise from the cup and thought of Barry's bonfires. An ache began in her heart, and she felt the sudden strong need to reach out to him.

Michelle came to sit at the table once the timer dinged. She brought a plate to hold the discarded tea bags. As soon as she sat down, Nina asked, "Would it be bad if I texted Barry?"

Sighing as she removed the bag from her mug, Michelle answered, "It wouldn't be bad, but it might look desperate. Keep in mind he walked out on *you*."

Nina groaned and put her head down. "I just want all this to be over. I need it resolved. I just … really miss him." She gave Michelle such a pitiful look that she almost took back what she said. But she couldn't.

"I know you do. I miss him, too, but in a different way. He will be back. Just a few more days." Michelle blew on her tea, avoiding eye contact, because she wasn't fully convinced of her own words. Barry had never walked away before. She hadn't expected that from him. Now, she had no clue what he might or might not do.

Chapter 55

Having slept well and avoided the temptation to text Barry, Nina felt she had emerged from some sort of fiery trial. She faced the day refreshed. A steady stream of customers kept her mind from straying to dangerous corners.

Something seemed familiar about the woman with the auburn hair who now approached the register with a fistful of shell jewelry. When the lady's gaze met her eyes, she said, "Nina?"

Then it hit her. This was a friend of her mother. "Rita?" Nina asked in amazement.

"I can't believe it's you! I haven't seen you in twenty years. You still look the same. Well, more grown up, but just as beautiful. How are you, dear?"

Nina's nerves were going haywire. "Fine, and you?"

"I'm on vacation, so, great! How is your mother? I haven't talked to her in about twenty years, either!"

Her stomach sank. She really didn't want to get into the painful details here. But she wasn't going to lie. "We don't talk. My parents disowned me when I married Donovan."

Rita gasped. "My word! I had no idea. I'm sorry." She scrambled nervously for a positive topic change. "So, you're married now. That's good! How is Donovan?"

"Divorced," Nina answered with direct eye contact to drive her point home. She needed Rita to catch on to the awkwardness further conversation would entail.

"Sorry," Rita whispered.

"That'll be $15.83."

Rita fumbled with the money. She handed it over to Nina while looking down at the counter.

Nina quickly printed out her receipt, handed it to her, and said, "Have a good day."

Offering only a nervous smile and a wave, Rita gathered her new belongings and made for the door. It was a good thing Rita and her mother weren't tight anymore. She would hate for her mother to gloat as Rita painted a pitiful picture of Nina's life. It would also be an inaccurate rendering. Nina's life was actually pretty good overall.

After work, Michelle agreed to go with Nina to photograph various seabirds. They headed to Johnson Beach, where they paid to park, and ventured off from there. Nina was interested in the Perdido Key Discovery Trail. She took several photos as they walked, mostly at the salt marsh, where a variety of birds stalked prey. She captured some of them taking off in flight.

When they finished hiking the boardwalk, they walked back toward the beach. Nina wondered aloud, "What's over there?" She pointed past the dunes to their right, on the opposite side of the road from the Gulf.

"That's Big Lagoon," answered Michelle.

"A lagoon? That sounds like a great place to photograph wildlife." They crossed the sand and found still, serene water. Nina walked to the water's edge. "I can see the fish!" she exclaimed.

"So can he," said Michelle, pointing to their left. Nina turned to find a big white egret about fifteen feet away. The look on his face said that they had disturbed his hunt, and he wasn't happy about it. He squawked and took one long step in their direction.

"Ooo, he's feisty! Let me snap him real quick and we'll get out of his hair." Nina photographed the egret from several angles. The angry bird took a few more steps, but they were slow and deliberate, so the motion didn't affect the quality of the photos.

When the bird got too close for comfort, Nina finally said, "I think I've got enough. Let's leave him alone." Glancing over her shoulder, she began to walk backward toward the road. No way was she turning her back on this riled up creature. She could envision that thing tangling its talons in her hair, ripping out chunks of it to use as nesting material, the price for scaring away his supper.

They got back to Michelle's car in one piece. "Wanna stop by the Shrimp Basket and get some dinner to go?" Michelle loved takeout and had convinced Nina, who preferred cooking at home, on multiple occasions to just grab something convenient.

"Sure." Strangely, Nina found herself in the mood for fried food. This almost never happened and surely had to do with the rollercoaster of emotions she had been forced to ride continuously for the past three days.

They got a couple of whitefish baskets. Nina actually looked forward to sinking her teeth into the crispy fish, hushpuppies, and fries. Tonight, salad was the furthest thing from her mind.

At home moments later, they dug into the food in the comfort of their dining room. Michelle laughed when Nina poured a Diet Pepsi over ice. "You're having a diet drink with this?"

Nina replied, "If you have a diet drink with fried food, it cancels out the calories. Right?"

Michelle laughed. "If only."

The food had substance. It filled an empty part of Nina. She took comfort in the enjoyment of it. That was all that mattered tonight.

Chapter 56

Thursday arrived, or as Nina called it, Day #3 Without Barry. She began to worry that he might never come back. Neither she nor Michelle had heard from him.

Her morning had been rather lonely. Michelle went off with her church crew to do volunteer yardwork, so Nina awakened to an empty house, where she must have her coffee alone. She was taking a half day, not going in to work until 1:00. She had slept until 10:00. Now, sipping her hazelnut brew, her spirits steadily sunk as her thoughts spiraled downward to a place where Barry no longer dwelled. It was an existence she might very well have to face.

So deeply immersed was she in these musings that she didn't hear the first knock at the door. The second knock, a bit louder, brought her up from despair. Could it be Barry? She ran to the door, but her heart sank from its momentary height as she glimpsed the short frame of a woman through the distortion of the glass window. She opened it and reality dropped from her grasp. "Mother?"

"Nina. It's really you," said the aged version of the woman who had raised and then rejected her. She reached out to hug Nina, who stood stiff in her embrace.

"What are you doing here?"

"Rita called me yesterday and told me she saw you working at that souvenir shop, and that you and Donovan were no longer together. I went to the shop, told the lady at the front who I was, and she told me where I could find you. Is it true? Are you and Donovan really over?"

Nina would have to thank Leslie later. "Yeah, we're done. But why would you care? I'm no longer your daughter, remember?"

Nina's mother shut her eyes against the blast. "We thought we were doing the right thing. We thought you would choose us over him. But we were wrong. So you see, there are two hurt parties here. We gave an ultimatum, but you made the choice that cast us from your life."

Considering the validity of her statement, Nina wavered a bit. She opened the door wider. "Come in." She didn't agree that what her parents had done had been the right thing by any means, but there was truth in what she said.

She motioned for her to sit at the table. "Coffee?"

"Oh, no, thanks. I'm nervous enough already. You can imagine."

Nina lowered herself into a chair. Not knowing what else to say, she asked, "How've you been?"

"Fine. Staying busy." She smiled and then her face grew serious. "Nina, why don't you come home? We'd love to have you back with us. I know there's no substitute for the years we've missed, but we could try to make up for lost time."

"Mother. I'm 37 years old. I'm not gonna come live back at home with you and Father." The words sounded strange when spoken aloud. She had called them "Mom" and "Dad" all her life growing up, but after the bond had been broken, she started referring to them by those more formal terms. Doing so put what seemed the correct amount of distance between herself and them.

"I see." Her mother leaned back in her chair. "Well how do you expect to make enough money working at that souvenir store to live on your own out here?"

Nina smiled as the first real bit of happiness she had felt all morning reached her face. "That 'souvenir store,' Seahorse Treasures, is the biggest one in all of Orange Beach. And I own it." She stared at her in satisfaction as she took a long sip of coffee.

"You what?! Did Donovan leave it to you in the divorce?"

Nina laughed and shook her head. "No. Donovan has nothing to do with the place. It's all based on contacts I made while living here. So, I think I'll stick around." She took another sip. "By the way, I own this house, too."

Her mother looked around in fascination. "Well. You've done well for yourself." A weak smile showed that Nina had turned the tables on her and come out on top. "I'll tell your father how well you're doing when I get home. I should be going."

Nina stood to see her out. "Thanks for stopping by. And for what it's worth? You and Dad were right. Marrying Donovan was a mistake. But my life with him led me to where I am today, and for that, I am grateful."

With a sad, sweet smile, Nina's mother turned to go. Nina shut the door and collapsed onto the sofa. The tremors she had experienced upon finishing her painting returned, claiming her limbs. But this time, no tears flowed. These were the shakes of triumph, the trembles of long-awaited resolution. The fifteen-year gap between her and her mother had been bridged, though with rope full of slack. They had made contact, no matter how flimsy.

Two important events had just occurred. Her mother had reached out, breaking the vow of disownment. And Nina had provided proof that she'd done better than okay on her own. The sheer magnitude of both overwhelmed her body. If life continued to be this eventful, she would have to look into training her mind to take control of her nerves.

By the time Michelle returned to shower, Nina had calmed down. She lit a candle and stared into the flame, concentrated on breathing in and out slowly, deeply. She felt Barry's presence, heard his voice telling her about fire therapy for the first time. Somehow, that soothed rather than saddened her.

Michelle walked in, saw Nina sitting cross-legged in what appeared to be a meditative state, and said, "Aw, you gettin' all zen up in here." She hurried through the room, whispering, "Don't let me bother you."

Nina cracked a smile. What would she do without Michelle? She brought laughter in the weirdest of moments and inspiration in the face of despair. Thinking of Michelle's idea to open up a corner of the shop to artists, Nina suddenly remembered her photo session from yesterday. She grabbed her phone and selected several to print for use as possible paint subjects. She needed to get on that. Her intention for taking the morning off had been to work on her art, but then she'd slept late and had a surprise visit from her mother.

It was 11:00. She could at least get a few preliminary canvas sketches done before work. Taking her printed photos back to her room, she set up to do that. She chose the threatening white egret on the sand, a great blue heron taking flight from the salt marsh, and a pelican on a pole from the same location. Using the pencil, she lightly sketched out the most important outlines of each subject onto the medium size canvases. She could easily knock out one of these paintings in a few hours after work.

The simple act of planning a new project lifted her spirits. Though the ache still persisted, it stayed in the background. Her creative juices lubricated the hinges of her artistic mind, preventing the creaks that came with lack of use.

By 12:15, she had completed all three sketches. She stopped for lunch. She ate a tin of mackerel filets, some saltines, and a small can of green beans. When Michelle joined her, she looked at the food, raised an eyebrow at the unusual choice, then said, "That looks good. I'm gonna have some, too."

Nina passed the sleeve of crackers across the table.

"So what gave you the idea to eat this? Weird craving?" Michelle took a bite.

"It was one of the cheap combinations I ate while I was living alone at the condo. When Donovan dumped me, I bought some canned food to save money. I wanted fish and vegetables, and this was the easy way to get them."

Michelle nodded. "Smart. It's really good. I could eat this for lunch a couple times a week and not get burnt out."

Nina swallowed, then asked, "How was yardwork?"

"Tiring, yet fulfilling. My muscles ache, but I feel good inside."

Gathering a handful of saltines, Nina asked, "Any more grandmotherly setups?"

Laughing, Michelle replied, "Not today. The people whose yard we worked on weren't home. I believe they were at a doctor's appointment."

"There's always next week."

Seeking a subject change, Michelle inquired, "So, what's new with you? Started any new paintings?"

"Actually, yes. I've got them drawn out and ready to begin. Oh, and my mother dropped by this morning."

Michelle dropped her fork. "What?!"

"Yeah. You know that friend of hers who came in the shop yesterday? She blabbed to my mother about my divorce, so she came to see if it was true. I confirmed it. She tried to get me to move home, asked me how I was going to make it alone financially. I got to tell her that I own a business and a house, and it was so liberating."

"Wow! What did she say?"

"Said I'd done well, and she'd tell my father."

"Is that it?!"

"Yep. No plans to get together in the future. Nothing." Nina had to admit she wasn't ready for an extended visit. She would be open to it down the road, but it would require a healing conversation that she wasn't sure her folks were ready to have.

"Dang, Nina. You are the queen bomb-dropper. The other day, you were like, 'I was kidnapped,' in the calmest voice. And just now, we're sitting here eating fish and beans for like five minutes before you're suddenly like, 'Oh, yeah. My mom dropped by.' Your deadpan delivery is excellent."

"Thanks," Nina said in her most vacant voice.

They finished eating, cleaned up, and walked to work. Today, it wasn't as hard not seeing Barry by the back door, due to the unusual time of their arrival. Still, she felt his absence keenly once inside the building, walking past the stockroom. She relieved Leslie of her post. Michelle approached Leslie before she left for lunch to tell her about the idea of the artist corner. She agreed that it sounded like a good plan. Michelle said, "I'm going to scope out an area I can rearrange to make space for it. Nina, could I get your input?"

No customers currently needed to check out, so Nina followed Michelle to the far left corner of the building. "I think we could easily move these kites over with the sand toys. We could scoot this shelf over perpendicular with that one, put some nails in the wall, and create hanging space. What do you think?"

Nina could see it. "I think that would work. That would open up plenty of room for art. Can you work on some signage? Maybe bring your laptop up here tomorrow and do your graphic design magic?"

Michelle gasped with delight. "I love it. Yes!"

Chapter 57

The flat rock skipped seven times to the center of the pond. "Not bad for a city boy," Barry's brother, Derek, taunted. Their father fished further down the bank.

"Now, you know I don't care a bit about the city. I moved there for the ocean, nothing more."

Derek replied, "Weeelll, and to get away from Jane."

"Fair enough," Barry admitted.

"Will you two be quiet? You're scaring the fish away." His dad was just irritated that they'd been here for two hours, and he hadn't gotten a single bite. The brothers had given up after forty-five minutes, but neither of them was a fisherman at heart.

"Wanna walk?" Derek offered, indicating the trail leading into the woods that they had hiked as kids.

"Sure." Barry had absolutely nothing better to do.

Derek purposely yelled, "Dad, we're going walking," as loud as he could.

Their father just frowned and mumbled. They ambled toward the forest of mostly pine and oak. The scent of pine sap filled the air, an aroma Barry had always found comforting, in part because it enveloped his hometown. It was one of his oldest olfactory memories.

"So, can I ask you a question?" Derek requested once they were out of their father's earshot.

"Yep."

"Why are you here?"

Barry stopped in his tracks. "That's no way to make a brother feel welcome."

Derek punched his arm. "You know what I mean. Other than for a friendly visit, why are you really here? You could be chilling on the beach, or floating in that sweet pool of yours. What are you doing at a pond?"

Barry considered how much he wanted to reveal. His brother was a lot of fun to be around, but when it came to matters of the heart, he could be rather flippant. "Just needed a reset."

"I get that. Needed a change of scenery to clear your head, right?"

Derek surprised him with that sympathetic comment.

"Right," Barry answered. "You sound like you've done this before."

He nodded. "I have. You remember Julie?"

Julie was Derek's girlfriend, or at least she had been when Barry left town. "Yes. What happened?"

Derek sighed. "Not long after you moved, she called me out on not being serious about our relationship. Said she needed to know where we stood. I told her I needed to take some time to think about it. So I went to the mountains for the weekend alone, just to really get in my head and examine what I wanted my future to look like. Every scenario I imagined had her in it. So I came home, prepared to propose. She had left a letter on my doorstep breaking up with me. I tried to call; she wouldn't answer. I stopped by her apartment; her roommate said she didn't want to see me. All because I took time to clear my head." Derek patted Barry on the shoulder. "If this reset is about a girl, man, you better fly back home. They don't always wait."

That filled Barry with dread. If he had messed up by leaving, it was probably already too late. He had been gone three days now. "Man, I'm sorry about Julie. My situation's different, but thanks for the advice. I believe I will head back tomorrow."

"Good plan," Derek assured him.

Barry needed to tell Nina what the painting meant. But he would have to feel her out first, make sure she hadn't distanced her heart in response to his sudden departure. The moment must be right, but he could let the opportunity slip away if he didn't do it soon.

Chapter 58

Michelle's church friends invited her to a movie, so Nina found herself alone once more. To keep the sadness at bay, she immersed herself in her craft again.

Though glad to discover that she still possessed the skill, Nina knew that if she continued using art as a crutch every single night to keep herself out of depression, it would eventually fail her. Barry had become, without her permission, the one who made her life interesting, with both the promise of emotional uplift and a sense of danger, but the good kind. The kind worth taking the risk to follow.

Nothing could replace him. She knew that. However, it appeared she might need to find something that could at least partially fill that void, as the days without him stretched on and on. He had told Leslie he would be gone a few days. How many were a few to him? Four? Ten? Thirty?

As Michelle spent more and more time with her new friends, Nina considered getting out there and finding an organization she could join. Simply following Michelle to her volunteer sessions wouldn't work. She didn't want to encroach on her life outside of their friendship.

For now, Nina was content to while away the hours painting. Perhaps once she had amassed a collection large enough to fill her share of the wall space in the newly created artist corner, she could allow herself to entertain other possibilities. Meet new people.

She didn't want to date. She could not see herself getting involved with anyone who possessed the fatal character flaw of being not Barry. That limited the sea of fish to one.

Nina knew one thing. If he ever came back, she was never letting him leave again. She would give him the "never again" he had hoped for when she'd made the mistake that caused all this. If he ever came back.

Chapter 59

Barry lay in bed, trying to rest up for the long drive in the morning. He wanted to reach out to Nina, let her know he hadn't run away for good, tell her she was all he could think about. But a text seemed too impersonal, a call perhaps too little, too late at this point. He was seven hours away, so rushing to her side wasn't an option at the moment.

Derek's story had gotten in his head. What if he had ruined the one chance he had with Nina? He should have just let her kiss him. So what if she broke his heart later by deciding it was too soon to move on from Donovan? He could have handled it. Eventually, she would have been ready to get on with her life, and he would have been there.

He considered the tangle of ironies in which he now tossed. She had needed time, which he'd given her, but she made him think she was ready and got his hopes up, then she dashed them, then he held back, resulting in her being suddenly ready, but he suddenly wasn't, all because he thought she was ignoring her own need by moving to fulfill his. A bitter laugh escaped his lips in the dark.

He sincerely hoped they could work through this. To do that, they needed to have the one thing they'd both been avoiding this entire time: an honest conversation. They needed to confront the elephant in the room together by telling each other exactly how they felt. Barry needed to ask her outright if she was ready to move on from her broken marriage.

It made so much sense. It was the simplest thing to do, yet they had made it the hardest in their minds. Time to stop the unspoken tug of war and just let go of the rope.

Since he had come here, his stomach had been in knots. Being away from Nina, not even talking to her, didn't feel right. He wondered if she was experiencing similar withdrawals. Or perhaps she had discovered how much painting she could get done without him around to distract her, and she would tell him to just stay gone so she could realize her full potential.

Hopefully, she missed him enough that his return would make her happy. He wanted nothing more than to see joy on her face when he came to her for the talk that would define their relationship. Everything hinged on tomorrow's discourse.

That night, Barry dreamed of being chased by a featureless shadow. It started after him in the forest of Mississippi, but the scene soon shifted to the Alabama beach, and then to the house where Nina slept. He desperately needed to see her, but he knew that leading this shadow to her door could only result in her death. So instead, he led it back to his own house, where it swallowed him whole.

He felt himself stop breathing. Everything faded to black. He awoke gasping for air. Looking around in a panic, he could not place his surroundings. As his eyes adjusted to the dark, his gaze fell upon the old rocking chair in the corner that had once belonged to his grandmother, and he realized he was in his old bedroom. He collapsed against the headboard in relief. When he had inhaled enough air to replace what the shadow stole, he lay back down and went to sleep.

Chapter 60

In between her tasks in the stockroom, Michelle worked on developing a sign for the artist corner. Her laptop rested on a table against the wall, and every time she got an opportunity, she plopped down on the stool in front of it and immersed herself in the art she had studied for four years. Though she enjoyed owning this business and even doing the grunt work, putting her degree to use felt right.

By 3 p.m., she was ready to show Nina three separate sign designs. Michelle carried her laptop to the front counter, where she found Nina staring at Barry's Facebook page. When Michelle put a hand on her shoulder, Nina said, "He hasn't posted anything the whole time he's been gone."

Michelle reassured her, "He's spending time with his family. He's not the type to be on his phone 24/7."

"Time with his family. Sure. You believe that? It's time away from me he wanted."

"If that's true, then he's somewhere thinking hard about what to do next. You really think he's going to be posting any of that to Facebook? He probably hasn't even logged on this week." Michelle knew that when she went through her time of crisis, that last thing she thought about was social media.

"You're probably right." Nina closed the browser. She caught a glimpse of Michelle's laptop on the counter. "What do you have there?"

"Some ideas. Come look." Michelle arranged all three of the signs on the screen in separate windows so Nina could compare them.

"These are great. You do good work."

"Thanks," Michelle glowed. "Okay, so we only need one. Which one best represents the theme?"

Nina leaned in close and studied the signs. She took her time examining all the attributes of each, which Michelle appreciated. It meant she was taking this seriously.

She pointed to the design with the slate gray background and white letters. "That one."

"Good choice," said Michelle. Of the three, it was the most refined. "I'll take a flash drive to Signs by Sam later and have it printed in a large format."

"Thank you for making that. And just, thanks, for pushing me to paint. I wouldn't have done it if you hadn't."

"You're welcome. I know I can be pushy, but sometimes, I help." Michelle shrugged, picked up her laptop, and disappeared into the back.

Closing time came, and Michelle emerged. "I'm going to go to the sign place now. Do you want to come?"

Nina had been sinking slowly all afternoon. In her hopeless state, she wanted to be alone. "I think I'm just going to go home."

"Okay. See you later." Michelle hopped into her car, and Nina started the journey across the sand. She made it all the way to the hedges before she saw the person sitting on her steps.

She stopped in her tracks as her heart and lungs temporarily malfunctioned. Barry now walked toward her, yet she struggled to believe it wasn't a hallucination. What if her eyes had joined the multi-organ momentary shutdown?

As he neared, her mind began to grasp that she was indeed in reality, not a dream, not a despair-induced vision. Barry really had come back. She had prepared for this moment, yet her body froze. She shook, and she couldn't speak. All she could do was wait and hope that he would do the talking. Maybe if he got the conversation started, she could find the power to respond.

He stopped about a foot from her. His eyes were both serious and friendly as he declared, "We need to talk."

Chapter 61

As he stood before Nina, it took every ounce of willpower not to take her in his arms and tell her how much he had missed her. There would be time for that later. Right now, he needed to clear the air between them.

When she spoke, her voice shook. "Okay. Do you want to talk on the beach or inside?"

"Let's go inside." He needed to be near the painting.

She led the way up the steps and unlocked the door. He followed her across the threshold and shut the door behind him, then motioned for her to sit on the couch. He sat near her without actually touching her. He had to keep his composure for the questions he needed to ask.

To his surprise, before he could say anything, she spoke. "I missed you."

His eyes met hers, and he saw regret there. She blamed herself for his departure, no doubt. Despite the temporary locked door he needed to keep between them until he had answers from her, he smiled and replied, "I missed you, too. A lot." Then he forced his eyes away from hers, for they linked directly to his heart.

He took a moment to compose himself. Then he stated, "I've been doing some heavy thinking, and I've found that I just need a simple answer from you to an easy question." He looked at her, and what he saw struck his heart. She was clearly terrified. Her eyes were open wide and covered with a veil of moisture, clouds that threatened to rain at any moment. A chill coursed through her, and she rubbed her hands over her arms, though it was not cold in the house. He couldn't continue like this. He paused his speech to say, "This isn't that question, but are you okay?"

She shivered once more. Her lips trembled, and the clouds began to sprinkle. "I think I messed up. I'm just hoping it wasn't a permanent mistake. Please tell me I can fix this."

That did it. He caved. Compassion poured out of his eyes. He took her by the shoulders gently, assuring her, "You haven't messed anything up. You didn't do anything wrong."

She was already crying. They may have been tears of relief. Either way, she needed to release them before they could have their important conversation, so he pulled her close and held her while she sobbed. He stroked her hair and said, "It's okay. There's nothing to be upset about." Still, sobs racked her body. All he could do was hold her and wait.

Several minutes later, her sobs had dwindled to sniffles. He pulled back far enough to grab a box of tissues and offer them to her. She took the box and went to the kitchen to blow her nose. She washed her hands, splashed water on her face, and dried both with a hand towel. When she returned to the couch, she seemed to have gained control of her emotions. She took his hand. "What did you want to ask me?"

He reached for her other hand. Looking in her eyes so that he could gauge her reaction, he asked, "Are you ready to move on from Donovan, more specifically, with me?"

Light like that of the sun emerging from behind a month of rain clouds filled her eyes. It lit her entire countenance. "Yes."

One word. One life-changing word held the key to happiness, and with it, Nina had just unlocked the door.

He put his hands on either side of her beautiful face. He leaned in and kissed her, finally free to release the feelings that had been such a source of torment these past few weeks. When she kissed him back, he reached a capacity of joy he had not known possible.

Though he didn't want the moment to end, he still had one very important thing to tell her. He gently pulled away. With a sparkle in his eyes, he said, "I want to show you something."

Slowly, he stood and walked to the painting that had belonged to his grandmother. He brought the framed piece back to the couch. With Nina watching intently, he flipped it over and slid the clasps on the back to an open position. He pulled the backing away from the canvas. As he tipped the painting out onto the cushion between them, he said, "The artist's name is on the side."

Nina spotted the signature along the right edge. Pulling it closer, she read it aloud. "Barry Sable."

Her eyes shot up to meet his, her shocked expression revealing she'd never suspected this. In an almost whisper, she asked, "You painted this?"

His face confessed with a smile. "I did. Fourteen years ago."

"But how did it end up here?" Nina asked breathlessly.

"That estate sale that Fred bought it from? It was at my grandmother's house. I gave her that painting. She taught me everything I knew about art, and she also lived here in its very subject matter. She didn't want to take it at first. She thought I should sell it or try to get it in a gallery somewhere. I refused, telling her I knew better than to try to make a career out of something that had a lot more likelihood of leaving me penniless than successful. So she kept it. But she said to me, 'Barry, I am convinced that one day, this painting will lead you to your destiny. Just be sure to follow it when it does.'"

Nina gasped. "That day, when you first saw it here. You looked as if you'd seen a ghost."

"Because I had, in a way. This painting on your wall was my grandmother showing me what I already knew."

Nina put the painting behind her and scooted toward him. "What is that?"

Barry pulled her close again. "You're my destiny."

They kissed once more. They were so wrapped up in the sacredness of the moment that they didn't hear Michelle opening the door. When she saw them, she gasped and dropped her laptop bag on the floor. They turned to look at her, and all she could think to say was, "Oops."

Chapter 62

No one spoke. They didn't seem to know what to say. When Nina shifted on the cushion, the painting tilted toward her, touching her leg as if to remind her.

Thankful for the nudge, Nina picked up the canvas and pointed it facing Michelle. Then, she announced, "Barry painted this!"

A thoroughly confused Michelle joined them on the couch at Nina's urging for an explanation. When Barry revealed to her the significance of this painting being in this house, Michelle cried out in amazement. She teared up with emotion. "We were just talking about coincidences the other day and how we don't believe in them. Nina and I both agreed that everything happens for a reason. This is a perfect example of too many things coming together in the right place and time for it to have happened at random. God did this."

She hugged Nina and Barry. Wiping away her happy tears, she declared, "Well, we have to celebrate. Let's go out for dinner, my treat. Where do you two want to eat?"

Nina looked at Barry, who left it up to her. "I hear The Crab Trap has pretty good food."

Michelle's stomach sank. How did Nina manage to pick the restaurant where Kevin had dumped her?

Recovering quickly before Nina noticed, Michelle determined to make a new, good memory there tonight to override her former devastation at that location. Why should she let Kevin take away her favorite place to eat?

They headed over to Perdido Key. After a thirty-minute wait, they were seated at an outdoor table facing the ocean. Michelle and Nina both ordered the shrimp skewers with confetti rice and black-eyed peas. Barry got the snow crab and shrimp with corn and new potatoes. Upon tasting their food, they all agreed it was some of the best in town.

As they waited on their check, Michelle stared at the sunset sky in much the same way she had on that fateful evening in the moments before her engagement dissolved. She marveled at all that had occurred between then and now. A twinge of sadness mixed with joy for the two friends at the table with her. Right now, they were talking and laughing about something she didn't overhear. They looked so in love. Michelle smiled and focused once more on the orange and purple clouds rolling like the day's credits across the screen of sky.

"Michelle?" An unfamiliar male voice drew her attention to her right side. She looked up to find a very attractive man with golden brown hair and blue eyes standing beside the table. She knew him from somewhere.

"Jace?" she asked.

"Yeah, you do remember me! Hey, I haven't seen you since we were sixteen! How are you?"

Michelle could hardly believe this was the same Jace Stone from high school. Evidently, he'd been working out and spending time in the sun. His good looks intimidated her, making it hard to focus on forming sentences. She settled upon a nod and the standard response, "Good. How are you?"

"Good. I'm living here now. I love it. What about you? Are you on vacation?"

Relieved that he asked a specific question to which the answer would be easy, she replied, "No. I live here, too."

"Really?" He smiled so beautifully she wanted to giggle like a teenager, but she stopped herself. She was sure she must have imagined his next words. "Well we should get together! What are you doing tomorrow?"

She could not remember in her current daze what she had planned. Fortunately, Barry was there to answer for her, "She has the day off." He then introduced himself and Nina. Michelle didn't know if she really had the day off tomorrow or not, but she'd take it.

Jace said, "Great. Would you like to go kayaking?" He looked to Nina and Barry, and an idea formed. "I've got a couple of two-person kayaks. We could all go."

Everyone turned to Michelle, who suddenly remembered how to talk. "Yes, that sounds like fun! Guys, what do you think?"

Barry and Nina agreed.

"Awesome. Let me give you the address and my number in case you have trouble finding the place," Jace offered.

Michelle pulled out her phone and typed both into her notes. Putting it back in her purse, she smiled at him. "See you tomorrow."

He walked through the door to the interior. As soon as it shut, Barry commented, "You're glowing."

Michelle became suddenly aware of the involuntary smile on her face. She tried to straighten her lips and look serious, but it kept returning.

Nina asked, "An old friend?"

"Yeah. Wow. I can't believe he's here. Jace and I were close in high school. We hung out all the time. Then his dad got a job somewhere in Alabama, so they had to move. I was sad to see him go, but I had just started dating Kevin, so he kind of filled the void. Wow. I haven't talked to him since we were sixteen. I can't believe he's here!"

Barry mentioned, "You said that already."

Michelle shook her head. Her state of happy confusion had her downright loopy. She was glad Barry had driven.

Chapter 63

Michelle was still smiling when they pulled into the parking lot where Jace wanted to meet the next day. Barry saw the look on her face when she got out of the backseat. He put a hand on her head and ruffled her hair. "I'm happy for you."

She squeezed his arm in return. Then her eyes darted over to the vehicle down by the water. Jace was unloading a couple of kayaks from the back of a truck. Barry jogged over to help him.

Michelle and Nina reached them just as the kayaks had been positioned for takeoff. Jace looked at Michelle, and he smiled like he had just been given good news. "Hey Michelle." There was a tenderness in the way he said her name, as if the word were precious.

"Hey Jace." Still couldn't stop smiling.

Everyone in their crew had kayaked before, so no instructions were needed. They each donned a life vest. Jace had Michelle sit down first, then he pulled the kayak into the water before boarding it himself. Barry followed his lead with Nina in the other boat.

They paddled out where the shallow emerald water was clear enough to see through to the bottom. Jace announced, "I thought we'd head out to the uninhabited islands. You can see a lot of cool wildlife out there."

When Michelle noticed where they were in reference to the Perdido Pass Bridge, she gasped. "Nina, this is where the dolphin cruise captain said we could see seahorses!"

Nina looked around. "You're right!"

Jace confirmed, "It's possible. They do live in the grass beds around Robinson Island."

Michelle wasn't sure the day could get much better.

They reached the island and secured their kayaks upon the sand. Though they spent a considerable amount of time closely inspecting the underwater grass, they couldn't find a seahorse. During her obsessive search, she wondered if Jace thought she was being rude for seemingly ignoring him, or even just plain weird.

She felt better when he said, "Next time, we'll bring nets and a small aquarium to put them in once we find them so we can get a good look at them before returning them to their home. You just about have to blindly scoop them up. They camouflage so well they're difficult to see."

So there would be a next time? That was a good sign.

"Thanks. I'm sorry I spent so much time looking for one."

Jace smiled at her. "It's good to be persistent when you really want something." His eyes stayed upon her. "Whatever happened to Kevin?"

She had wondered when Jace would ask about him. She explained, "We got engaged. Then he broke it off two weeks before the wedding."

Jace's eyes widened. "Oh, I'm sorry."

Michelle waved it off. "Don't be. I'm better off."

Jace sat in the sand. He had a faraway look in his eyes, but a smile still held his lips. "Did you know I had a huge crush on you back in high school?"

Michelle's heartbeat slowed. The world around her seemed to spin a little. "What?"

"You really didn't know?" he said with disbelief.

"I had no idea. We were such good friends. I never picked up on that vibe from you." Michelle thought back to all the time they'd spent together, with her going on and on to him about her crush on Kevin, who didn't seem to know she was alive back then. "Why didn't you tell me?"

Jace looked off to the side. "I was about to. Right before you told me Kevin finally asked you out. You were so excited. Your dream had come true. I wasn't about to put a damper on it."

Michelle's jaw dropped. She thought back to that moment. Jace had seemed a little less thrilled than she thought he should be. She had wanted him to celebrate the momentous occasion with her, and though he smiled and said he was happy for her, he seemed distant. She thought at the time that he must have his mind on things at home. His dad had just told the family he had a job interview in Alabama, and Jace was scared they might have to move away.

She sat down beside him. "Oh, Jace. I'm so sorry. That must have hurt." She wanted to cry just thinking about the pain she caused him.

"It's okay. The heart wants what it wants, right?"

She sat there speechless, still aching from what she had done. "The heart can be wrong sometimes."

He looked at her for a long moment. She wondered if he was thinking about leaving her here on the island for revenge. Then he asked something she didn't expect. "Do you go to church anywhere?"

Michelle felt suddenly self-conscious. She had to admit, "No. I haven't gone to church services since I lived in Georgia. I have been doing volunteer community outreach with a group affiliated with Christian Calling Church, but I haven't actually been in the building."

Astonishment covered his face. "That's the church I go to!"

"What?! Really?" Michelle could hardly believe it.

"Yes! I would like to do the outreach program, but with the hours I work, I just can't get there in time. Wow. Small world." When he recovered from the realization, he asked, "Why don't you come to church with me tomorrow? You'll already know a few people."

She had been considering attending before she had run into Jace. However, her past experience at her old church had made her reluctant to try another one. Now she had no reason to hesitate. "Sure, I'd love to."

Chapter 64

The sound of piano music reached the parking lot as Michelle stepped out of her car. She had been a ball of nerves all morning thinking about coming here. Jace told her that he would meet her outside so she wouldn't have to walk in alone, but a part of her worried that he wouldn't show.

"Michelle!" a female voice yelled out. She turned to find Alicia, Alfred, and his new woman walking toward her. Alicia ran up and gave her a hug. "I'm so glad you decided to come!"

"I'm meeting someone here," she explained just as she saw Jace approaching from behind the group. "And there he is."

Alicia turned her head. "Jace!" she exclaimed. "You know Michelle?"

Looking at Michelle with a warm smile, he replied, "We go way back."

She found herself smiling at him, unable to look away. He stepped forward and put his hand on her back. "Shall we go inside?"

"We shall," she answered. Something in her tone reminded her of how she'd described Nina's voice when she talked to Barry: "full of syrup." Oh, well. There was nothing wrong with a little sap in a sweet moment.

They entered the sanctuary, and Michelle instantly sensed the presence of goodness. People weren't sitting stoically, facing forward ten minutes before church began. They were talking. Laughing. She felt overwhelmingly here what had been missing at her old church: joy. On the front of the bulletin, 2 Corinthians 3:17 read, "Now the Lord is the Spirit; and where the Spirit of the Lord is, there is freedom." These people were free.

Jace spotted a group standing by a pew on the far left. She felt his hand on her back again as he said, "Come over here. There's someone I want you to meet."

He led her toward the gathering of three people. They approached the nearest one, an elderly woman with curly white hair, from behind. Jace put a hand on the woman's back, stepped in front of her, and gave her a hug. "Grandma, there's someone I'd like you to meet."

The woman turned to face her, and Michelle gasped. "Mrs. Betty!"

"Michelle!" The sweet old woman whom Michelle had brought casseroles for the past two weeks opened her arms wide for a hug. Then she whispered, "I told you that you two would hit it off." As she pulled away, she winked.

Michelle's heart pounded. She looked from Mrs. Betty to Jace. "You're Jason?"

He shut his eyes. "My full name is Jason Everly Stone. Everyone calls me Jace." Then he opened them. "But my grandmother insists on calling me Jason."

Mrs. Betty wore a look of confusion. She asked Michelle, "Well, didn't you ask for Jason when you went to his work to meet him?"

Jace looked puzzled. "You were supposed to meet me?"

Michelle explained, "Mrs. Betty wanted to set us up. She wanted me to go to your workplace. I had no idea who you were. I wasn't going to go track down a stranger for a date, no offense, Mrs. Betty." She turned to the woman and continued, "Jace and I were close friends in high school. We just ran into each other at a restaurant Friday and reconnected. He invited me to church, and here I am."

Mrs. Betty laughed with delight. "How wonderful. God works in mysterious ways, doesn't He?"

Jace gave Michelle a look that melted her heart. She had seen it before. It was the same look Barry gave Nina every time he laid eyes on her.

The parallels in their lives were undeniable. Barry had been shown his destiny through his grandmother, who played matchmaker from beyond, with a painting from his past. Jace's grandmother had picked Michelle out for him, not realizing they had a past. Nina and Michelle had emerged from broken relationships to find a job at the same place and live in the same house. Though all of them had spent a large portion of their lives miles apart, God had brought them together with a series of miracles. Each of them realized the sanctity of what they had been given.

Later that night, after another day exploring the islands together, Jace walked Michelle home. They held hands as they traversed the cool sand. Being with him just felt right. Much like her new church compared to the old, she sensed with Jace what had been missing with Kevin.

He walked her up the steps to her door. She turned to say goodnight, and he looked at her as if she were a treasure, like the seahorse she had sought so diligently at the beach. "Goodnight," he said. Then he leaned in and kissed her gently, as one would touch a butterfly. He retreated down the steps. Her sudden lightheadedness caused tiny purple shapes to dance before her eyes like flower petals on the breeze.

Some would say it was too soon to tell, but Michelle already knew she had found her destiny in the most unexpected way. She thought of that day on the beach when loneliness had so fully consumed her that she wished for death over continuing to live with that pain. Then God answered her prayer with a simple piece of paper to let her know He cared. She knew that joining the outreach and meeting Mrs. Betty had been a wink from God, who knew all along that she would run into Jace and make the connection once she got back in church. The myriad of experiences that had forged the path to now would forever serve as a reminder that she was never alone.

Have you read these other books by Kathy Wile?

Red Redemption
Sunflower Solstice (a novella)

<u>The Kate Adams Series</u>:
Shifting Seaward
Drifting Inland
Sloping Southward

Night Visions
Psychological Potluck
The Characters of Sardis Lake
Gulf Shores Godsend

About the Author

Kathy Wile lives in Mississippi with her husband, three dogs, and one cat. She began writing at age 35. Though she has always loved the written word, Kathy merely minored in English. She received her degree in art with an emphasis in graphic design from The University of Mississippi in 2001, and she put it to use first as a graphic designer for The Oxford Eagle newspaper. Her hobbies include painting landscapes, writing songs, and exploring nature, particularly bodies of water. Sardis Lake, The Tennessee River, Pickwick Lake, and the Gulf of Mexico are some of her favorite spots, as is reflected in her writing.

Visit **kathywiletheauthor.com** to learn more and to subscribe to her mailing list.

Facebook: facebook.com/kathywileauthor
Instagram: instagram.com/kathywileauthor/
Rate and review on Goodreads and Amazon.

www.ingramcontent.com/pod-product-compliance
Lightning Source LLC
LaVergne TN
LVHW091003190425
809083LV00008B/157